PROPHECY

PROPHECY

THE CHARMED CITY™
BOOK TWO

KELLI ROBYNS

MICHAEL ANDERLE

DON'T MISS OUR NEW RELEASES

Join the Florid Romance email list to be notified of new releases and special promotions (which happen often) by following this link:

https://floridromance.lmbpn.com/about/sign-up-for-our-newsletter/

Published by Florid Romance
an imprint of LMBPN Publishing
2375 E. Tropicana Avenue, Suite 8-305
Las Vegas, Nevada 89119 USA

Version 1.00, May 2025
eBook ISBN: 979-8-89354-810-5
Print ISBN: 979-8-89354-811-2

Lila Matthews entered the Council's secure briefing room with a tightness in her chest that refused to ease. The corridor leading there had been deathly quiet, despite the muffled hum of city traffic far above. The entire room glowed with subdued lantern-light that sparked and crackled against the rigid ward lines along the walls, as if preparing for a demonstration of authority. She noticed five Council elders gathered at a large round table, along with several watchers holding stacks of papers, runic sheets, and half-rolled maps depicting magical hotspots in Manhattan. Marcus Steele stood at the helm with a firm posture, beckoning everyone to sit.

Caleb Blackwood walked at her side, gaze keen as they approached the table. His fingers kept brushing against hers whenever she shifted, stirring warmth at the base of her neck. It was only the second time she had been asked to attend a briefing this pressing, and the heaviness in the air reminded her how capable illusions had become at upending the city's fragile balance.

A quiet fell over the gathering as a tall woman stepped forward. She wore a midnight-blue robe embroidered with silver crescents and swirling lines that resembled lunar phases. Her inky hair was piled atop her head in a loose bun, strands falling forward to frame a face that held gentle confidence. Though new to Lila, the woman's presence seemed to command immediate respect from the watchers. Marcus cleared his throat and gestured to her.

"This is Keira Costa," he said. "A Luna witch. She serves as the principal guardian for some of the city's most important nexus points. She has critical news about an alarming breach on her watch."

Lila had heard whispers about Luna witches: magic-wielders who derived power from phases of the moon. They specialized in harmonizing mystical energies in wards and nexus sites where magic flowed like underground rivers. Luna witches rarely arrived at Council gatherings, preferring to do their work quietly at night, but it seemed the rising wave of illusions had forced new alliances.

Keira took a measured breath, her hand resting on the back of an empty chair. "Thank you, Marcus," she said. Her voice was calm, with a softness that soothed yet hinted at unspoken strength. "The city's nexus lines have been disturbed. I have tracked disruptions near four locations, each site showing evidence of sabotage. Generally, I oversee them alone, but this is beyond anything I have encountered."

She paused, eyes traveling the room. Lila saw sympathy beneath the witch's calm demeanor. In that quiet moment, it felt as if Keira could sense each person's worry and grief, storing it like moonlight for safekeeping. The watchful silence remained unbroken until one of the elders, a man with a perpetually furrowed brow, muttered, "Sabotage implies an inside hand. Which means traitors."

Another council member murmured agreement. Several watchers exchanged uneasy looks. Weary as she felt, Lila recognized tension welling at the edges of the table. Everyone had theories, but no one wanted to name them aloud.

Keira inclined her head. "If illusions or dark spells tampered with the nexus flow, they could destabilize wards across Manhattan. Whoever is behind it has advanced skill, likely from within our ranks or allied factions. My wards are undone in ways that defy random assault."

Marcus's stern face darkened. "We cannot afford a splinter in our defenses," he said. "We need a plan of action before illusions seep into every street corner. Any suggestions?"

Silence weighted the air. Lila felt her pulse hammer. She finally cleared her throat. "Maybe we can cross-reference the times and locations of these sabotaged nexus points with reported illusions in those same areas. The illusions have been popping up more frequently, so the overlap might reveal a pattern."

Her own voice surprised her. She heard how steady it

sounded despite a thousand nerves. Caleb glanced at her with unmistakable admiration in his eyes. The faint press of his foot against hers, hidden beneath the table, made her breath catch. For a heartbeat, she recalled the night she had triggered illusions in midtown. He had shown up, unwavering, to help. He always did.

An elder coughed, drawing everyone's attention. "Cross-referencing illusions with sabotage would require full disclosure of our watchers' logs. That has its own risks."

Marcus's gaze flicked to the watchers. "We are far past worrying about what is private or not," he said. "We must unify our data if we are to expose whoever is tampering with the nexus lines."

"And if sabotage shows Council involvement?" asked a different watcher, arms folded tight.

Keira lifted her chin. Her voice, though calm, carried gravity. "I realize none of us want to believe that. Yet the illusions in the city are too orchestrated to be random. My wards do not fail so completely unless someone actively tears them down. I suspect infiltration."

She lowered her head slightly, as if sympathizing with the Council's predicament: betrayals, illusions that appeared anywhere at any hour, wards faltering under pressure no one predicted. Lila's chest constricted. Part of her wanted to demand the watchers trust her plan, but she swallowed the impulse, mindful that she was the newest voice in a deeply traditional institution.

Marcus nodded at Lila's suggestion. "We will compile a thorough cross-reference," he said. "Keira, we would like you to help. Our watchers will pool their logs, and the novices in training can assist. Each known illusion event will be matched against times the nexus lines failed."

Murmurs rippled across the table. One elder with a pinched mouth looked uneasy, but he nodded. Another shot Lila a look she could not easily read—suspicion or grudging acceptance, maybe. Still, the atmosphere shifted to cautious agreement.

Lila let out the breath she had been holding. She caught Caleb's eye. In the low glow of the lanterns, he looked proud, and that silent encouragement wrapped her in warmth. The feeling of gratitude tangled with the tension in her chest, reminding her that the threat had not gone away. If sabotage truly lurked among them, illusions could strike again in places they assumed safe.

Marcus ran a hand along the table's edge. "Then we move forward. Keira, you will remain in the city for a time. We could use your expertise."

"I am at your disposal," she said. "I only ask for enough freedom to mend or reinforce the sites under my care."

The watchers agreed. A mood of frenzied relief rose, though no one called it a victory. Everyone was aware that illusions could overtake them at any moment. They had only taken the first step toward a solution.

Marcus's gaze darted around the room. "That concludes our immediate business. I want updates on the cross-reference by tomorrow evening. We must act quickly if we hope to prevent further sabotage."

Encouraged by Keira's presence and Lila's practical

idea, the watchers gathered their papers. Keira bowed politely to Marcus, then offered Lila a warm smile. For a moment, Lila felt that gentle empathy again, as though the Luna witch sensed the swirl of anxiety beneath her calm exterior. Keira's parted lips suggested she wanted to say something else, but the watchful tension in the room pressed them all into motion.

After they scattered, Lila fell into step beside Caleb, whose quiet presence drew her attention more than anything else in that corridor. A swirl of relief rushed through her veins. She spotted a flicker of pride in his eyes. He placed a hand lightly on her lower back, guiding her beyond the doorway before letting it fall away. Even that small contact sent shivers through her.

They emerged into a narrower hallway lined with tall columns. The wards buzzed overhead, casting flickers of runic light along the ceiling. Lila brushed a strand of hair from her eyes. The meeting's tension still hummed through her body, and her pulse raced with adrenaline she could not quite shed.

Caleb started to speak, but a pair of watchers strode by, interrupting them with greetings. Once the watchers disappeared around a corner, he exhaled. "You were remarkable in there," he said. "Hearing you offer that plan gave me real hope. I was too caught up in worrying about sabotage to think so practically."

She felt her cheeks warm. "I just blurted out what made sense. You know illusions, I know a bit about patterns. I never told you I majored in math, did I?"

He nodded. "Well, that explains everything. Thanks for stepping up."

They headed through one final door, stepping out of the Council's labyrinth into a quiet side exit near Greenwich Village. The cool night air hit them, ripe with the scents of car exhaust and city living. They exchanged a look before descending the stone steps leading to the main street.

All around them, tall buildings framed the sky. Neon lights flickered, hinting at the bustle of New York further downtown. Despite the tension inside the Council, the city appeared almost serene under the moonlit sky, at least on the surface. Lila let the late breeze wash over her face, banishing the last taste of worry.

Caleb slid a hand into his coat pocket. "It is late, but I cannot stand the thought of going straight home," he said. "I don't think I can sleep with so much on my mind, with you so close."

She rubbed her arms. The night chill seeped through the thin sleeves of her shirt, but she felt more alive than tired. "Me either. Maybe we could... get dinner?"

His mouth curved into a small, genuine smile. " We never actually sat for a proper meal together, have we?"

Her breath caught on a soft laugh, remembering stolen bites of café pastries, or quick sips of coffee when illusions threatened to break loose around them. But a quiet, real meal in a normal restaurant felt like the one thing they had not managed. "No, we never have."

He offered his arm, and she looped hers through it,

leaning against him more than she expected. She blamed it on the residual tension and adrenaline coursing through her. Yet the warmth of his body felt grounding in a way no ward ever had. They walked along the sidewalk until they found a small restaurant tucked on a side street, its windows glowing gold, only a modest sign above the door announcing its name.

Caleb opened the door for her, and they stepped into a space filled with conversation, the smell of roasted herbs, and a faint sound of jazz music from hidden speakers. A hostess ushered them to a small table near the back. Soft light glistened off Caleb's dark hair as he pulled out her chair. They sat in comfortable silence until a server approached.

The server brought them water, leaving them to decide. Lila noticed the restaurant specialized in Italian dishes. She skimmed the menu, trying to focus on entrée descriptions instead of the nervous flutter in her stomach. This was the first time she and Caleb had ventured into something so... ordinary. No wards, no illusions flaring. It felt dangerously cozy, an unguarded breath of normalcy after the intense tension at the Council.

She glanced up, and he was watching her with that measured, quietly reverent look that always made her flush. "Any favorites?" she asked, tilting the menu so he could see.

He considered her question, then shook his head. "Order for both of us," he said. "I trust your taste."

A tiny smile curled at her lips. She appreciated the

sincerity in his voice. She settled on a pasta dish in vodka sauce for herself and a hearty, peppery risotto for him, adding a side of fresh bread. When the server left to bring their order, an unspoken comfort stretched between them.

She fiddled with the napkin, letting the clinks of silverware and low murmur of other patrons fill the background. Eventually, she dared to speak. "I was a little terrified in the briefing," she admitted softly. "All those watchers who have done this for decades, and me, a novice who can hardly hold illusions back half the time."

Caleb reached forward and covered her hand gently. She felt the calluses on his fingertips, evidence of training, repeated wards, endless vigilance. "I know how intimidating it can be," he said. "But seeing your composure made them listen. You proved you deserve that seat at their table today."

Her cheeks warmed, but she refused to look away. "I want them to trust me," she said. "I need them to. Otherwise, how do we ever fix the sabotage or keep illusions from overrunning everything?"

His expression turned more serious. "We will keep pushing," he promised. "Marcus values results more than formality. Once we uncover a lead on those tampered nexus sites, I suspect the truth about sabotage will come to light."

She felt a tremor of apprehension mixed with hope. "I just want to make a difference and... not live in fear all the time."

A shadow flickered across his gaze, but he caught her

hand tighter. "I will help ensure you do not have to. You have me at your side, always." He hesitated, as if considering his next words. "If you want me there."

Emotion fluttered in her chest. Warm affection spilled through her veins, so sudden and potent that she struggled to frame a response. She simply nodded, swallowing the lump in her throat.

The server arrived with their food, placing steaming plates on the table. Fragrant herbs wafted up, mixing with the cozy ambient lighting. For a few blissful moments, they focused on delicious pasta and savoring the fresh flavors. Lila exhaled in a contented sigh, letting the spiced sauce and warm bread chase away the last edges of tension. She had forgotten how nice it was to pause, put aside the weight of illusions and sabotage, and just taste normal life.

He took a bite of the risotto, eyes half closing at the first forkful. The faint lines on his brow smoothed out, and a small grin tugged at his mouth. She giggled, relieved that he liked her choice. Silence cradled them again, though peaceful now. She caught herself watching how his hair fell across his forehead, how the flex of his fingers around the fork made her pulse skip. She could look at those manly lips and feel deep desire.

They lingered over their meal, talking in low voices about small, easy things. They chatted about normal city life, concerts in the park, an odd coffee blend Lila wanted to try at her café, and a fleeting mention of upcoming Council tasks. Each time their gaze locked, the rest of the restaurant seemed to fade. Every sense sharpened: the gentle rustle of tablecloth, the glow of candles in the corner, the taste of fresh tomato on her tongue. This moment felt anchored in reality, a rare sanctuary from illusions and hidden truths.

When they left the restaurant, it was without discussion. His hand slid into hers as they walked beneath the dim glow of streetlamps, the city humming softly around them. They didn't speak—didn't need to.

He hailed a cab, and she followed him to his hidden oasis in the basement of The New Yorker Hotel without question. The air between them buzzed with anticipation, with all the things they hadn't said but had long since started to feel.

His apartment was quiet when they stepped in, the city's noise muffled by thick windows and distance. He locked the door behind them, then turned and looked at her as if asking one final time for permission.

Lila didn't answer with words. She stepped in close, rising on her toes to kiss him. The moment their lips met, it was as if the entire night collapsed inward. Her fingers slid into his hair, tugging him down to her as his arms came around her, firm and wanting.

Their kisses turned greedy, heated. He pressed her back against the wall, his mouth exploring hers, hands tugging her shirt free of its tucked edge. Fabric rustled as they undressed each other in pieces, revealing skin in a slow, frantic unveiling that made her ache.

Caleb swept her up into his arms with a soft grunt and carried her to the bedroom, setting her down like she was something precious. Then he joined her on the bed, and they came together like gravity had made them—mouth to mouth, skin to skin, hands roaming and claiming.

He kissed her throat, her collarbone, the swell of her breast, worshipful and hungry at once. His fingers traced down her ribcage, along her waist, learning every inch of her with reverent precision. She arched beneath him, gasping when his lips found the spot behind her knee, then moved upward with agonizing care.

"Tell me what you want," he whispered, his voice rough.

"You," she breathed, pulling him up, over, into her. "Now. Just... *you.*"

When he entered her, the world narrowed to the place their bodies met. Their rhythm started slow, deep and consuming, each thrust a silent vow. His forehead pressed to hers, sweat-damp and trembling, and the way he said her name—like a prayer, like a promise—made her fall harder.

They moved together with rising urgency, bodies slick and attuned, until everything crested in a burst of sensation so intense she cried out, hands gripping his back. He followed her with a low groan, burying himself deep as they unraveled in each other's arms.

Afterward, they lay tangled in sweat-damp sheets, her head on his chest, his heartbeat still wild beneath her ear. His hand stroked down her spine, slow and grounding.

"In case it wasn't obvious," he murmured, pressing a kiss to her temple, "I'm in this—for all of it."

Lila smiled against his skin, her body deliciously

spent. "Good," she whispered. "Because I'm not letting you go now."

Outside, the city kept moving. But in the quiet of that room, beneath cooling sheets and twined limbs, nothing else existed but the two of them—and the promise of what came next.

CHAPTER

TWO

Lila stirred to the muted glow of early sunlight seeping through the blinds. The room was quiet, save for the steady rise and fall of Caleb's chest beneath her cheek. His arm was draped around her back, their legs tangled in a lazy knot beneath the rumpled sheets. She felt sore in all the best ways, her skin still tingling from where his hands had lingered long after the heat of their bodies had cooled.

She turned her head slightly to look at him.

He was already awake, watching her with the softest expression—his hair mussed, jaw shadowed, eyes heavy-lidded but clear. He brushed a strand of hair from her face and let his thumb graze her cheek. "Good morning," he said, his voice rough and warm, like flannel against bare skin.

"Morning," she murmured, stretching just enough to make her muscles hum. "I think I just slept harder than I have in weeks."

"You needed it." His gaze dropped to her mouth, and he kissed her gently, thoroughly, like they had all the time in the world.

When she pulled back with a sleepy smile, she wrinkled her nose. "I probably need a shower more."

Caleb laughed, low and delicious. "Me too." He slid out of bed and held out a hand. "Come on. We'll save water."

She arched a brow. "Is that your best environmentalist pickup line?"

"I have better ones," he said, already leading her toward the bathroom, "but they're less appropriate before caffeine."

The bathroom filled with steam as the water warmed. Lila stepped in first, groaning softly as the heat soaked into her sore shoulders. A moment later, Caleb joined her, his hands sliding around her waist from behind. He nuzzled into her neck, his scruff brushing her skin.

For a while, there was no urgency. Just the rhythm of warm water falling, the gentle glide of hands on wet skin, the occasional laugh between soapy kisses. He lathered shampoo into her hair with a kind of reverence that made her close her eyes and lean into him completely. She returned the favor, running her hands across his back and shoulders, memorizing the tension and strength there.

Eventually, she turned to face him, water running between them, her hands flat against his chest.

"Last night was beyond magic," she said quietly.

"It was pure magic." He kissed her again, slower now, with less hunger and more heat.

They made love under the water, slow and drenched

and beautiful—more sensual than frantic this time, their bodies moving with the kind of familiarity that didn't need permission. The world outside the tile walls disappeared. It was just skin, steam, and the sound of their breath filling the space between.

Afterward, they toweled off in silence, exchanging glances that said more than words could. She stole one of his shirts and padded barefoot into the kitchen. He followed, still damp, running a hand through his hair and watching her like he couldn't quite believe she was there.

As the coffee brewed, she leaned against the counter, holding her mug with both hands.

"We still have to save the city," she said, voice dry but fond.

Caleb grinned and took a slow sip of his coffee. "Let's start with breakfast and go from there."

LATER THAT EVENING, Lila stood on the worn stone steps of a long-forgotten corridor beneath Grand Central Terminal. Holding a small orb of witch light in her left hand, she glanced at Keira Costa, who hovered just ahead. The Luna witch brushed a few dark strands from her face and gestured toward the darker stretch of tunnel. Lila's throat felt suddenly tight. She could almost taste the stale air, tinged with a metallic tang that hinted at old wards and deeper enchantments.

"These passages were sealed decades ago," Keira said softly, her voice echoing. "The mortal authorities called them structurally unsafe, so the Council took advantage. It made sense to hide them from casual explorers."

Lila inhaled, pushing back her nerves. Around her, the walls flickered like half-seen ghosts, stones rippling out of focus every time she shifted. Even the cold was strange: it rose in waves, then vanished, as if illusions tested each visitor's resolve.

Caleb stood at Lila's shoulder, his tall form an anchor in the confusion. She caught a glimpse of his gloved hand forming a subtle ward sign, the faint glow of runes dancing across his fingertips. She was grateful he was with her, especially when the corridor flickered in and out of existence, warping the perspective so the floor seemed to tilt.

Keira stepped forward first. "Follow exactly where I walk," she said. "Sebastian left behind layered spells. Some are illusions meant to trap intruders. Others might be decoys." Her black robe fluttered around her ankles, embroidered with crescent shapes that caught the meager light of Lila's orb. Without waiting for confirmation, Keira moved ahead at a measured pace.

Lila glanced at Caleb. The tension in his expression did little to reassure her. He nodded, a silent message that they should keep going. She let out a breath and followed Keira into the labyrinth. Each step revealed a new distortion: the bricks along the corridor bent inward, or else parted in swirls of dim color. Twice, Lila nearly stumbled when what appeared to be a stable patch of floor turned translucent beneath her feet.

"This is worse than some of the illusions we've faced

before," she murmured. A flicker of unease coiled in her stomach. Although she had grown more confident in her abilities, nobody told her illusions could push reality so close to the edge that walls appeared to melt. Caleb reached for her hand, guiding her around a spot where the ground dipped abruptly. She squeezed his fingers in gratitude.

He gave her a half-smile. "Keep your guard up. Sebastian used to talk about how illusions are an art. This is a masterpiece of chaos."

Keira paused at a junction where two corridors intersected. The echo of dripping water lingered on the air, though no visible source existed. "We head right," she said, her gaze trailing along a faint shimmer etched into the stone. "Sebastian's signature. He was here."

Lila eyed the scorch marks that cut across the bricks. Partially burned runes glowed faintly like embers. It looked as if someone had tried to scrub them away, only to leave ghostly silhouettes behind. The uneasy sense of stepping through a half-real dream tightened around her lungs. The air felt denser here, and her mouth was dry from breathing dust and lingering magic.

They continued, every footstep echoing a moment too late, like the sound was caught in a slowed reflection. Lila braced herself with small wards when she sensed reality shift. Once, a swirl of illusions formed a wall of mirror fragments that shattered as soon as she tried to look closely. Keira dispelled the shards with lunar-based incantations, the silvery glow of her magic rippling against the gloom.

Suddenly, the corridor dipped downward. Lila didn't see the hazard until she stepped directly onto a sheen of conjured water. Her foot slid out from under her, and she pitched forward. She let out a startled gasp, arms flailing for balance. The cold burn of the water soaked her palms, but then the illusion vanished as quickly as it had appeared, and her own momentum carried her downward.

For a heart-stopping second, an entire chasm yawned in front of her, black and bottomless. She gasped, convinced she was about to plummet into darkness. She tried to form a ward, but her energy felt tangled, her mind reeling from the abrupt shift. Her pulse thundered in her ears.

Caleb lunged, his arm hooking around her waist. The impact knocked the breath out of her, but at least she wasn't falling anymore. She clutched at his coat, eyes wide. For a moment, she couldn't tell which direction was up. Her illusion sight blurred the edges of everything, and every flicker of light seemed to dance.

He dragged her away from the illusory chasm, heart hammering against her side. She felt the hardness of his forearm around her body. When reality caught up, she realized they were still in a corridor—there was no true pit. She found her footing, breathing shakily.

"Better hold on until we stabilize this area," Caleb managed, voice tight. He kept a firm hold on her, as if afraid she might vanish the instant he let go. Lila's cheeks flamed from the contact, but she nodded, letting him support her. Keira stepped closer, chanting softly to dispel the last remnants of water illusions so no one else would slip.

Lila leaned her forehead against Caleb's shoulder for a moment, focusing on the steady drum of his heartbeat. That small tether of warmth helped steady her own pulse. She reminded herself that these illusions fed on disorientation and fear. She would not give them that power.

Keira motioned for them to continue once the path felt stable. They pressed deeper, only to find new illusions swirling around a broad archway. The air crackled with tension. Half-formed illusions slid across the walls, flickering from one shape to another—a swirl of faces, a coil of text Lila couldn't read, cracks in the floor that vanished when she blinked. She concentrated on the earthy resonance in her chest, using the grounding techniques she had practiced so many times. Beside her, she sensed Caleb weaving a net of illusions to counter Sebastian's spells.

After what felt like hours, they reached a rusted metal door jammed tight from disuse. The faint odor of stale rust clung to the handle. Keira tested it, murmuring a brief incantation, and the door groaned open. A wave of fresh air, comparatively free of illusions, rolled in. Lila inhaled deeply. Her limbs trembled from the extended tension, and a trickle of sweat beaded along her hairline.

Caleb released a quiet exhale. "That might be our exit." He guided Lila over the threshold. When she stumbled again, he caught her elbow, concern flickering in his gaze.

"I'm fine," she said softly, though the adrenaline still coursed through her body. Her cheeks felt warm, and each breath seemed to cling to the memory of his arm around her waist.

They emerged into an abandoned service corridor lined with dust-caked maintenance signs. Only the occasional flicker of overhead bulbs offered illumination, but to Lila, it felt like stepping from a nightmare into the pallid light of day. She spotted a few battered crates and rolled-up tarps strewn against the wall, likely from whatever mortal crew had worked here long ago. Outside, traffic rumbled in muffled waves above the terminal's main concourse.

Keira heaved a sigh. "We've done enough for one day. I'll report these illusions to the Council. They'll want to send watchers to purge or seal the area completely."

Caleb nodded. "We need to revisit the runes we saw. Certain patterns might reveal the illusions' anchor points." He cast a glance at Lila, seemingly worried about her exhaustion. "We can meet tomorrow to go through the details."

Keira studied them, and her lips curved in a gentle, knowing smile. "Alright," she said. "But rest first. That labyrinth was no small feat."

She parted ways with them in the next corridor, leaving Lila and Caleb to climb the stairs toward the main terminal exit. Constellations painted across Grand Central's ceiling glimmered far above them. The vast space hummed with mortal life, unsuspecting travelers bustling with luggage and half-finished phone calls. Lila winced at how normal everything appeared, considering the illusions whirling only floors below.

Caleb rested a hand on her shoulder. "Let me walk you out. I know we have a lot to cover, but do you want to come over? I can cook something that isn't cafeteria food for a change."

At first, Lila meant to decline. A swirl of nerves still jittered in her limbs, but the idea of returning to her apartment alone after that unnerving labyrinth left her uneasy. She smiled gratefully and nodded. "That sounds perfect. I could use something hot and... normal."

Caleb's apartment welcomed them with soft lighting and protective wards that kept illusions at bay. Slight arcs of ward light glowed in the corners, verifying the space was secure. He showed her to the kitchen area, rummaging through the fridge with a thoughtful frown.

"I'm thinking tomato and basil pasta," he said, pulling out fresh ingredients. "Plus, some garlic bread, if that suits you. But first, let me pour you some of my favorite wine."

Relief spread over Lila like a warm comforter. "Garlic bread sounds heavenly. Wine sounds divine."

She settled in at the bar counter and watched him as he decanted and poured the wine, taking great care by choosing the perfect glass and explaining how it helped the wine breathe. Then he started on dinner by tossing chopped tomatoes and basil into a saucepan. She let the homey scents soothe her frazzled mind. She watched him cradle a small jar of spices, sprinkling them in with the graceful focus that reminded her of how meticulously he cast illusions. The sizzling pan smelled of fresh herbs and onions. Her stomach rumbled, a sharp reminder she hadn't eaten since early morning.

"Need a hand with anything?" she asked.

He shook his head. "I have it covered. Just catch your breath." He cast a half-smile her way, a private warmth lighting his eyes. "You nearly fell into that illusion back there. How do you feel now?"

She closed her eyes briefly, recalling the sensation of empty air beneath her feet. "I'm still shaky," she admitted. "But I'm managing. Thank you for... saving me."

He turned off the flame. "Anytime. And I mean that."

The softness in his voice teased her heart with a tender ache. She couldn't ignore how simply being near him made her feel safer, even when illusions buzzed just beyond these walls. Crossing the kitchen, she placed a hand lightly on his arm. The breath stalled in her chest when she saw the concern flicker behind his eyes.

They ate their dinner at a small table beside a window that offered a partial view of the city lights. Conversation flowed in low undertones. They discussed potential leads in the labyrinth, the half-burned sigils, and the sense that Sebastian was accelerating illusions throughout Manhattan. Yet when the meal finished, Lila couldn't deny the gentle undercurrent of their closeness had grown unstoppable.

Caleb stood to clear the plates, then paused, gaze lingering on her. "You did well today," he said. "We faced illusions that skilled guardians would normally tackle in larger teams."

"Felt like I almost crumbled," she mumbled. "You saw how badly I slipped."

He returned the plates to the sink and stepped closer.

"You didn't crumble. You faced it, even when it felt impossible."

Her throat tightened. She was still sweaty, still heart-worn from the danger, yet a new tension filled the gap between them. The apartment carried the charge of unspoken emotion. She looked up into his steady gaze and felt the last of her walls break. When he brushed his thumb across her cheek, her heart leapt in anticipation.

"Lila," he murmured, voice just above a whisper.

She didn't wait for him to finish. She leaned in and pressed her lips to his. All the fear and adrenaline of the day poured into that single kiss, wild as a storm. His free hand slid around her waist, pulling her flush against him. The heady scent of basil still clung to her senses, mingling with the quiet hum of wards. He kissed her back with fervor, as though they were starved for the power of that tenderness.

They broke apart for only a breath. She saw the wariness in his eyes shift to hunger, and an answering thrill danced up her spine. He guided her toward his bedroom. She noted the subtle runic symbols on the doorframe that kept illusions from crossing the boundary, and her heart pounded with the realization that tonight, she wanted more than just the reassurance of safety. She wanted him.

Inside, the lights were low, the bed neatly made. Colors from the city's glow filtered through gaps in the blinds, painting drifting shapes over the walls. Caleb paused only to brush his thumbs across her flushed cheeks, and the sweetness in that gesture unraveled her composure. Their kisses deepened, slow yet insistent, each murmur between them a promise that brushed away the echoes of illusions.

He slipped off her jacket and tossed it aside. She tangled her fingers in his hair, responding to the heat that flared between them. The day's grime and tension fell away with every caress. When his lips found the curve of her neck, she gasped softly, her tensed muscles finally releasing. They undressed with trembling hands, laughter arising when she got momentarily tangled in her shirt. He helped with a gentleness that melted her lingering caution, the warmth of his hands stirring her pulse.

They sank onto the bed together, lost in each other's taste and touch. The sheets felt cool beneath her, contrasting the steady fire in her veins. She arched against him, reveling in the sensation of bare skin against skin. Each slow kiss carried an unspoken vow: they were safe here, illusions could not reach them, and neither would let go of the other without a fight. His hand trailed along her side, and she heard a soft sound escape her—a half-laugh, half-moan at how genuine this moment felt.

It was not frantic, although it teetered on urgent. Their movements guided one another deeper into the intimacy that grew each time they touched. Coherent thought dissolved. Lila let herself enjoy the way he whispered her name, how he held her as though she were the only real thing in a world built on illusions. She felt the strength of his arms, kinder than any magical barrier she had ever known.

When they finally came together, it was with breath-less determination, a meeting of desire and relief that pulsed through Lila's entire body. She clutched at his shoulders, lips parted in silent encouragement. The pleasure crashed in waves that tore her from the memory of dark corridors, anchoring her firmly in this safe, electric present.

THREE

Lila's shoulders ached as she trudged down the sidewalk, bracing herself for the early-morning bustle of Manhattan. Barely six hours had passed since she wrapped up a grueling round of late-night training, and the lack of decent rest tore at her ability to mask the telltale signs of exhaustion. Still, The Daily Grind needed opening, and she had rent looming at the end of the month. She forced her feet to keep moving, hoping the brisk pace would clear her mind.

She reached the café's chipped front door and stalled with the keys in her hand, noticing how her fingers trembled from fatigue. It took three tries to fit the key into the lock. She exhaled, pushing through a wave of dizziness, and stepped inside. The interior lights buzzed to life with a flick of the overhead switches. For an instant, the café looked harmless: rows of tables, battered wooden chairs, the clunky espresso station. The air smelled faintly of roasted beans and sugar. Yet tension coiled in her chest, just waiting to spark.

She dodged the crates of supplies Maya had ordered, letting them sit until she found the energy to organize them. With a grimace, she fired up the espresso machine. A hiss from its boiler echoed her own short fuse. "Please cooperate," she muttered, tapping a button to run a quick rinse cycle. The machine sputtered, then quieted to a gentle hum.

She inhaled deeply, resisting the urge to rub her eyes, which already felt gritty. Each small motion sent twinges through her arms and back, thanks to the rigorous illusions practice she'd endured. Caleb's voice from the night before still echoed in her memory—steady instructions to keep her hands raised and body centered whenever illusions jarred her. Though he'd insisted on calling it a "necessary step," she couldn't help feeling pushed to her limits. The city's illusions were multiplying, and the Council had made it abundantly clear that novices like her needed to adapt or risk letting Sebastian's infiltration overwhelm them.

The shop's open sign flickered to full brightness, and she sighed in relief that at least that piece of equipment still worked. Maybe, if she was lucky, she'd survive the morning rush without magic bursting into the open. Ten minutes later, the first customers trickled in: bleary-eyed office workers, an older woman with a black tote bag, a pair of college students studying on their phones. Lila greeted them with a strained smile, punching orders into the register and pulling shots of espresso with mechanical efficiency. She had done this dance for so long that her hands operated on muscle memory. Even so, her chest felt off-balance, and the faint tingle in her fingers suggested her magic was anything but calm.

The trouble began when the overhead lights started dimming in and out, a halting flicker that made customers glance upward. One woman frowned at the sudden brightness shift, but Lila hastened to play it off as a faulty circuit. She made a mental note to call the landlord, though her finances hardly covered repeated maintenance calls. Still, ignoring the malfunction was risky if illusions or raw magic were behind it.

As if on cue, a small flare of green light crackled at the base of the espresso machine. Lila almost dropped the pitcher of milk she was steaming. She clenched her teeth, struggling to impose calm on whatever magic flitted around her. The last thing she wanted was random illusions taking shape for everyone to see.

"It's probably just the wiring," she said to the startled man waiting for his latte. The words tasted like a lie. She knew the difference between a mundane glitch and the shift of magic bristling along her skin. The man gave her a skeptical look, but he accepted his drink and moved aside. Lila tried to slow her racing pulse. She hated feeling this close to losing control.

A few minutes later, the lights jerked off entirely, plunging the café into dim gloom. Customers exclaimed in confusion or mild alarm, and someone asked if the building had lost power. More flickers of green-sparking energy threaded near Lila's fingertips. She forced her hands behind the counter, out of sight. Anxiety made them tingle, threatening to betray the real cause. She couldn't afford a full-blown magical display in front of everyone.

She hurried to tap the circuit breaker switch on the wall, forcing the lights to hum back to life. "We've been having issues all week," Lila claimed in a louder voice, hoping no one pressed her further. She could hear the tremor in her laugh as she added, "Sorry for the inconvenience, folks."

Yet the tension in her gut climbed higher with each passing moment. The fluorescent tubes overhead resumed their normal brightness, only to waver again a few seconds later. Lila swallowed, aware that her presence under stress was making it worse. The illusions or magic swirling around her seemed to feed off her ragged state, prying at her emotional guard. She needed to settle herself or risk a spectacular meltdown in front of unsuspecting customers.

A new wave of arrivals jostled in, ordering cappuccinos and croissants. She plastered on a smile and forced her gaze anywhere but the flickering lights. She managed to serve four or five customers without incident, though a few cast worried glances around the café, unsettled by the repeated lighting shifts. Then, a startled gasp sounded from near the pastry display. Lila twisted to see a faint green spark dancing across the glass case.

"What the—" an older gentleman murmured, stepping back so abruptly he bumped into a table. Half of him looked intrigued, the other half leery. The spark vanished, leaving no scorch marks, but what settled was more damning than any physical evidence. She saw her reflection in the glass, eyes ringed by exhaustion.

Before the murmuring escalated, Lila slid over and drew the display's curtain, hiding the interior from view. She cleared her throat. "Electrical short," she said, voice wobbling. "I'm sorry for the inconvenience. We'll have to close for maintenance if it keeps happening."

Customers fidgeted. Some looked at the exit, apparently nervous. Another spark darted near the stacked espresso cups, and Lila's heart lurched. She realized that no amount of half-truth was going to keep this calm if the flickers kept leaping across corners of the café. She could try to will her magic into submission—Caleb had taught her a few grounding techniques—but controlling this mounting energy felt like trying to dam a rushing tide.

An embarrassed heat flushed her cheeks. She hurried around the counter, forcing a polite smile at a cluster of confused patrons. "I'm sorry," she repeated, louder. "There's a... well... an electrical surge we need to address." She inwardly cursed that the Council wards meant to protect The Daily Grind from random illusions had clearly faltered. Possibly the city's entire magical infrastructure was diminishing under Sebastian's trickery. If the wards were trembling, no place in Manhattan was guaranteed stable anymore.

Uneasy with the crowd's stares, she made her decision. "We need to close early for repairs," she announced, ignoring the pang of lost income. "Everyone, please feel free to take your drinks on the house if you haven't paid yet."

Protests murmured through the crowd, but curiosity and mild alarm helped usher them out. One or two demanded an explanation, though Lila dodged specifics, chalking it up to a hazard that required immediate attention. Inside, her stomach churned at how easily illusions might keep escalating to the point that her café—her last link to normalcy—could become a spectacle. The cost to her finances weighed on her, but she refused to risk her patrons' safety.

When the door finally clicked shut behind the last customer, Lila exhaled in a trembling rush. The emptiness of the café felt hollow. She slumped against the counter, resting her forehead on her forearm. She watched the overhead lights sputter and realized she was likely the cause. She reached for calm as best she could, steadying her breathing the way Caleb had coached: slow inhales, controlled exhales. Eventually, the flickers died down a little, leaving only a faint buzz of tension in her limbs.

Her phone vibrated in her apron pocket, but she ignored it. She didn't have the energy to talk to anyone, not even Maya if she was texting some question about the new pastry order. Instead, she busied herself with an attempt to tidy the counter, wiping away stray drips of milk and scattered coffee beans. The repetitive motion helped ground her, each swipe of the cloth a reminder that life could still be normal if only illusions would leave her alone.

She had just turned to check the front door when she

sensed a stirring of magic from the entrance. Her pulse spiked. For one dizzying second, she feared Sebastian or some twisted specter had come to taunt her. Then she saw Caleb's tall figure through the glass. He let himself in silently, his deep blue eyes scanning the shop. Relief and exasperation clashed in Lila's chest. She shot him a tired stare, trying not to snap. It wasn't his fault she was this strung out, but her patience was nearly gone.

"Are you okay?" he asked softly, voice gentle as he flicked his gaze from the half-dimmed overhead lights to the shuttered pastry case.

She set down the cloth with a thump. "Define okay," she said in a brittle tone.

His mouth curved in a sympathetic frown, and he approached her, crossing the empty café to lay a careful hand on her shoulder. Warmth radiated from his touch in a subtle wave, and for an instant, she felt the illusion-laced tension recede. He leaned in and pressed a soft kiss to her temple, the brush of his lips a silent show of support.

"You're running on fumes," he said, worry shadowing his eyes. "Marcus told me you'd had a rough night, but I didn't realize it was this bad."

She let out a short, humorless laugh. "Rough? I can't keep the lights on for ten minutes without them flickering like some haunted carnival ride. A random spark danced across the pastries. I had to close the shop, probably losing another day's worth of sales I can't afford. Meanwhile, illusions are swirling around the city. And the wards—"

She cut herself off, aware that frustration edged her

voice to near desperation. Caleb's brow furrowed. He shifted his hand from her shoulder to the back of her neck, a tender gesture that made her eyes prickle with sudden emotion. She had grown used to his stoic calm, but right now she needed that reassurance. For a moment, she let herself indulge in the closeness, inhaling the faint mix of soap and ward incense that lingered on his jacket.

"I know," he said quietly. "The wards are trembling everywhere, not just here. We're seeing illusions bloom in random places with no clear pattern. It's getting harder for watchers to keep track. Some suspect Sebastian's stepping up his infiltration. Others think he's just testing how much the Council can handle." He paused, seeing how her hands clenched into fists at her sides. "You don't have to handle this alone."

She offered a shaky nod. "It just feels like everything is unraveling, and I'm stuck trying to keep it together with duct tape and excuses about faulty wiring."

He released a soft exhale and glanced around. Even with the shop emptied, the tension felt thick as soup. "I can place a temporary ward here, if it helps until we figure out a more permanent fix."

She nodded again, relieved. "Thanks. I'd appreciate that."

They walked toward the corner behind the counter, where he rummaged for a piece of white chalk, etched with small runic symbols. He knelt and drew a circle on the floor, murmuring a series of protective incantations under his breath. The air tingled as pale blue lines of magic traced outward from the chalk lines, radiating across the threshold where customers normally stood. Lila swallowed, noticing how the overhead lights flickered once and then stilled.

She whispered, "That's better."

She watched him rise, brushing chalk dust from his hand. The swirl of wards left a faint shimmer in the air that only she or another magic user might notice. Having a barrier between the outside world and her raw, unsteady power made it easier to breathe. She wished she could lock up illusions the same way, but Sebastian's infiltration was far too widespread for one simple ward circle to repel completely.

Finally, she pulled off her apron and folded it with more force than necessary, tossing it on the counter. A pang of guilt flashed through her at the knowledge that closing early would slash into her already tight finances. But she couldn't keep scaring her customers. Even if no illusions ignited again today, rumors had already started swirling. She'd probably have to offer a discount or a free coffee tomorrow to smooth things over with her regulars.

Caleb's eyes flickered with concern, and he offered a quiet, "We'll find a way. The Council's crisis aside, you shouldn't have to watch your livelihood crumble."

She shrugged, forcing a half-smile. "I'll manage. Right now, it's probably the least of my worries, but it still sucks." She tried to release some tension by rubbing her forehead, only to realize how clammy her skin felt.

He stepped closer and wrestled gently with the urge to pull her into a firmer embrace. She relented, resting her cheek against his chest for a moment. The steady rhythm of his heartbeat slowed the pounding in her ears. That moment of warmth steadied her more than any ward or circuit-breaker fix.

A muffled rattle from the street outside drew her attention to the front windows. In the daylight, she noticed a faint glow dancing several blocks away, swirling just over a distant storefront. Her stomach lurched at the sign of illusions creeping around the neighborhood. She squeezed her eyes shut, bleak acceptance settling in. "They're everywhere," she muttered. "I swear, I can't walk five minutes without seeing or sensing illusions these days."

Caleb's hand slid to her arm, his grip reassuring. "The city's magical infrastructure is fraying, so illusions spread. Sebastian likely wants to push us until something snaps. He's counting on the wards failing so the Council is left scrambling."

She clenched her jaw. "Why can't he give the city a break?" She knew how naive that sounded. Sebastian seemed intent on toppling the old system piece by piece, sowing discord in the process. But the question slipped out, raw frustration leaking through.

Caleb responded with a gentle shush, brushing a second kiss across her temple. "I wish it could be that simple. But you and I both know he won't stop until he either gets what he wants or we knock him down."

She raised her chin, letting her anger burn bright enough to chase away her lingering weariness. "We will stop him. He isn't cornered yet, but neither are we." Her voice sounded bolder than she felt, but the fleeting spark of conviction steadied her.

She glanced around the café, noticing how quiet it was without the usual midday chatter. Instead, the air felt charged, as if illusions might creep under the windowsills at any moment. Her attention drifted back to the swirling glow in the distance. She remembered the scalding dread from earlier as green sparks leapt across the espresso machine, threatening to out her secrets to unsuspecting locals. If illusions weren't contained, she'd have to do more than close early. She'd risk losing everything she'd built.

Caleb's arm tightened around her in a supportive squeeze. "You're not alone, Lila," he murmured. "We'll face this together, no matter how many illusions spring up."

She sighed, letting herself accept the comfort of his words. At least for a moment, it staved off the lingering fear that the wards were only a temporary patch on a dam about to break. "I hope we have enough time," she said, voice subdued. "Because if these wards collapse, the whole city might see more than just flickers of party lights. And Sebastian—he's waiting for that chance."

Caleb gave her a solemn nod. "Then we'll keep searching for better ways to reinforce the wards and track him. Marcus is ramping up the watch squads, and we have some leads on how illusions are piggybacking through the city's old networks."

She brushed her hand against the neckline of her shirt, where the small silver amulet—the heirloom from her grandmother—rested just out of sight. Its subtle warmth reminded her that she did have a trump card for illusions, if only she could refine her control. But that kind of advanced synergy with her family's magic needed time, and time was exactly what Sebastian seemed intent on denying them.

She stilled, noticing again the faint shimmer of illusions dancing across the building across the street. The swirl of color looked almost pretty—like auroras in broad daylight. Yet the sight made her stomach twist, a nagging reminder that the magical realm was inching closer to open chaos. Caleb followed her gaze, and she sensed his worry doubling her own.

"Come on," he said softly, coaxing her hand into his. "Let's get some air. You can lock up, and then we'll figure out the next step."

She hesitated, scanning the café with a hollow ache. Closing early was the right decision, but it felt like a small defeat. The financial hit wouldn't be crippling yet, but if illusions kept interfering, she wasn't sure how she would bounce back. Still, there was no point lingering.

"All right," she whispered, and she escorted him to the front door. She locked it, her key rattling in the deadbolt. Outside, the midday sun was brighter than she expected, the city's noise continuing seconds after she stepped onto the sidewalk. A warm breeze carried the smell of car exhaust, pretzels from a street cart, and beneath all that, the faint metallic tang of magic. She glanced at Caleb, uneasy.

He traced a thumb over her knuckles. "We'll rally," he

said, a quiet promise in his tone. "Don't let this break your resolve."

"I won't," she answered, despite the shaky note in her voice. The closeness of him gave her courage, even as she spotted swirling illusions far above. Neon wisps coiled at the edges of an old office building, like drifting ribbons waiting to pounce on unsuspecting watchers. She recognized the signs of advanced illusions—spectral shapes that changed color in slow pulsations. Part of her wanted to look away, to pretend none of this was real, but it wouldn't help.

She raised her gaze, meeting his concerned eyes. "I'm just... tired. Sometimes it feels like the entire city wants to tumble into chaos, and all I have is a bunch of wards and a half-baked skill set."

He squeezed her hand. "You've got more than that. You have determination. You have that family heritage, your grandmother's wisdom, your own instincts. And you have me."

A hesitant smile touched her lips at his sincerity. "Thanks for reminding me. I just wish I could make it all stop. The illusions, the suspicion, the city on edge..."

Caleb wrapped an arm around her shoulders, guiding her away from the closed café door. "It'll ease once we figure out Sebastian's next move. We're making progress, even if it doesn't feel like it."

She nodded. Together, they began walking down the sidewalk, leaving The Daily Grind's flickering lights and swirling anxieties behind. She couldn't ignore the sense that illusions were creeping in from every direction, but for a moment, the comforting feel of Caleb's arm buoyed her spirits. With each step, they put distance between themselves and the café's confusion. Yet that distant glow of illusions never faded. It only deepened, painting the side of the building ahead with unnatural shades of green and violet.

Lila swallowed. The city's wards were trembling more than ever. If the Nexus Prism remained out there—still feeding Sebastian's illusions—then time was running short. She squared her shoulders, allowing the swirl of fear and anger to fuel her resolve.

Caleb seemed to read the tension in her rigid posture. He leaned close to whisper, "We'll face it together, remember?"

She offered a firm nod, though dread lingered in her mind. Together or not, they had to act fast. The illusions' presence loomed like a storm cloud on the verge of unleashing havoc. With the city's magical infrastructure wavering, they couldn't afford many more close calls. If these illusions spread unchecked, if Sebastian pushed even harder, the wards might dissolve completely. And then everyday life in Manhattan would shatter.

She looked up at Caleb, who gave her a reassuring smile that didn't fully mask his own worry. The remains of her tension flared again, reminding her of how quickly everything could fall apart. She exhaled sharply, clinging to the hope that they would find a solution before the illusions claimed the upper hand. Despite their shared fatigue, they both recognized the looming stakes.

He brushed a final, soft kiss across her temple as they

turned a corner. "We'll do whatever it takes," he said. "We won't let him tear the city down."

In her chest, her heart pounded with a mixture of exhaustion and fragile determination. She curled her fingers around his and held on. No matter how precarious the situation felt, she refused to let Sebastian's illusions snuff out her resolve. Beneath that unwavering resolve, though, lay the gnawing truth: if the wards collapsed, the entire magical veil would crumble, leaving them—and the city—utterly exposed. She and Caleb would need every ounce of skill and courage to stand a chance.

She nodded at him, words escaping in a hollow laugh. "We've got a mess, but we'll keep going."

Lila emerged from Caleb's apartment in a flush of early sunlight, warmth still lingering in her cheeks. Her heart thrummed with the afterglow of a sweet, secret night and the promise that maybe life would not always revolve around illusions and Council tensions. She still felt the faint press of his lips from the hurried goodbye at the door. Despite everything happening in the city, that kiss grounded her in a sense of normalcy—fleeting, yes, but potent enough to make her feel brave.

She adjusted the strap of her worn messenger bag, determined to get to The Daily Grind on time for once. The city's usual clamor rose from the streets, mingling with the sounds of nearby buses and a chorus of impatient car horns. Even in the bustle, subtle traces of magic prickled along her arms, a caution she could not entirely dismiss. She wove through clusters of pedestrians in front of the historic New Yorker Hotel, stepping onto the sidewalk with her mind already halfway to the café. She scolded herself for letting the swirl of romance distract her from the city's dangers.

Yet the steadiness she felt leaving Caleb's apartment still made her smile. She pictured the way his hair fell across his forehead when he was too exhausted to lock it back. She recalled the kindness in his eyes as he asked if she felt safe to walk alone. She had teased him for being overprotective, but deep down she appreciated his concern. That memory glowed in her chest, driving away the chilly morning air.

But as soon as she reached a less crowded block, the air changed. The noise of the city dimmed unnaturally, as though muffled by an invisible hand. The bright sunshine dimmed in her peripheral vision. She slowed, turning in a small half-circle to see if something was wrong behind her. Concrete buildings, shops, and the swirl of normal Manhattan life continued, but there was a smear at the edges like a painting left in the rain.

Her pulse skittered. This felt like the illusions she had battled under Grand Central, where reality warped at an instant's notice. She gripped her messenger bag tighter, stepping carefully into the middle of the sidewalk, scanning the vicinity for any shimmer of conjured magic. People still rushed by, but they seemed oddly oblivious, as if they looked past her. A prickle of dread rose on her neck.

In a single disorienting blink, the cityscape twisted into a stretch of pitch-black gloom. It was as if the bustling street had been swallowed by a void. Her breath caught, and she lost all sense of direction. One moment, she stood beneath a bright morning sky; the next, she was caged in darkness so thick it weighed on her lungs. Her own heartbeat drummed louder than the faint echoes of traffic and footsteps—now muted and distant.

She tried to whisper a ward, "Abscindo illusio," shaping the phrase carefully, but her words echoed back, vanishing into a black haze. A cage of illusions pressed in from all angles, crushing the last anchor points of the real world. She felt her feet grow unsteady as though the ground itself might fall from beneath her. Pressure pounded in her ears.

Fear trickled in, unbidden. Her training with Caleb had taught her that illusions this potent did not spring from inexperience. Someone skilled—and malicious—had targeted her. Her mind flashed to Sebastian's cunning illusions. But was Sebastian here, or had he sent a hidden accomplice? She forced herself to concentrate.

She tried to recall the grounding technique that Caleb repeatedly drilled into her. Settle your breath. Remember what is stable and real. She planted her feet, despite the sense of emptiness under them. Her fingertips tingled with awakened earth magic, urging her to find a connection in a place that felt stripped of life. Her hands shook, but she closed her eyes and pictured tactile details: the grain of the sidewalk, the faint ridges in the concrete, the texture of a broken curb somewhere nearby. An echo of real ground surfaced in her mind.

For a moment, the pressure eased. Then an abrupt laugh coiled through the darkness. It was low, silky, and undeniably familiar. Sebastian's voice, mocking and calm, drifted as though from a great distance. Her stomach twisted. She heard him whisper her name with an amused lilt, as if welcoming her to this private show of illusions. He urged her to surrender, claiming the shadow was stronger than anything her earth magic could muster.

She pressed her lips together, refusing to feed her fear. She recalled how Caleb had once told her to channel her power through her hands and summon a barrier like a living ripple of energy. Doubt clawed at her, but she forced it aside.

Green sparks flickered along the insides of her wrists as she pulled in a deep breath. She visualized vines emerging from within her pulse, weaving outward in a protective shell. Her nails bit into her palms. Slowly, a faint glimmer of emerald light formed around her hands. It wasn't a brush of quick magic. It was raw potential, built on the knowledge that illusions, no matter how vivid, were still illusions.

The swirling gloom intensified, pressing at her shoulders, her chest, her throat. Her breath caught, and she felt a vertiginous drop in the pit of her stomach. Panicked, she almost lost focus, teetering on the edge of giving in to that sinister laughter that seemed to taunt her from all sides. But her stubborn streak flared, fueled by her frustration that Sebastian dared to threaten her so boldly. She refused to yield.

Green light burst from her palms in a sharp flare. She thrust her arms forward, fingers splayed wide. Magic roared up like a wildfire through a dry forest. The emerald glow collided with the blackness, and she sensed the illusions shred under its force. She pictured it like a physical wave, tearing through the void, ripping apart Sebastian's layered conjurations until they peeled away from her body.

The void cracked into strands of half-formed shadows. She almost wavered, but she clenched her jaw and focused her mind on the sidewalk. A stinging pressure flared at her temples when a final surge of illusions tried to suffocate her from behind. She gasped, forcing her magic to spin around her like a shield. A swirl of bright green sparkles fanned out, and in a sudden whoosh of displaced air, the darkness crumpled.

She stumbled to one knee, blinking rapidly as sunlight invaded her vision. The pounding of the city's real noise returned, jarring her senses after the illusions cape. Still dizzy, she forced in a shaky breath. Passersby stepped around her, several halting to ask if she was all right, but their voices blurred, as though her mind couldn't process them quickly enough.

"Lila!" Caleb's voice cut through the confusion, snapping her back to reality. In the next moment, he was beside her, panting. His wide eyes skimmed her face, and his wards shimmered around them in a faint circle of runes. She realized that heavy illusions still clung to the corners of the block, but his presence calmed them with swirling lines of magical script.

"You—" she started, throat too constricted to speak more.

He gripped her arm, hoisting her up with a gentleness that contradicted the alarm etched into his features. "Are you hurt?" he demanded, eyes never leaving hers.

She shook her head, coughing out a half-laugh sharp with leftover panic. "No, I think—no, not hurt." Her body trembled from the adrenaline that still coursed through her veins. "Someone attacked me. The illusions were thick, so thick I could barely breathe."

He nodded grimly. "I felt the surge of dark magic halfway down the street. It was like a beacon." His voice shook just enough to reveal how worried he had been. "I got here as fast as I could."

She realized she was clutching at his sleeve with white-knuckled intensity. She released him, flushing at her obvious desperation, and took a moment to steady her stance. Her lungs still caught on every breath, as if the illusions had carved a groove in her airflow.

A faint ripple of leftover conjurations wavered at the curb, distorting the edges of a lamppost. Caleb flicked his wrist, sending a faint ward that dissolved the final threads of false blackness. Her ear still rang with phantom echoes of Sebastian's laughter, but the city's real sound returned in full force. An approaching taxi honked. A street vendor pitched the name of his pretzels. The world spun briefly, then settled.

He nudged her away from the crowd, guiding her toward the gap between two buildings, where an old, barred doorway offered a slice of privacy. She leaned against the chipped brick, forcing her lungs to cooperate. Tension coiled in her chest. She let her eyes drift shut, remembering how it had felt to have her reality overwritten by pitch darkness. It rattled her in more ways than she cared to admit.

Caleb pressed a hand to her shoulder. "Look at me," he murmured. She obeyed, meeting his gaze. "Focus on something that's real." His fingertips brushed her cheek, warmth steadying her. "You drove it back. That was your own power, your barrier. Remember that."

She exhaled shakily. "I do. It was just—" Her voice cracked before she could finish. She realized that tears pricked at the corners of her eyes, a mixture of fury and relief. "He was in my head again," she whispered, hating the vulnerability in her tone.

Caleb's face hardened at the mention of Sebastian. His arm slid around her, and she let him hold her for a few seconds, pressing her forehead to the coarse fabric of his jacket. The busy city rumbled around them, but for that moment, all that mattered was regaining the steadiness illusions had tried to steal.

"You did well," he said softly. "I swear we will stop him."

She nodded, letting a quiet wave of gratitude wash over her. Every muscle still felt tinged with tremors, but the knowledge that her earth magic had stood firm brought a flicker of pride. She was not helpless. She recalled the times Caleb had coached her on how to anchor illusions to something tangible, how to coax power from the city's very bones. She had done just that now, even as her fear threatened to swallow her.

He pulled back slightly, letting his arm settle around her waist. "Your hands," he said, tilting his head. "They're shaking."

"I know," she answered, trying to laugh it off. "I'll be

fine." But the quiver persisted, coursing through her fingers until she tucked them against her coat pockets. "I just need to come down from that rush. It felt like everything was collapsing."

They paused in shared silence. Concern flickered in his gaze. She expected him to coax her into going home, or to the Council, but he surprised her by saying, "That was Sebastian's magic. He wants to corner you, to exploit your fear. I cannot let that happen. I have to stop him for good."

She swallowed hard. "He singled me out, Caleb. I recognized his voice, but I still don't know if he was physically here. It might have been a projection, or someone under his command."

She spotted how he clenched his jaw. "Regardless, it is too close for comfort." A swirl of frustration laced his tone as he glanced toward the street. "We do not know who might be lurking nearby." Then his expression softened. "I love you. I need you to know that no matter what illusions he summons."

Her breath caught at the quiet weight of those words. Her heart thudded in her chest with an almost dizzying sense of relief that, after so much tension, he had voiced it plainly. She felt the fragile silence between them—an acceptance of something she had been certain of in her heart but hearing him say it still felt electrifying. Her lips parted, questions mingling with gratitude and unspoken warmth. Then she saw how his eyes shifted with determination.

He inhaled, each syllable sounding pained but resolute. "I have to find Sebastian. He grows bolder every day, and if I do not track him soon, these illusions will only get worse. I need to keep you safe. The best way is to stop him at the source."

Her entire body tensed at the thought of him going after Sebastian alone, yet she heard the unyielding ring of necessity in his voice. She closed her eyes briefly, torn between wanting to protest and knowing he was right. She forced her fingers to release the tight grip they had on his sleeve, though anxiety flooded every corner of her chest.

"Go," she whispered, voice unsteady. "Find him before it's too late."

FIVE

Lila pushed through the front doors of The Daily Grind with leaden limbs and a raw ache in her lungs, as though the claustrophobic illusions still clung to her every breath. The cacophony of espresso machines and squeaking shoes welcomed her, but each familiar sound felt strained through a haze. Over the course of the day, customers came and went in their usual rush-hour waves, yet something in the café's electric hum felt off-kilter. She tried to hide her trembling hands behind the register, but every now and then, she saw the worried expressions from coworkers who had known her too long to miss the tension in her posture.

The smell of fresh coffee grounds normally comforted her. Today, the dark roast's bold fragrance churned in her stomach, stirring queasiness instead of calm. She steeled herself to greet the next customer in line, forcing her lips into a half-hearted smile as she rung up a latte. Her gaze snapped to the corner of the café at the slightest flash of movement. Nothing suspicious lingered there now, but the memory of illusions that could twist shadows haunted her thoughts.

"Lila, are you alright?" asked Kelly, another barista they had just hired. Her tone was hesitant, as though tiptoeing around a deeper concern.

"I'm fine," Lila lied. She adjusted the apron strings at her waist. "Just not sleeping well, I guess."

Kelly studied her with open concern, but a flood of impatient customers prevented any deeper questioning. Lila clung to the nearest distraction, busying herself with the espresso machine. She felt relief that Kelly's shift would end soon, meaning fewer questioning eyes on her. That relief mingled with the unyielding heaviness in her chest. She had never liked lying. She hated it to her core, but explaining illusions to a coworker—especially illusions that threatened to shatter everything if they got out of control—seemed impossible.

She finished steaming milk for a cappuccino, wincing when a bit of froth splattered on her hand. The sting registered a heartbeat late, like her body was lagging behind her mind. She wiped it off with a clean rag, ignoring the twinge of pain, and tried to focus on the next order. Yet the memory of swirling darkness felt lodged behind her eyes. All day, she worked on autopilot, half-expecting an illusion to materialize around the pastry display. Whenever she glimpsed her reflection in the glass case, she saw faint bruises peeking out near the collar of her shirt—remnants of that frantic struggle to break free of illusions. She tugged the fabric higher, hoping no one else noticed.

As late afternoon approached, the steady rush of patrons thinned. A few stragglers remained, tapping on laptops or scrolling through endless messages on their phones. The café's lights took on a softer glow just before dusk, and the sounds dulled to clinking spoons and occasional footsteps. Lila wiped the counter and started the closing routine, chasing away crumbs that barely existed. Being left mostly alone in the shop made her hyper-alert; she had no desire to face an ambush. She exhaled slowly, reminding herself that illusions had no reason to target a mundane coffee shop today—at least not if she kept her head down.

She glanced at the back hallway. Maya would still be finishing inventory in the storeroom. They had barely spoken all day, except for a few clipped exchanges. Conflict stirred in Lila's chest whenever she pictured Maya's furrowed brows and concerned questions. Maya knew something was wrong. Lila felt that knowledge like a weight she could scarcely carry.

An older couple approached the counter, and she forced a friendlier expression. She took their takeaway orders—an herbal tea and a caramel latte—trying to seem normal. If they noticed the strain in her smile, they gave no sign. After she handed over the cups, they wandered out the door, whispering quietly to each other. Lila's shoulders slumped as soon as they turned away. How long could she keep up the pretense that everything was fine?

Eventually, she turned the sign on the door to "Closed". The café was quiet, save for the low hum of overhead lights. The silence pressed against her eardrums like something tangible, refusing to let her pretend anymore.

She grabbed her phone from beneath the counter, noticing no missed calls. She tried not to dwell on the frustration that Caleb hadn't shown up, but her mind still flickered with the concern that illusions might have rattled him too. With a clumsy press, she locked her phone's screen and pocketed it, reminding herself that their connection didn't require constant reassurance. He was probably occupied with Council details that she hadn't even begun to understand. Still, she couldn't push away the longing to feel him at her side the way he had been in that final rush of illusions. She was too tired to talk herself out of the comfort his presence offered.

She sauntered toward the dusty storeroom to fetch more cleaning supplies, but the moment she pushed open the door, she saw Maya waiting inside, arms folded, eyes already locked on her.

"Hey," Lila said with a weak attempt at casualness. "You were taking inventory, right? Need help with anything?"

Maya shook her head, expression grim. "No, I'm done. Now, I need you to tell me what the hell is going on."

Lila froze in the doorway. The small storeroom was cramped, with stacked boxes of coffee beans and paper cups lining the shelves. A faint fluorescent light overhead gave the space a harsh glare. Maya's stance bristled with determination, and her tone left no room for small talk. The door clicked shut behind Lila, sealing them in near silence.

Lila glanced over her shoulder, suddenly worried someone else might listen in. But they were alone in the café. She swallowed hard and stepped farther into the storeroom.

"You look like you've been in a fistfight with shadows," Maya said, her voice tight. "And I can't just smile and act like nothing's wrong. You're jumpy, you've been bruised all week, your eyes are red, and—" She inhaled sharply, pain flickering across her face. "You vanish at odd hours with no explanation. Today, you can hardly keep your balance. Lila, I am not an idiot."

The earnest concern in Maya's eyes nearly broke Lila's composure. She pressed her lips together, rummaging for a half-truth that might satisfy her friend. Guilt weighed heavy on her chest. The two of them had been close since Lila's first day at The Daily Grind, when Maya taught her how to froth milk properly. They had joked with each other through lost pay checks and broken machines. Lying—truly lying—felt like a betrayal she couldn't sustain.

"Maya..." Lila's voice cracked. She balled her hands into fists at her sides, forcing herself to meet Maya's gaze. "I'm sorry. I wanted to explain, but—"

"You wanted to explain, but you didn't." Maya's jaw clenched, voice trembling with concern rather than anger. "That means it's big. You're scaring me."

"I..." Lila's pulse hammered as she took a step closer. She glanced at the shelves, gaze momentarily landing on a box labeled with the café's brand of coffee beans. She needed to keep calm, to keep her voice steady. "It's dangerous," she admitted at last, though every oath she had taken with the Council shouted warnings in her head. She sensed her vow pressing on her lungs, telling her to be careful with her words.

Maya's hand tightened around the edge of a cardboard box. "Dangerous how? Are you mixed up with criminals? Because if so, let me remind you that I have an aunt who works for the DA's office—"

"No, it's not that," Lila interrupted, appreciating Maya's fierce protectiveness but knowing this was not the typical kind of threat one could nail down with a simple legal approach. She inhaled slowly, trying to calm her galloping heart. "I wish it was something normal like that, but it's... complicated. People are messing with me, threatening me—and others—because apparently I'm part of something I never knew existed."

Maya's dark eyes widened, alarm flickering there. "So, that guy who turns up, is hurting you?"

The memory of illusions so tangible that they nearly choked her resurged, twisting her stomach. She closed her eyes briefly, forcing composure before responding. "No, not him. He is actually my protector and now my lover. I can't explain every detail, but I swear I'm not involved in anything illegal. It's more... a family thing, I guess. Something old that's catching up to me."

Maya studied her, worry carving lines in her brow. She reached out and gently tapped Lila's arm. "Don't lie to protect me. If you're in danger, I want to help."

"I'm not lying," Lila said, voice trembling despite her effort at calm. "I'm telling you what I can. I found out some stuff about who I am—about my family. Turns out some people want to use that for their own ends." She paused, lips pressed together. "That's why I'm so jumpy. I don't know when they might come after me again."

She couldn't dare mention illusions or the Council by name, not when the vow she'd signed clearly prohibited revealing the magical realm outright to a civilian. Even so, Maya deserved something tangible. Lila tried to gauge what the minimal truth looked like without crossing the line. "I ended up in over my head," she continued, voice low. "There's a group—people with power, let's call it. I stumbled onto something they need, and they've been showing up to intimidate me. Sometimes... the intimidation gets physical."

Lila's cheeks burned with guilt at the half-baked explanation. But Maya's expression had already sharpened into something fierce. "Physical? As in, they laid hands on you?" She glanced at Lila's bruises. "Why haven't you called the police?"

"It's not the kind of thing the police can solve," Lila said. She hated how hollow it sounded. "Not easily, anyway. These people slip away before they can be caught. They're... good at hiding."

Maya's grip on Lila's arm tightened. "That's all I need to know. They're hurting you. So, I'm not letting you face them alone."

"Maya, please," Lila whispered, tears threatening to surface. "You don't understand—this is dangerous stuff. Some of them are unbelievably strong. I would never forgive myself if something happened to you."

Maya's eyes flared with resolve. "And what about me

never forgiving myself if I stood by and did nothing? You think I'm going to walk away, let you get bruised and shaken by these creeps? No." She clenched her fists. "You're my best friend, Lila. I don't care if this is some top-secret business or the next apocalypse. You don't get rid of me just by telling me it's dangerous."

Lila's breath caught, relief colliding with apprehension. She wanted to protest, to remind Maya that illusions —which she couldn't even describe properly—could swallow them both. Yet her chest clenched at the unconditional loyalty in Maya's voice. Lila's entire body trembled, and she placed a hand on Maya's shoulder, meeting that unwavering gaze.

"I never wanted to shut you out," Lila said, voice soft. "I hated doing it. I just... it's not something I can talk about freely. I'm sorry."

Maya's features softened at Lila's obvious distress. She glanced around the cramped storeroom, stacked with coffee supplies and cleaning detergents that smelled faintly of bleach. "Look, if there's more you can't tell me, I won't push for details." She swallowed hard, frustration briefly marring her expression. "But I want you safe, and if that means taking a few extra steps, so be it. Hell, let me walk you home every night. I'll do it."

The mirrored devotion in Maya's words overwhelmed Lila with gratitude. In that shivery moment, she realized just how badly she had needed an ally who wasn't tangled up in cloaked rituals or grand illusions—someone normal, but fierce. Tears threatened at the corners of her eyes. She blinked them away, refusing to give in to raw emotion.

"Maya..." she began. She hesitated, then forced the next words out. "I've gotten mixed up in some dangerous stuff... I can't say everything, but people are messing with me."

Her friend's voice wavered with heartbreak and anger. "I hate the idea of you facing them alone. I only know a fraction of whatever this is, but I'm not leaving you."

Lila's throat tightened. She recalled the vow of secrecy echoing in her mind, as if the Council's eyes were every-where. Her gaze darted to the storeroom door. No illusions lurked there—only the skeleton of a normal workday that had finally ended. Should she push Maya away for her own protection? That instinct warred with the desperate need to keep her closest friend close. If illusions struck again, having someone watch Lila's back might prove priceless. Yet the thought of Maya stepping into that dark-ness made Lila's stomach churn with dread.

Maya must have sensed the conflict in her eyes. She wrapped warm fingers around Lila's wrist. "Hey. I'm not going anywhere," she said in a quiet vow. "If these 'dan-gerous people' come for you, they'll meet my wrath too. Got it?"

A short laugh escaped Lila's lips, sounding more like a sob. Relief crashed through her, mingled with the gnawing realization that Maya still had no clue how bad it really was. But Maya's kindness was a lifeline, anchoring Lila to a semblance of normal friendship. For a heartbeat, the storeroom's fluorescent lights felt less harsh and more hopeful.

She placed her hand over Maya's, nodding firmly. "Got

it. Thank you." Her voice shook. She exhaled her gratitude, letting herself savor the promise of not being alone. If illusions or threats came next time, at least she had a friend who refused to disappear at the first sign of trouble.

Maya looked ready to hurl curses at any invisible menace that dared to harm Lila. She set her jaw, fiery resolve in her eyes. Lila recognized that unwavering stance from the many times Maya had fended off rowdy customers or cocky street vendors. Maybe this was the kind of loyalty that transcended the lines of magical and mundane, the spark that made Lila believe she could still protect people worth protecting.

She still felt the oath's pressure in her chest and the swirl of guilt for withholding multiple truths, but for now, it had to be enough. As the storeroom's light buzzed quietly above them and the scents of cardboard and cleaning fluid hung in the air, Maya's vow seemed as solid as any ward Lila had tried to conjure in recent days.

Lila swiped the back of her hand across her eyes. "I'm sorry I've worried you," she murmured. "I'll... keep you updated the best I can, okay?"

"I'll hold you to that," Maya replied. She brushed stray hair out of Lila's face, studying her bruises with a grimace. "First, we'll get you cleaned up. Then, if you want, I'll walk you home."

Lila's cheeks warmed. She gave a small nod, her limbs too drained to argue. Outside, the hum of the city persisted, muffled by the coffee shop's glass doors. A flicker of worry that illusions might lurk in the night shadows still pricked at her nerves, but Maya's unshake-able presence steadied her.

They walked out of the storeroom side by side, switching off the lights behind them. The café itself appeared oddly tranquil—rows of empty tables, chairs stacked along the walls, the overhead bulbs casting a gentle glow. Lila felt the day's tension linger like a dull ache beneath her ribcage, but new resolve mingled with her apprehension. She had told Maya the partial truth, enough to share the burden. If the illusions came for her again, she would not stand alone in silence.

They paused at the doorway, trash bags and cleaning tools piled in a neat corner. Maya locked up behind them. The final clang of the gate over the entrance rattled into place, and night air brushed Lila's face with a gentle chill. The streetlights stretched across the damp pavement, and the usual hum of traffic flowed in the distance.

Maya's features hardened again. "You're sure you're alright to walk? I can sign us up for a rideshare if you want."

Lila inhaled, letting a shaky smile curl the edge of her mouth. "No, I'm good now that I have my best friend here. Let's go." She forced her shoulders back, ignoring how the bruises protested.

Maya looped an arm around Lila's. Lila's steps felt a bit steadier with her friend clinging at her side. The vow that Maya would stand by her throbbed in the back of Lila's mind, and she wondered if she deserved such loyalty when she couldn't share the full truth. For better or worse, Maya had made her choice, and Lila could only accept it with gratitude and a faint, quivering hope that it might be enough.

She cast one final glance at the closed café, recalling the illusions that had shaken her earlier in the day. The memory still raised goosebumps along her arms, but now she had Maya's voice echoing in her thoughts. If these dangerous people come for you, they'll face me too.

The promise stirred warmth in Lila's chest that no illusions could douse. She squeezed Maya's arm to convey silent thanks. Deep down, she knew her best friend had only touched the tip of a very sinister iceberg. That knowledge sent a tremor through her, but in the quiet glow of a streetlamp, she found enough courage to keep walking.

CHAPTER
SIX

The next day, Lila's phone buzzed late in the afternoon, just as she tried, and failed, to steady her nerves behind the café's pastry case. Her heart lifted the instant she saw Caleb's name flicker on the screen. She quickly excused herself from the front counter, ignoring a coworker's quizzical look, and ducked into the storage closet to answer.

"Come to my place," Caleb said, his voice low. "I know it's last minute, but I'd like to see you."

Relief mingled with anticipation. Lila had been hoping for exactly this invitation all morning, itching for a reason to slip away from the humdrum routine of The Daily Grind. After telling Maya she was going to meet Caleb, she left early and hopped the subway, bracing for potential illusions in any corner of the city. Yet the trip passed without incident, and soon she was standing at the handsome door of Caleb's apartment in the New Yorker Hotel's hidden wing.

The classic hotel corridor smelled of polished brass and the faint tang of old carpet. Even so, Lila sensed Caleb's woven wards. A subtle shimmer settled on her arms, confirming that the illusions that had tormented her previously were kept at bay here. She knocked once, and the door swung open almost immediately. A beautiful girl, tall and poised with a stern tilt to her mouth, was the first person she saw.

She ushered Lila inside with a soft murmur, taking her arm as she guided her into the warm glow of the living room. "I'm Caleb's sister, Zoe. You're hurt," Zoe said, eyeing the darkening bruises on Lila's forearm. "Let me help."

There was no prying in her tone, only clear concern. Lila's heart constricted as she remembered illusions so thick they had nearly choked her a day earlier. She nodded gratefully, letting Zoe lead her to a tidy loveseat near the corner lamp. The lamp's amber glow revealed just how mottled the skin around Lila's wrist and elbow had become. Though the bruises looked worse than they felt, a dull ache radiated from each spot where an illusory trap had cinched around her.

"Where's Caleb?" Lila asked, voice low. She glanced around the neat apartment. Several books lay open on the coffee table, complicated runic notes scrawled in the margins. The flicker of half-burned candles hinted that he might have tried a protective ritual earlier.

Zoe bent over a small kit she had retrieved from her bag. "He'll join us in a moment," she said briskly. "He was checking something in his study."

Lila watched as Zoe pulled out a faintly glowing ointment, the swirl of pale pink pungent with herbal extracts. Zoe pressed gently, smoothing the ointment over Lila's bruises with a delicate touch. A tingling heat spread through Lila's skin as the balm sank in, easing tenderness that she hadn't fully realized was throbbing.

"You should have called me as soon as you felt that sting," Zoe said. Her voice carried both warmth and reproach.

"I figured I'd tough it out. But thanks. This is amazing." The ache receded, slipping away like a dream.

Zoe's eyes flickered with empathy. "It is no trouble." She ran her hand one more time over the bruised skin, then glanced toward the door leading to Caleb's library. "I'm glad you're here, Lila. You might end up being the voice of reason tonight."

Before Lila could ask what that meant, the door to the study eased open. Caleb appeared, shoulders stiff, gaze sharp. He paused only a beat before joining them in the living room. "How bad are the bruises?" he asked quietly.

"Better now," Zoe responded, her voice crisp. She snapped the lid back onto the ointment jar and turned to her brother. "Which is more than I can say for your sense of caution. Have you even slept? You look half-alive."

A flicker of guilt pulsed in Caleb's blue eyes. Lila stood, reaching for his hand. "I'm alright, truly. Zoe's taken good care of me." She prayed her attempt at calm would soften whatever tension lurked in the air.

For a moment, Caleb's mouth quirked in a faint half-smile. Then Zoe exhaled sharply and rose from the loveseat. In her posture, Lila saw a storm gathering. "Glad that's handled," Zoe said, voice tight. "Because we need to talk about Sebastian."

Caleb's attention snapped to her. "Zoe," he warned.

She shook her head and crossed her arms. "No. I've kept quiet long enough. The illusions plaguing Lila lately —Sebastian's brand is all over them. His illusions are disturbingly bold, and you know it." Her gaze cut to her brother, fierce and unyielding. "This didn't happen overnight. You let him slip through the Council's cracks back then. You knew his fascination with illusions was veering dark, and you turned a blind eye."

Caleb looked ready to retort, but he hesitated. Lila could feel the tension spark between them as surely as a live wire. She tightened her hold on Caleb's hand, willing him not to lash out. Yet the next moment, his composure broke.

"I hardly 'let' him do anything," Caleb said, voice measured, though anger thrummed beneath. "I pitied him, Zoe. Sebastian was... misguided." He glanced at Lila as though searching for words. "But I never trusted him enough to help him sabotage the Council. I never supported his madness."

Zoe's jaw tightened. "Pity can be as destructive as trust. You saw him flirting with forbidden illusions, and you never warned anyone. Maybe you thought you could fix him, or maybe you assumed he wouldn't go this far. But look around you now. He threatens novices and tears at the wards. He nearly strangled Lila in illusions the other day. It's too big, Caleb. You can't keep rationalizing it."

Lila's heartbeat quickened at the mention of her near-disastrous run-in with Sebastian's illusions. She cleared her throat softly, trying to sound gentle. "Zoe, we—I appreciate your fear. I do. Caleb has been working tirelessly to stop Sebastian ever since the Council realized how dangerous he is."

Zoe's attention flicked to Lila. "I know that." She shook her head. "But you can't pretend his guilt isn't playing right into Sebastian's hands. Sebastian feeds on vulnerabilities. If he senses that Caleb still feels responsible, he will exploit that. He will twist it."

Caleb bristled. "I'm not so easily manipulated," he said, each word clipped.

Zoe's expression was pained rather than angry now, though her tone only grew sharper. "Can you swear that? I'm asking because the next time Sebastian surfaces, I don't want to watch you hesitate. I can't watch illusions tear you apart piece by piece." Her voice wobbled, if only slightly. "You know I would die before letting him wreck this city, but I'm worried you'll be the one who gets hurt first."

Lila tried to place a calming hand on Zoe's forearm. "He won't let that happen," she murmured. "Sebastian is cunning, yes, but we're training. We're reinforcing wards. Caleb is the last person who'd fold under pressure."

Zoe's shoulders sagged, relief and frustration mingling. Her gaze still pinned her brother, searching his face. "Forgive me for not believing that wholeheartedly. I've known you for at least my lifetime, and I've never seen you this on edge." She set the ointment kit down on the table with a clatter and momentarily closed her eyes. "I'm sorry. I just— I can't stand by and watch illusions spread without speaking up."

Caleb ran a hand through his hair. He looked wearier now. "I'm sorry you feel I failed Sebastian. But I don't regret trying to help him back in the day. I regret not stopping him sooner. I regret not telling Marcus everything I observed."

She gave a short, bitter laugh. "Which is exactly the guilt Sebastian can manipulate. I warn you, that weakness might cost you." Zoe inhaled slowly, then faced Lila. "I'm glad you're healing. Take care of him, if you can, because he still doesn't know how to protect himself from his own regrets."

Without further words, Zoe turned and left the room. Her footsteps tapped down the hallway, then the front door clicked, leaving an echo of unresolved tension. Lila stood frozen, feeling her pulse roar in her ears. She glanced at Caleb, whose eyes tracked the closed door until silence served as the only companion in the apartment.

He exhaled, shoulders drooping as though the confrontation had drained what little strength he had. "I'm sorry you had to see that."

She shook her head. "Zoe worries about you. She isn't wrong that guilt can make us vulnerable. But you're doing everything in your power to keep Sebastian from harming anyone else."

He didn't answer, only sank onto the sofa. The dim lamplight cast shadows across his face, highlighting the tension in his jaw. After a heartbeat, he stood again, almost restless, and walked toward the library. "I need a minute," he whispered, voice thick with shame.

Lila waited a few moments, then followed quietly. Through the open doorway, she saw him in the library, perched on the edge of a tall leather chair. His hands shook, white-knuckled, pressed against his knees. Books with swirling runic scripts covered the table, scattered notes revealing frantic research. Candle wax dripped onto the polished floor near the hearth. The scent of extinguished incense lingered in the air, swirling near half-drawn wards chalked onto the library's walls.

She crossed to him, each step deliberate, and knelt by the chair. Gently, she rested her hand on his thigh, coaxing him to meet her gaze. The flicker of anguish in his eyes cut right through her.

"Hey," she said softly. "I'm here. Talk to me."

Caleb closed his eyes, pressing his trembling hands over hers. "I did fail him once," he whispered. "I saw the strange illusions he was conjuring. I should have told the Council earlier, but I held out hope. Perhaps I was arrogant enough to believe I could fix him with friendship instead of turning him in."

Lila's chest tightened. "We all make choices with the best intentions. That doesn't mean you created the monster he became."

He let out a shuddery breath. "Zoe's right about one thing. Sebastian might try to use my regret against me. I can't let him. I can't let illusions destroy us."

She slid her arms around him, leaning in until she felt his heartbeat thrum beneath her cheek.

For a while, he said nothing. The two of them sat close, the fireplace embers glowing with barely a flicker. Eventually, he pulled her tighter. His arms coiled around her waist, pressing her close until she felt the frantic beat of his pulse slow.

He turned his face toward her hair, voice raw with longing. "Stay with me tonight."

She lifted her head, meeting his gaze. They both felt safe here, nights etched with half-restrained desire and whispered confessions. The tension in his shoulders eased slightly when she nodded.

She kissed him gently at first, coaxing him away from guilt and worry. He paused, capturing her breath in a trembling exhale, then kissed her deeply in return. The soft lamplight made the library's shadows dance. She felt the press of his fingers as he slid them under the worn edge of her jacket, helping her peel it off. There was no hurry, only an undercurrent of unspoken need, a craving to remember that there was light, even in the darkest illusions.

He rose, tugging her up with him. They navigated back toward the library's plush rug, stepping over scattered books without a second look. A gentle tumble brought them onto soft pillows near the smoldering fireplace. Heat flared low in Lila's abdomen when Caleb leaned in to press feathers of kisses along her jawline. She answered with a soft moan that rose from deep in her chest, her hands sliding beneath his shirt, feeling the muscles in his back tense and relax.

Each touch erased the ache of past illusions, replaced by a slow awareness of how desperately they wanted each other. She relaxed under his movements, consciousness narrowing to the sound of his breath and the faint crackle of coals in the hearth. His heartbeat pounded in sync with her own, strong and determined. When he murmured her name, she curled her fingers deeper into his hair.

His kisses grew bolder, and she let out a soft gasp. Her day's exhaustion transformed into sparks of renewed energy as they cast aside tension and caution alike. Her bruises felt distant now, soothed by the earlier balm and by the warmth of his body. The scent of candle wax and ancient tomes mixed with the salt of tears neither had realized they were shedding. Grief, fear, and relief tangled together in each sigh.

He whispered something about how he needed her, how her presence had become the anchor he had never known to seek. She stroked his cheek, urging him to keep speaking, to let the guilt unravel, if only for tonight. Their clothes soon lay in a muddled heap. Gentle touches turned urgent. Lips trailed lower. Murmured breaths caught on the edges of whispered promises.

The fireplace offered a gentle glow across their entwined silhouettes, painting them in gold and shadow on the tapestry of the library floor. She responded to every deep kiss, bracing a hand against his chest to feel the steady drumming of his heart. The moment stretched, vivid and incomplete, like a cherished secret. Her own heartbeat fluttered with a mixture of tenderness and raw desire.

They moved in unison, letting passion flow freely. The lingering tension from Zoe's earlier anger and from Sebastian's threat blended into a bittersweet chord of longing. Each press of his lips on her skin calmed the leftover tremors from illusions that had plagued her dreams. She reveled in the certainty of his arms around her, a desperately needed refuge in a world twisted by trickery and fear.

At last, they sank together into the pillows, bodies sated, breath shallow and warm. Their fingertips remained tangled in a quiet vow of connection. She could feel his chest rising and falling beneath her cheek. In the silence that followed, neither needed words. Guilt, regret, warnings from Zoe—they all receded into the dim corners. For this one moment, they found solace in each other's acceptance.

When her eyes fluttered open, she saw Caleb's gaze fixed on her. His hand brushed a lock of hair away from her face. The hint of a smile touched his lips. "Thank you," he whispered.

She leaned up and pressed her forehead to his. "Always."

They remained like that, wrapped in each other's arms, letting darkness gather gently around them. The library's final candle gave a small sputter and went out, but neither of them moved from their makeshift haven on the floor. With only the embers' glow remaining, Lila curled closer. She refused to let illusions—or guilt—claim him tonight. In that intimate setting, she promised herself she would stand firm, no matter what new trials might come.

They fell asleep in the circle of each other's warmth, lulled by the last crackling sparks in the hearth and the lingering promise that together, they could face whatever danger lay beyond tomorrow.

CHAPTER

SEVEN

Lila rubbed at a stubborn espresso stain on the café counter, trying to keep her mind off the day's mounting tension. The shop's late-morning lull had replaced the earlier clamor of regulars clamoring for cappuccinos. Sunlight draped over the tables, illuminating dust motes and the soft hum of the air conditioner. She began rinsing the steam wand in preparation for an afternoon wave of customers. Any sense of calm, though, was short-lived.

Her phone buzzed on the shelf by the pastry display. At first, Lila assumed it was a notification for a missed call or an annoying advertisement. She frowned when she picked it up and read a text message from an unfamiliar number: Meet me at the Murray Hill Tunnel, between 33rd and 40th. I need you. – Caleb.

It took her a stunned pause to register that Caleb had only texted a few times before and usually in response to her reaching out to him. He preferred spells, wards, or personal visits, making each meeting discreet. Nothing about him was casual enough for standard digital messaging. The fact that he used such a direct channel felt like an alarm bell in her head.

Her heart thumped with renewed urgency. Confusion flashed through her. Why contact her this way if he could invoke one of the usual wards? Was he in danger? She glanced at the café's entrance, then at her reflection in the pastry case glass. Her cheeks were still flushed from the morning's usual hustle, but now adrenaline spiked her pulse.

She forced a shaky breath and approached Maya, who was reorganizing napkins at the condiment station. Maya's eyes narrowed with concern. Lila hated lying or half-truths, but she did not have time for explanations. "I have to head out. Something... came up." She tried to keep her voice steady, tapping a brief apology into the air. "Cover for me, please."

Maya pursed her lips, but her stance softened. "I'll manage. Go. Be safe, alright?"

Lila grabbed her shoulder bag, muttering thanks, then hurried into the midday heat. She all but jogged to the nearest subway station, ignoring the jostle of passersby who seemed far too slow. Tension twisted in her stomach with each step down the station's worn steps. Clutching her fare card, she slid through the turnstile and caught the next 4 train heading downtown. Nerves jangled in her veins, every rattle of the subway tracks amplifying her sense of unease.

When she reached 33rd Street, Lila hopped off the

train, weaving through the thin weekday crowd. A musty smell clung to the station, reminding her all too well of past illusions that lurked beneath the city. She swallowed hard. Had Sebastian set another trap? Or was Caleb truly waiting for her?

At the foot of a tall service ladder was a tunnel sign with chipped paint, marking off-limits territory for non-authorized personnel. She crept carefully inside, following the text's instructions. The air was stale, and flickering overhead lights cast shifting shadows against old concrete. Her footsteps echoed, sounding too loud in the gloom.

"Caleb?" Her voice wavered, but she called out anyway, scanning the dim corridor for that familiar silhouette. Only silence answered. She walked farther, senses prickling at every flicker of the long overhead fluorescent lights.

Then she saw him.

Not Caleb.

A figure stood at the end of the tunnel, tall, dressed in dark clothing that blurred into the shadows. The face resolved first: pale skin, hair dark as midnight, and eyes that seemed to glow with a cruel amusement. Even before clarity struck, Lila recognized him from the photos Caleb had reluctantly shown her. Fury and mockery mingled in his stance. Sebastian.

Her pulse slammed. She stopped so abruptly that she nearly lost her balance. The floor felt unsteady, as if illusions coiled beneath her feet. She tried to tear her gaze away, but her eyes locked onto his. He cocked his head like a predator considering prey. She could almost hear his voice in her mind, whispering half-formed words: come closer, explore the magic the Council fears. Let me show you the power they do not want you to have.

She jerked back, fighting the compulsion to step nearer. Heat flared across her cheeks, and her heart drummed so hard she felt it in her temples. A crawling chill slid up her spine, the same dread she felt when she thought she was falling down into an abyss under Grand Central. Voices in her ears, urged her to bend, to scorn the Council's rules. Her skin prickled as though illusions were weaving around her. She reminded herself to breathe. This was not real. This was Sebastian's trick. It had to be.

The figure advanced a single step, lips peeling into a mocking half-smile. The moment he began to speak— though no actual sound left his mouth—she glimpsed flickers along the edges of his shape. Like smoke, he rippled. The corridor pulsed with violet light, disorienting her. She clenched her fists, grappling to recall the grounding techniques. The presence was so intense, so tangible, that her rational mind scattered.

"Get out of my head," she muttered through clenched teeth. Her voice echoed pathetically in the tunnel.

The silhouette shimmered, and she swore it whispered her name. Then a bright surge of false light blinded her. She yelped, stumbling backward. When she forced her eyes open again, the corridor was empty. No sign of Sebastian, no illusions drifting. She was alone, gasping for breath, the faint hum of the overhead lights mocking her frazzled nerves.

Attempts to steady herself failed as dread settled in, heavy as iron. She turned on her heel and sprinted out, back toward the bustle of the station. She ignored the confused stares of a janitor and a lone commuter, focusing only on escaping that oppressive place. If that was truly Sebastian's doing, he was testing her directly. Or, worse, forging a mental link she had unintentionally brushed.

Caleb, she thought. I need Caleb.

Careening onto the next available train, she rode in numb silence until she reached the station nearest the New Yorker Hotel. She jogged the remaining blocks, her lungs burning and heart battered by adrenaline. At the building's discreet side entrance, she punched the operator code on a panel that Caleb had shown her weeks ago. The door opened with a faint click, and she hurried inside, crossing the hallway leading to his hidden apartment.

He was in the library, bent over a broad wooden table covered in runic charts. Candles flickered at the corners, wards shimmering faintly along the walls. His head snapped up when she entered, worry etched on his face.

"What happened? Are you hurt?" Caleb's voice was taut. He stepped around the table and placed a hand on her arm. She almost collapsed into him. The concern in his blue eyes made her breath hitch, but she needed to speak.

"Sebastian," she said, forcing the word out. "I got a text from you, or someone posing as you, telling me to meet in the Murray Hill Tunnel. When I arrived, I saw... I saw him. Or something like him. He taunted me. It felt real, but it was not."

Caleb's features hardened, and the color drained from his cheeks. "I never texted," he murmured. "He must have manipulated any wards that block normal phone signals. That is cunning, even for him."

He gently guided her to a nearby chair. A muscle ticked along his jaw as he listened while she recounted her terrifying vision. She felt tremors in her stomach recalling the phantom words creeping into her mind. Caleb's anger cast tension into the room, and the candles flickered harder, almost reacting to his turmoil.

"Sly illusions," he said quietly. "He wanted to see how you would respond, to test how strong your defenses are." His voice cracked with anger. "He is done hiding. This was a direct message."

Lila clenched the arms of the chair, struggling to rein in the leftover panic. "He is reaching out, trying to exploit me. Maybe he thinks I am—" She exhaled, recalling talk of her lineage. "He thinks I can somehow help him break the boundary with illusions. He wants me frightened or... enthralled."

Caleb's gaze flared with fury, but Lila also spotted dread lingering behind that anger. "He will not have you," he said. "We will step up our searches, renew wards, and I will not let him twist your power."

She nodded, absorbing the promise in his words. Anxiety still gnawed at her, but his determination lent her a fragile sense of calm. He retrieved a small bottle from an adjacent side table and poured a measure of amber liquid into a tumbler. Handing it to her, he offered a tentative smile.

"Drink," he said quietly. "It will calm the shaking."

She took a careful sip, letting the warmth glide down her throat. It tasted like a potent whiskey or brandy laced with subtle magical notes. At least it steadied her trembling voice. She felt more alert now, ready to anchor herself in this quiet, lamp-lit sanctuary.

"I also brought something to eat," Caleb said after a moment. He set a small dish of caviar and crisp crackers on the table, urging her to take a few bites. The sight was oddly normal in the midst of crisis, yet that normalcy comforted her. She swallowed a piece, the salty tang distracting her from the memory of Sebastian's half-real presence.

Caleb cleared the plates when she was done and left her for a short while. Lila leaned back on the chair, letting out a breath. She studied the flickering wards along the library walls, letting that rippling magical energy reassure her that Sebastian could not simply waltz in here uninvited.

When Caleb returned, his expression held a softer strain of concern. "I prepared a bath in the marble bathroom." He spoke gently, but his eyes flicked over her posture, noticing how tense she still was. "You can use the sea salts if you like. The scent might help you unwind."

She hesitated, feeling a twinge of self-consciousness. A short bath would do wonders for her battered nerves, though. She nodded gratefully. He guided her to the bathroom, lighting more candles along the tiled counters. Soft, low music drifted from a discreet speaker. The tub steamed with rose petals floating on the surface, releasing a fragrant swirl that helped her breathe easier.

He left her with a brief squeeze of her hand. Once alone, Lila peeled off her clothes, shivering as the night's anguish seeped back for a moment. She stepped into the hot water, the combination of sea salts and roses enveloping her in gentle warmth. The tension in her shoulders ebbed as she sank deeper, resting her head against the tub's edge. She tried to focus on the present, letting go of Sebastian's mocking silhouette and focusing on the calm of the water around her.

Sometime later, with pruned fingertips and a calmer heart, she emerged from the bath. Toweling off, she found a plush robe hanging by the sink. She slipped into it and made her way back to the library where the fire crackled in the ornate fireplace. Shadows danced along the bookshelves, and Caleb stood near the hearth, stirring embers with a poker. He looked up at her approach.

Her throat felt tight as she watched the flames reflect in his eyes. The tension that lingered in the atmosphere was no longer just anxiety from Sebastian's illusions. Something else pulsed between them, a heady awareness that simmered whenever they were close. She walked to him, letting the robe hang loosely around her shoulders. His gaze traveled over her in quiet invitation.

She pressed her lips together, then let the robe drop. Candlelight played across her bare skin, illuminating every inch of vulnerability. A faint blush heated her cheeks, but she did not shy away from that moment.

Caleb's breath caught, and his own composure wavered. She caught the flicker of desire that lit his eyes, merging with all the protective warmth he had shown her.

He set aside the poker, taking a single step forward until their bodies nearly touched. Sparks seemed to crackle in the air, akin to the magical hum she felt when illusions churned—but this was different. This was an intimate spell woven between them, a shared understanding that after all the sleepless nights and violent illusions, they deserved time of human connection.

"Lila," he murmured, voice raw, "you're beautiful."

She placed her hands against his chest, feeling the steady thrum of his heartbeat. "And you're beautiful too," she whispered. Then she leaned in to kiss him. Their lips met firmly, a searing contact that dispelled the last vestiges of her lingering fear. He cradled her face, returning the kiss with a tenderness that managed to chase out every haunting memory of the tunnel.

She felt his warmth against her skin, his arms sliding around her waist as they sank onto the soft rug before the fireplace. The crackle of flames underscored the heady silence that enveloped them. They found comfort: his sigh against her ear, her whisper of his name, each unspoken promise fueling the press of their bodies. Her pulse roared as she savored the contrast of his clothes against her bare skin.

They came together in slow, reverent motions. Fingertips traced over every ridge of muscle, every curve and soft place, as though rediscovering the reality that they were both alive and safe here. She felt every exhale, every shift of muscle under her palms, while he showered her with careful, measured caresses that made her shiver with need. Their kisses grew more intense, building a shared rhythm that grounded them in the simple, undeniable fact that they were no longer alone in this quiet fight against illusions and fear.

CHAPTER

EIGHT

Lila tugged on her jacket collar as she and Caleb stepped into a high-ceilinged Council Hall, its torches casting jittery gold light across marble columns. Her nerves had simmered since dawn, ever since the summons arrived with curt instructions to present themselves immediately. Now, the heat in her cheeks was impossible to hide. Accusations tumbled across the chamber before Marcus even finished calling the meeting to order.

Elder Marwood, frowning with disapproval, pointed a quivering finger at Caleb. "We have let this... complication go on too long. Your history with Sebastian Shell is turning into a liability."

Others voiced agreement, nodding or muttering about illusions spreading through the city in unsettling patterns. Lila noted how shadows flickered at the corners of the hall, illusory remnants that still leaked through wards. She gritted her teeth, wishing the Council would focus their energy on stamping out the illusions rather than scape-goating the people actively containing them.

"Is that so?" Caleb asked quietly, crossing his arms. He held himself with a detached calm, but Lila saw the tension in his shoulders. His eyes flashed at the mention of Sebastian's name, a reminder of regrets he rarely voiced.

Elder Farnese made a clicking sound. "We all know you were close to him. That personal entanglement could compromise everything."

"He is not compromised," Lila spat, heart thudding. She refused to stand by while they put Caleb on trial for a matter he could not change. "Sebastian is out there, yes, but it is not Caleb's fault." Her frustration spiked at the locked expressions around the chamber.

A wiry, gray-haired witch glowered at her. "And your family ties are not much better," she said stiffly. "Evelyn Matthews was powerful once, but she walked away from Council duties. Perhaps that is part of the reason Sebastian singled you out. Your grandmother's influence could draw him right to us." Those last words landed with a scornful edge, setting Lila's jaw tight.

Her gaze flicked toward Marcus Steele, who stood on a slight dais at the chamber's far end. He had not intervened in the back-and-forth argument, his lips pressed in a thin line. Lila suspected he was weighing how to keep order without fueling further chaos.

One Council member shook her head in dismay. "We are risking exposure. The illusions are becoming bolder, and novices like Lila are at the center of it. She has not even consolidated her control; she is newly awakened. If her grandmother was once so influential, that attention alone places a bullseye on the city's wards."

Lila's skin burned. She hated the idea that her grandmother's past life might become an excuse to blame her for everything. She had chosen to stay quiet until now but watching them question Caleb—and labeling him unfit—forced a rising anger through her veins.

"He is the only one who noticed Sebastian's strategies early." She spoke carefully, voice trembling. She locked eyes with a stout warlock who was sharpening his complaints. "If you had possessed half his vigilance when all of this started, we might have caught Sebastian a long time ago!"

Her retort rang in the marble chamber like a bell. For a moment, no one spoke. Whispers broke out, accompanied by the shift of robes and the squeak of boots on polished floors. The stout warlock rose in indignation, color creeping up his neck as he bristled. A quiet fell, as though the entire Council held its collective breath in shock.

"You dare—" he began, voice rising.

Marcus cut him off with a curt gesture. "Enough," he commanded. The single word echoed. Tension vibrated through the hall. Lila's heart pounded so hard she wondered if everyone could hear it. She saw a flicker of grudging respect in Marcus's gaze before he returned to the business of controlling the uproar.

"You have all made your positions clear," Marcus said, scanning the circle of elders. "This is not the time to tear each other apart. We are in crisis. If we cannot unify, illusions will overrun us." His tone carried a finality that quieted even the most vocal elders.

Lila inhaled unsteadily. She glanced over at Caleb, who was standing silent but resolute. The faint tension in his jaw remained. Sometimes, she could guess exactly which regrets were circling in his mind—that he had known Sebastian once, that he had missed certain warning signs. She gave him a tiny, encouraging nod.

His gaze softened, acknowledging her defense. Yet her outburst had not dispelled the doubts swirling between Council members. Low murmurs started up again, pairs splitting off into private discussions. Lila's instincts told her it would not be wise to stay. Her tongue felt raw from her angry retort.

Caleb bent closer, voice low. "Want to step out for a moment?"

She mouthed the word yes without hesitation.

They slipped to the edge of the gathering, ignoring the pointed stares of two elders conversing near the main entrance. The massive, rune-etched doors stood guarded, but a side walkway angled away, winding past racks of warding stones and leading out to a narrow balcony. Lila remembered glimpsing it once—a private overlook seldom used except by Council scribes who needed fresh air.

Once outside, the night pressed in around them, unexpectedly cool. The city sprawled below, a mosaic of lights and distant horns. Lila exhaled, trying to release the tension coiled in her chest. She leaned over the stone railing, shoulders sagging as she peered at the labyrinth of streets. In a distant corner, a flicker of illusion glowed—a reminder that they could not pretend normal life reigned entirely. Still, the breeze felt like solace after facing so many judging eyes.

Caleb stood beside her, so close his arm brushed hers. She sensed the weariness in him, the weight he carried. They had been training furiously, chasing faint leads on Sebastian's whereabouts, and fending off illusions that threatened civility in pockets of Manhattan. Now they faced hostility within the Council too.

She pressed her lips together. "They are all so suspicious," she whispered, letting her thoughts slip out. "I get that illusions are scaring them, but blaming you—blaming me—"

His hand found hers. "They are running out of patience with a crisis they cannot fully contain," he said, voice quiet. "Sebastian has them cornered. He attacks their pride as much as the wards."

She turned, studying the serious lines of his face. In the faint wash of city light, his eyes carried a softness that made her chest tighten. "We will handle it," she said determinedly, though fear still nipped at her. "They are not going to tear you down because you once showed Sebastian compassion. That compassion is what makes you a better mentor than half the people in there."

His jaw tensed, but gratitude gleamed in his gaze. For a moment, they allowed themselves the luxury of simple closeness. The breeze carried the faint tang of car exhaust and wet pavement, yet out here, the city felt almost distant. Lila realized how desperately she needed the reassurance of his presence.

She watched the shifting glow of passing headlights on the building opposite them. "I hate the Council's bickering. When will they realize Sebastian is the real threat?"

"They know," he murmured. "They are just scared that he is unstoppable."

She squeezed his hand. "He is not unstoppable."

Their shoulders brushed again, a deliberate welcome. She felt something fragile and certain in that contact. The memories of illusions, bruises from training, and every tension-laden meeting coalesced into a single raw truth: they needed each other. Despite the swirl of politics and fear, they had found a corner of solace.

She searched his eyes, voice barely above a whisper. "I hope I did not make more enemies by standing up for you."

He shook his head. "Even if you did, that kind of loyalty is... rare." Lips curving in a faint, warm smile, he stepped closer. The subdued brightness of the city skyline outlined the curve of his jaw.

Their fingertips touched on the railing, and a trembling surge of relief coursed through her. In all the chaos, she had found someone eager to stand at her side—not just to protect her, but to share the risk and the fight. She could not hold back the pulse of longing that soared in her chest.

She leaned in. Caleb exhaled, eyes flickering with desire that he tried to control, but failed. The moment ignited in a heartbeat. Gentle tension snapped into a desperate kiss, his mouth pressed to hers with the urgency of everything they could not say. She felt the warmth of his hand cradle her cheek, a subtle enough gesture but thrumming with possession. The taste of possibility mingled with her own vulnerability in that single moment.

Her heart pounded, and the city's distant hum seemed to fade beneath the rush of blood in her ears. She clutched his jacket, letting the solidity anchor her. When they pulled back, the electricity between them radiated with unspoken need. She drew a shaky breath, tasting the lingering spark of that kiss. He rested his forehead against hers, eyes closed, inhaling sharply.

"We'll figure this out," she murmured. "Together."

He nodded, tension melting long enough that she glimpsed the man behind the vigilant warlock—the man who cared for her with an intensity she never expected. "Yes," he said. "Together."

They lingered there, gazing at the skyline, until the chill wind sank in through their clothes and reminded them the Council meeting still waited inside. She gave his hand one final squeeze, then they slipped off the balcony and back through the corridor, hearts pounding far differently than before.

THE NEXT EVENING found them in Caleb's apartment, seated at a small table in the softly lit dining space. Lila had insisted on preparing a simple meal—mostly reheated leftovers—but it felt good to share something normal. Their conversation circled around illusions they had dispelled that morning near a half-abandoned subway station, and the odd flickers of magic that now haunted random city corners. Caleb's expression was weary, but he tried to smile as he reached for another spoonful of steamed rice.

Candles cast a gentle glow against the apartment walls. Although the day's tension weighed on both of them, Lila felt a sense of safety here, away from the Council's suspicious stares. She wanted to lose herself in the domestic quiet—only the sound of the city outside and the occasional drip of the kitchen faucet.

That illusion of peace shattered the instant the door swung open. The wards recognized Marcus's signature, Lila realized, because the door had unlocked without warning. She practically jumped from her seat, confusion flooding her chest. Marcus strode in with three senior guardians close behind, their faces lined with worry. The older man did not wait for an invitation. He scanned the table, mouth set in a grim line.

"Apologies for barging in," Marcus said briskly, "but we have no time for formality."

Caleb stood, brow furrowing. "What has happened?" He kept his voice measured, though Lila felt him shift protectively in front of her.

Marcus pressed his fingers to his temples. "We are facing infiltration attempts near critical wards throughout Manhattan. The illusions are getting bolder. Key watchers nearly got tricked into disabling entrance seals at the

Council's main chamber. We suspect it is Sebastian or a ring loyal to him."

The mention of illusions made Lila's stomach drop. Caleb's jaw tightened, but he remained quiet, letting Marcus continue.

"We are done waiting," Marcus went on, voice resonating in the quiet dining area. "The Council is launching massive protective wards in three days. A rare cosmic alignment will allow us to seal the city's borders—magically speaking—and reinforce every major nexus so illusions cannot tear through. That operation demands nearly every resource and warlock we have. If we do not lock down at that time, illusions might overwhelm us."

One of the guardians beside Marcus, a severe man with a neatly trimmed beard, narrowed his eyes. "Which means that if you two fail to deliver solid, actionable evidence on Sebastian's whereabouts—proof we can act on—within seventy-two hours, the Council will divert all its energy to fortifying wards. We will not have the manpower to chase illusions or traitors. The city will slip deeper into chaos." His gaze flicked to Caleb. "This is a grim reality, but we cannot indulge personal hunts any longer."

Lila's blood stirred with anger. She could hardly stand the insinuation that their efforts were somehow "personal hunts," especially after all they had done to push back illusions. "You are effectively saying that if we do not catch or pin down Sebastian in three days, you will abandon that search altogether?" Her voice came out sharply, but she did not regret it.

Marcus's gaze slid to her. "We will not abandon it, but we will have no resources left to allocate. Our wards are failing faster than we can repair them. The alignment is our best shot at preserving the city from a complete meltdown of illusions. If you fail to find leads before then, we cannot delay the operation. Our priority must be to keep illusions from ripping open the boundary."

Lila opened her mouth, flustered. Anger accompanied the cold certainty that the Council had cornered them. The ultimatum might be the only plan they could manage, but it felt incredibly unfair. Caleb pivoted to face Marcus, his face grim.

The older warlock sighed. "This is not about punishing you. It is about stopping illusions from plunging Manhattan into irreversible chaos."

A graying elder behind Marcus stepped forward, his gaze firm on Caleb. "We cannot ignore your connection to Sebastian. You should have known sooner. It might even cloud your judgment now."

She watched Caleb's posture stiffen, his muscles taut. He kept his voice level, though. "My only objective is to stop him from harming more lives."

Marcus gave a stiff nod. "We trust that." Then his expression steeled once more. "But you must act quickly. The illusions will not wait for us to debate."

Silence settled, broken only by the low hiss of the apartment's ventilation. Finally, Lila swallowed her frustration. "We will do whatever we can," she said, meeting Marcus's gaze. "I promise."

Marcus inclined his head. "See that you do." He

stepped back, letting the tension in the room subside slightly. "There is one resource you can tap immediately: Isabel Ramirez at the New York Public Library. She has compiled data from old records and newly uncovered references to partial illusions in Midtown. I have asked her to assist you. Use her knowledge. If we can map Sebastian's pattern, we might corner him."

Lila only nodded, grappling with equal parts anger and urgency. The guardians withdrew, leaving the apartment door ajar as the last of them exited into the hallway. When the click of footsteps faded, she pressed a hand to her temple.

Caleb exhaled, raking a hand through his hair. "They are forcing our hand." His frustration glinted in the lamplight, but beneath it, determination rose. "We have fought illusions day and night. Now they demand results in three days, or everything changes."

"They are scared," she murmured. "And I suppose they should be. If illusions keep multiplying, maybe none of us will be safe." She looked down, noticing how her half-eaten dinner sat abandoned. Her appetite had vanished.

She turned her head, catching his gaze. A flicker of heat danced between them, a shared understanding that no matter how the Council judged them, they stood on the same side. She placed her hand over his, absorbing the quiet strength in his touch.

"We only have seventy-two hours," she repeated softly. Anxiety churned in her stomach. "That is so little time."

He nodded, expression hardening. "We start tonight.

We will visit Isabel. We will cross-reference every thread of information. Sebastian cannot hide forever."

They each took a moment, glancing at the scattered plates on the table. She moved to clean up the meal, but he stopped her with a quiet suggestion that they leave it for tomorrow. More pressing matters beckoned.

At the threshold, they paused, searching each other's eyes. Outside the window, the city lights cut a path through the dusk. Lila imagined illusions flickering near those unsuspecting streets, mocking the Council's last illusions of security. They had to act quickly if they wanted to prevent more havoc.

They stood there, entwined, a quiet moment of unity amid the swirl of dangerous forces. She squeezed his fingers, letting the closeness remind her that she was not alone in this fight. Their shoulders squared, renewed determination pulsing through the air. Then, dispensing with any further hesitation, they left to gather what they needed, resolved to hunt for the answers that would lead them to Sebastian. If the Council only gave them three days, they intended to make every hour count.

NINE

Caleb opened the passenger door to a black sedan that pulled up to the curb. She slid inside, feeling a tightness in her chest when he settled next to her and nodded silently at the driver. They reached the New York Public Library soon after. Night had fallen fully, and the building's facade shone under multiple spotlights, turning the iconic marble lions at the entrance into silent sentinels. Lila gazed up at the massive pillars and the famed stone lions named Patience and Fortitude. She remembered visiting this place as a little girl; back then, she never could have imagined stepping inside to consult a hidden wealth of magical texts.

Caleb pulled to a stop near the sidewalk. "We should hurry," he said. His voice was quiet, but she heard the urgency there. He nodded again at the driver who pulled away from the curb.

Lila felt a comforting brush of his fingers against her elbow. He didn't linger, but she registered the gesture all the same. Together, they approached the lion on the right —Fortitude. Its stoic face regarded them as though it guarded the building from all manner of secrets. Caleb pressed his palm to the lion's head. The stone under his fingertips gleamed faintly, and the statue's eyes flickered with latent magic.

A faint line crackled down the marble facade behind the lion, revealing a hidden door that none of the passersby seemed to notice. She and Caleb stepped through, entering a corridor with faded wallpaper and a single dusty bench. In an instant, the secret entrance closed behind them, and the quiet of an enchanted library replaced the distant traffic noise.

A single orb of enchanted light bobbed in the passage, guiding them deeper into the building's restricted wing. They reached a small desk, where a young man in a gray uniform raised his eyes in mild curiosity. Upon seeing Caleb's Council sigil pinned to his jacket collar, the guard only nodded and pointed to a winding staircase that spiraled downward.

The moment Lila's boots touched those steps, she detected the tang of old books and something sharper—a dryness that hinted at protective spells laid into the walls. She recognized runes carved into stone archways, flickering pale blue whenever she passed. Each step descended them into deeper gloom until an antechamber spread out before them. She could see floor-to-ceiling shelves, all filled with thick, tattered tomes. The shelves rose so high that the upper reaches disappeared into shadows.

At a central table, a woman in a fitted maroon blazer

stood surrounded by floating orbs of light. She used their glow to leaf through what looked like a massive leather-bound volume. Lila recognized her from a brief mention in past Council notes: Isabel Ramirez, the librarian temporarily granted special research access. Her dark, curly hair was pinned back, and she wore wire-rimmed glasses that perched on her nose.

When Isabel spotted them, she smiled in greeting. "You must be Caleb Blackwood and Lila Matthews. Marcus alerted me to expect you tonight." Her voice was welcoming, though her polite expression carried a hint of fatigue, as though she had been poring over ancient texts for hours already.

Caleb approached with a measured nod. "Thank you for agreeing to help on short notice. The Council seems to believe your knowledge of arcane records could be the key to unraveling Sebastian's next move."

Isabel lifted the thick volume and set it aside. "Keys and codes, yes. I have sorted the volumes by era and region. But the references to illusions, particularly relic-based illusions, are scattered across centuries. Some have been transcribed incorrectly. Others are just fragments." She turned to Lila, extending an earnest gaze. "We must do our best to piece them together."

Lila smoothed her hand over the edge of the table and mustered a grateful smile. "I appreciate all of this, Isabel. We have only so much time before illusions cause serious damage out there."

Her words hung between them like a reminder of the crisis beyond these walls. Caleb placed a steadying hand on Lila's shoulder. His warmth seeped through the fabric of her jacket, anchoring her in a moment that felt too big to handle alone. She exhaled and forced her focus back on the books around them.

"Alright," Isabel said, gesturing to several piles. "Let me show you the relevant sections I identified. They describe earlier attempts to harness relics akin to the Prism. Not all are illusions-based, but we might find parallels that Sebastian could exploit."

Stacks of books grew as they began sorting them into neat piles. Lila kept one ear trained on Caleb's low voice as he read lines from a medieval treatise out loud. Occasionally, he paused to consult an obscure dictionary Isabel provided. The words included old references to illusions so potent they mimicked entire landscapes, illusions that men revered like living gods. Dampness pricked Lila's palms at the notion of illusions that entire boroughs believed real.

Over time, Lila fell into a steady rhythm: scanning a brittle page, summarizing any mention of illusions, passing important details to Caleb. Although the room felt cool, sweat gathered at the back of her neck. She couldn't stop imagining Sebastian rummaging through these same accounts if he had gained access. With every frightening detail they uncovered, her heart sank further. Yet she pressed on, determined not to let fear derail their work.

"Here," she finally said, lifting a thin folio that had turned yellow with age. The text was partially in cursive script, partially in archaic runic scrawls. "There is a mention of catacombs under Manhattan that once housed wards to boost illusions. The wards apparently let illusions remain stable for days. That might explain how entire city blocks are flickering with illusions now."

Caleb's gaze flicked up. "It does align with rumors about Sebastian's infiltration into older Council outposts. The catacombs might be a perfect place to embed illusions in the city's magical infrastructure." He tapped a finger on a line of text that described collapsed corridors. "The record insists that nobody fully charted them. The Council gave up on the attempt decades ago. If Sebastian found a method to navigate them, he could hide illusions anywhere."

Isabel rubbed her temple. "Yes, that's consistent with what I've sifted through. These references are scattered, but they all point to the same conclusion: Those tunnels are ancient and extremely unstable. If someone tampered with wards down there, illusions could spread like wildfire across the city above."

Lila felt a tremor of dread. "We need to find out how he might have adapted the wards. If he's discovered a way to replicate illusions in uncharted areas, it explains why we can't pinpoint his location."

Caleb's brow furrowed with concern. "This is precisely the supercharged magic Sebastian always chased. Creating illusions powerful enough to rewrite reality on a local scale. If these old wards remain, even partially, he could amplify them by bridging them with modern illusions. It puts all of Manhattan at risk."

Isabel scooted another tome across the table. "Try this. It's from the mid-1700s—notes from a Council attempt to reestablish control in those catacombs. The scribe mentions relic spells for illusions, but the language is incomplete." She opened the book to a page where complicated diagrams nearly filled the entire spread. The lines curved like blueprints, mapping partial tunnels that ended abruptly or overlapped with scribbled question marks.

Lila leaned closer, peering at the sketches. She recognized a few runes. Some resembled the old wards used around the Council vault, but the shapes were twisted, almost corrupted. Her pulse pounded with every new realization. If Sebastian had found a conduit through those passages, maybe he was using layered illusions to keep the Council in the dark while perfecting his hold on the city's magic.

A thick silence settled among them as they flipped from page to page, occasionally voicing half-formed theories. Isabel paused every so often to jot notes onto separate parchment, cross-referencing the coordinates of abandoned Council stations with rumored chasms in Manhattan's underbelly.

In front of Lila, enchanted orbs overhead offered most of the light. Months ago, she used to worry only about rent and café hours. Now, she was shoulder-deep in lost magical records, fighting illusions as the city brimmed with invisible threats. She swallowed a guilty knot that formed in her throat. She knew Maya was covering shifts at The Daily Grind again, probably lying through her teeth to baffled customers irritated by Lila's repeated absences.

"Are you alright?" Caleb's soft question broke through her thoughts.

She lifted her gaze from the musty pages. Her eyes settled on his, drawn by the quiet concern there. "Yeah," she managed. "Just thinking of how quickly everything changed."

A trace of a smile reached his lips, though his eyes carried a worry she recognized well. "I promise we'll make it right," he whispered. His hand inched toward hers, stopping just shy of actual contact. "We're close to a breakthrough. We won't let illusions consume this city."

She nodded, the warmth of his presence helping her fight back the chill that crawled up her arms. Clearing her throat, she returned her attention to the folio. She turned a page and found a curious line describing illusions not just as illusions, but as "untethered realities." Reading it sent a nervous flutter through her chest.

Isabel claimed the text was partial, and passages jumped from warnings about unstoppable illusions to references of wards that had collapsed under the city. Pieces were missing. Some lines ended in mid-sentence. The script turned illegible in places, as if the scribe had run out of time or simply lost the ability to record what they saw.

They studied well past the hour Lila guessed they would finish. The library's silence magnified every sigh, every faint rustle of paper. At one point, Isabel excused herself to retrieve a set of referencing catalogs stored in a side alcove, leaving Lila and Caleb momentarily alone among the towering shelves.

Lila stretched her stiff muscles, glancing at the ceiling where shadows flickered. She could hardly tell how many hours had passed. After the tension from earlier Council gatherings, she half expected someone to barge in demanding progress. Instead, there was only the hum of protective wards and the soft light shining on rows of texts. She inhaled deeply, looking over at Caleb. His posture spoke of quiet determination, and she remembered how often he had urged her to pace herself. She offered him a small, tired grin. He returned a look that held affection beneath his seriousness.

Eventually, Isabel returned, carrying two more thin volumes. She read aloud from the older one: "Here, it cites the catacombs as uncharted for good reason. The wards have fizzled or changed over time, so even the Council's advanced reconnaissance spells failed to map every corridor. Many attempts ended in devastation when illusions tricked explorers into labyrinths that caved in."

Caleb cursed under his breath. "Sebastian might exploit illusions that hide structural weaknesses. If he sets the wards to reflect illusions of stable passages... we might be walking into a trap the second we step down there. Lila walked into one the other night."

Lila's skin prickled at the thought. She remembered Sebastian's cunning approach to illusions. He had a knack for turning the simplest environment into a disorienting nightmare. The battered pages gave them only partial insight, but at least now they understood that the catacombs had the potential to amplify illusions far beyond typical spells.

Time slipped by as they continued digging, piece by piece, bridging the knowledge gaps. In one moment of discovery, Lila found a note referencing a "dark conjurer" from centuries ago who nearly managed to trick an entire Council unit with illusions so tangible that the line between reality and magic dissolved. She paused to read the old script carefully, heart hammering. That conjurer must have failed, or else the city would have fallen back then. She wondered what final measure had stopped him. The text offered no explanation, only a single word: "buried."

Caleb cleared his throat, interpreting her silence. "Maybe the illusions turned on the conjurer, or a group of guardians sealed him away. Either way, it's a grim parallel to Sebastian's path."

Lila swallowed hard. "So, history threatens to repeat itself. We need to trust we can do what they did. Or do better."

He gave a resolute nod. "We will."

Not long after, the orbs above them dimmed, signaling the lateness of the hour. Isabel closed the final tome she had checked and rubbed her eyes. "I think we have gathered all we can in one night. If Sebastian is harnessing these old wards, then the city's in greater danger than we realized." She stacked the books, careful not to damage the fragile edges.

Caleb rose from his seat, rolling his stiff shoulders. "We know more now than when we first walked in. That's progress." His voice held a calm determination that Lila found oddly soothing.

She stood, helping them return the books to protective sleeves or to the neat row at the edge of the table. "Thank you for your patience, Isabel. We appreciate all of this," Lila said softly, tucking a stray hair behind her ear. Anxiety still churned inside her, but at least they had a clearer sense of how Sebastian might be operating.

Isabel gave a weary smile. "Any time. The Council rarely lets me do field work, so archive research is my way of contributing." She caught Lila's gaze. "Be careful when you investigate those catacombs. They can fool the eye as well as the mind. Don't go alone if you can help it."

"We won't," Lila answered, sharing a look with Caleb. She felt the cool weight of the amulet against her collarbone. Perhaps it would help them cling to reality in those tunnels. She prayed that would be enough.

They bade Isabel farewell, promising to return if they needed more cross-referencing. The orbs of light flickered behind them as they climbed the spiral steps. Lila felt each footstep in her bones, a reminder of her fatigue and the pressing urgency that still hovered around them.

When they emerged from the hidden corridor, the night sky above Manhattan had grown darker. The library's main halls were locked up for the evening, with only a distant security guard visible on the far side of the marble steps. Lila suppressed a yawn, stepping into the open air.

Shoulder to shoulder, she and Caleb descended the front steps past the statues of Patience and Fortitude. The city's glow spread out in all directions, neon lights coloring the sidewalk. Her thoughts crowded with images of catacombs, illusions, and half-forgotten wards waiting to be twisted into unstoppable threats. Yet, as she adjusted the collar of her jacket, she felt new resolve kindling inside. At least now they possessed information nobody else had pieced together. That had to count for something.

Caleb brushed his knuckles lightly across her sleeve. His expression held a quiet spark of reassurance. She recognized the loyal confidence there, the same straightforward devotion that told her she wasn't alone in facing this. She gave a small nod, letting that unspoken bond steady her frayed nerves.

A calm silence lingered until they reached the sidewalk, where traffic hummed in the distance. She exhaled a breath she hadn't realized she was holding. He took one more glance at the hidden door behind the lion's stone mane, then turned to her.

"How do you feel?" he asked.

"Like I've got five different storms building in my head," she replied, forcing a half-smile. "But also... I feel certain we're on the right track. Sebastian won't see us coming."

They exchanged knowing looks. The tension in Lila's chest eased a fraction, replaced by a determined readiness. They had just unearthed centuries of secrets in a single evening—secrets that might explain how illusions threatened to swallow Manhattan whole.

They walked together into the night, heading for the next step in their plan. The crisp air bit at Lila's cheeks, but she lifted her chin and kept stride with Caleb. She carried the knowledge that the catacombs would likely be their next battlefield, their next gauntlet. Yet with these dusty texts echoing at the back of her mind, she clung to the conviction that they could turn Sebastian's own illusions against him.

They did not look back at the library as the car and driver magically returned. Their breath mingled in thin, moonlit air. By the time they slipped into the sedan once more, Lila had no doubt that she, Caleb, and the Council had taken a necessary leap toward preserving Manhattan from the illusions devouring its edges.

Before long, the streetlights blurred past again, and she glanced at the quiet set of Caleb's jaw. They shared a long silence, letting the magnitude of their new discoveries settle. Finally, she caught his gaze and found the same glimmer of conviction that thrummed in her own veins.

They had uncovered references to catacombs none of them truly understood. They had found hints of illusions so potent they almost defied belief. And they had gained a plan—or at least the kernel of one—to unearth Sebastian's methods.

"Do you want to go to your home or mine?" Caleb asked with a glint in his eye.

"I think I need to go home to check on things there. Do you mind?"

Caleb grabbed her hand and kissed it. "Yes, I mind but I also understand. We both need to be focused and we need some real sleep." He gave the driver Lila's address. By the time the car pulled in front, both of them carried a renewed sense of purpose in their eyes. Lila kissed Caleb on the check and grabbed the last few copied notes and references from the library, fueling her determination to face whatever illusions waited for them next.

Caleb walked her to her door and made sure the wards were intact.

"Goodnight my lovely one. Dream about me," Caleb smiled as he turned smiling.

TEN

Lila jolted awake to a soft knock at her apartment door. The clock on her phone showed a time that hovered on the edge of dawn, that strange hour when the city outside felt both restless and half-asleep. She rubbed her eyes and blinked into the faint glow of a single lamp she had left burning overnight. Whoever was outside knocked again, the sound more urgent now. Her body tensed.

She pulled on a loose sweater over her tank top and padded carefully toward the door, annoyance bubbling under her chest. She had expected Caleb—maybe he had sensed another disruptive illusion swirling around her building—but the presence on the other side of the door did not feel like him. She closed her eyes, took in a slow breath, and roused a minimal ward to make sure no hostile magic lurked in the hallway. The ward revealed a distinctly human silhouette, bones and breath unaccompanied by the telltale shimmer of illusions. Still, the knock felt weighty with meaning.

Lila opened the door by a cautious inch. At once, her heart leaped. Evelyn Matthews stood in the dim corridor, wisps of her auburn hair plastered to her forehead as though she had raced through wind or rain. Her jacket looked dusty with a faint residue of dried leaves clinging to the hem. Lila's pulse aired a frantic staccato, uncertain whether to worry or be relieved. She and her grandmother rarely met at such an in-between hour.

"Grandma..." Lila began in a disbelieving whisper. "What are you doing here?"

Evelyn's lips quirked into a gently apologetic smile. "May I come in, dear? I have something for you." She hugged herself as if chilled by more than the hallway air.

Lila nodded and opened the door fully. Evelyn slipped inside, shutting the door behind her with surprising caution. The older woman rested against the wall, breathing as though she had climbed several flights of stairs too quickly. Lila tried to disguise her concern as she guided her grandmother toward the worn couch.

"What happened?" Lila asked softly. She flicked off the ward she had raised in the entry and allowed the small lamp's glow to frame Evelyn's face. Her grandmother's eyes showed the faint lines of worry or exhaustion, maybe both.

Evelyn inhaled slowly, then looked around the cramped apartment. She glanced over the pile of mismatched books, a leftover pastry container from The Daily Grind, and a scattering of notepads in which Lila had scrawled runic sketches. The older woman seemed to take in every detail.

"I had to use an older warding technique from our family," Evelyn explained quietly, smoothing a strand of hair that clung to her temple. "It allowed me to slip past and even avoid certain watchers from the Council. I doubt anyone but a Matthews could manage it."

Lila felt a chill scrape down her spine. She wondered if that was the same skill Evelyn had once mentioned in passing, the method for crossing hidden thresholds that had never been properly recorded in Council logs. Had her grandmother traveled like a phantom through the city's wards? It was a disconcerting idea, yet typical of the Matthews line and its history of earth-based magic.

"Why take such a risk? Grandma, you could have asked Caleb or even me to come to you." Lila's voice cracked with concern.

Evelyn sighed. "This needed to be done quietly. No prying eyes and no illusions meddling with the truth." She gently patted Lila's arm. "I have a feeling your apartment is safer than the Council halls right now, especially at this odd hour."

Lila's stomach twisted. She wondered what it meant that her grandmother had chosen to trust these four walls more than the labyrinthine corridors that boasted the best wards in the city. She suspected it had to do with the infiltration rumors swirling around the Council, or the knowledge that illusions had compromised entire wings of their domain. Anxiety pinched between her eyebrows.

Evelyn reached into the tattered canvas bag slung over

her shoulder. With slow reverence, she scooped out bundles of yellowed pages bound in rough, worn leather. At a glance, they appeared to be diaries or journals. Small cracks ran along the spines, suggesting they had been stashed in an attic for decades.

Lila counted six volumes in total, each marked with a range of years in Evelyn's sweeping handwriting. A swirl of excitement and nerves made her heart pound. She had recently learned from members of the Council that her grandmother had walked away from extensive Council duties years ago. Apparently, these journals were a relic of that time.

She lifted the first book. The cover bore the dates 1938–1943. Inside, many pages contained only a sentence or two recording mundane details: delivering herbal remedies to neighbors, a trip to a local grocery store. Then she turned a few leaves and found multiple pages filled with neat diagrams, swirl after swirl of intricate runes. Scattered among them were sketched illustrations of plants, arcane symbols, and short paragraphs detailing measurements for potions. She paused on a page describing an **Illusion Displacement Spell**, but the text abruptly broke off at the bottom.

Exhaling slowly, Lila placed the journal on the table and reached for the next one. The sense of discovery lulled her tired mind, as if each page was an anchor to her grandmother's younger self.

She opened the next one and two pages of pages fluttered out. She gasped, heart jolting at the sudden movement. Carefully, she bent down and scooped up the fallen sheets. Their edges felt brittle against her fingertips.

Sprawled across both pages were cryptic runes, deeply black and somehow more deliberate than the casual notes scattered through the journal. The lines looped in a way that made Lila's skin prickle. An itch of recognition teased her memory. She had just seen this rune at the New York Public Library in their research there.

"This is it, Grandma" she breathed. Her pulse thudded with sudden energy, all fatigue swept away. When she brushed her fingertips over the runes, she felt a mild tingle, the dormant hum of old magic that had lain hidden in her grandmother's attic for decades.

"Oh, you already found something helpful?" Evelyn laughed. "That's good, dear. I've got a taxi waiting downstairs and I'm tired so I'm going to leave you with all of this and go to my hotel I booked for a few days. Let's plan to get together later and discuss what you've found."

Lila gave Evelyn a big hug walking her to the door. "Thank you so much for trusting me with all of this incredible knowledge, Grandma."

As soon as Eveyln was gone, Lila grabbed her phone from the table, snapping a clear photo of both pages. She glanced at the phone's screen; the runes were captured with decent clarity.

She opened a message thread with Caleb.

Typing in a rush, she sent: *Does this look familiar? Just found it in Evelyn's journals. She just popped in with a treasure trove.* She attached the photo and tapped send. Usually,

Caleb took a while to respond at such an early hour, but her phone buzzed almost immediately.

"Yes," the text said, followed by a single request: "Come for breakfast and show me what you have."

Despite her anxiety over illusions roiling the city, a small smile curved her lips. Caleb's invitation felt like a promise that she wasn't alone. She carefully packed the loose pages back into the journal, setting them in her satchel so she wouldn't leave anything behind. She flipped off the light and went back to bed, her mind whirling with possibilities.

In the darkness, she clutched a pillow and tried to drift off to sleep. The faint hum of her ancestral magic, awakened by those runes, made her veins buzz with restless warmth. She inhaled deeply, focusing on the knowledge that in just a few hours, she'd show Caleb. That glimmer of hope carried her into uneasy dreams.

She woke before her alarm, feeling groggy but determined. After a quick shower, she made sure to tuck the precious pages in a protective folder along with several journals. Her phone kept vibrating with news updates about minor illusions flaring up near Times Square, though city officials shrugged them off as *experimental holograms*. Lila ignored them for now, focusing her attention on the immediate clues from her grandmother.

She picked up her satchel and headed out. The morning air was chilly despite the soft sun, and the usual bustle of Manhattan surrounded her: honking taxis, bleary-eyed commuters, the tang of roasted peanuts from street carts. She boarded the subway, ignoring the press of tired bodies around her, and exited near 34th Street to walk the remaining blocks to the New Yorker Hotel.

She found the discreet door marked 481-U. A faint shimmer of magic brushed over her as she pressed a palm to the metal placard. The handle, disguised moments before, appeared as if coaxed by her presence. She stepped through into a modest hallway lit with a single orb. At the far end, an elegantly carved door greeted her, etched with subtle runes that glowed when she approached. She remembered the first time she had stood here, heart racing with uncertainty. Today, the feeling was more controlled, but no less intense for how deeply the stakes had grown.

The door swung open soundlessly. Caleb stood inside, dressed in a casual sweater and dark jeans, his eyes brightening the moment he saw her. She noticed the silver ring on his finger catch the morning light. "Come in," he said, his voice low and warm.

His apartment felt as organized as ever, though a few stray books scattered across the coffee table betrayed late-night research sessions. The gentle aroma of coffee mingled with something sweet—fresh fruit, maybe. Lila found herself relaxing a bit, letting the domestic atmosphere soothe her.

"Thanks for meeting me this early," she said. She set down her satchel and took off her jacket, feeling the pleasant warmth of the space. He guided her toward the small dining area where a bowl of yogurt with sliced berries awaited her. Beside it, two mugs of coffee steamed, the aroma rich and inviting.

"You said you had new pages of runes," he replied. He

gestured for her to sit, then took a seat across from her. His gaze kept flicking to her face, as if assessing her level of tension.

Her heart thrummed with anticipation. "Evelyn suddenly showed up early this morning with a bag full of papers, diaries and journals. She thinks something in them might help me." Hunched over the table, she eased the journal out of her satchel and extracted the two parchment sheets. "These fell out of the 1938–1943 book."

She laid them carefully on the table. The runes spiraled across the pages in looping arcs, interspersed with cryptic glyphs that reminded her of wards she had practiced.

Caleb leaned forward. The tension around his eyes told her that he recognized certain elements. "Your grandmother's note said she kept daily logs. Did she mention if these were a formal spell or more of a reference?"

"She left almost as soon as she arrived so I didn't have time to ask her," Lila answered. "Her handwriting's definitely all over these journals, but these runes feel different from her normal style. It might be something she copied."

Caleb nodded thoughtfully, tracing one symbol with the edge of his fingertip, careful not to smudge the ink. "I see the same archaic stroke we found in that old catacomb record about illusions. We only had fragments of it. This is definitely more extensive."

Her pulse kicked. "Are you sure?"

He lifted his gaze. "Yes. The library's partial transcripts showed a few repeated glyphs that never fully translated. And here"—he placed a fingertip along two curved lines on Lila's parchment—"this is the same swirl we saw in the neglected ledger referencing illusions anchored by wards older than the Council itself."

"So... does that mean this might be our missing piece? Some way to neutralize illusions?"

"Possibly," Caleb said. His voice trembled with the same mixture of relief and worry that churned in Lila's stomach. "We can't know for sure without cross-referencing more texts. But it could be a key. Something to anchor illusions to a stable point or unravel them at their source."

A swirl of excitement and dread fluttered through her. She remembered how the city's illusions kept intensifying, how the Council had grown desperate for any advantage in the race against Sebastian's cunning. "You think Evelyn knows more than we thought?" she asked. "Like she's been waiting for me to awaken?"

His expression softened. "I don't think she withheld it on purpose to make you struggle. She might have simply kept these and planned to share them if you had magical inclinations. Sometimes older witches gather references without fully comprehending how crucial they might be to the next generation."

Lila tucked a lock of hair behind her ear. She thought of her grandmother's phone call weeks ago, mentioning only bits and pieces about the family's heritage. "She never told me about half the spells I started reading in her journals. It's a treasure trove of knowledge. But I wonder if she worried the Council would try to claim it as their own."

The gloom behind Caleb's eyes told her he had similar suspicions. The Council had become jumpy, mistrusting, and selective in how it distributed resources. He rubbed his thumb over the ring on his finger and studied the runes once more. "If these cryptic outlines fit with the illusions we've seen in the catacombs, it gives us a direct lead. But we'll have to go down there ourselves."

Lila nodded, swallowing a lump in her throat. The catacombs were rife with precarious wards, half-collapsed passages, and illusions that lurked in every echo. The labyrinth's darkness had an otherworldly weight to it, as if centuries of hidden spells pressed in on all sides. Even the Council had rarely ventured there in full force.

She touched the parchment. "We only have half a puzzle, though. What if we need more lines of incantation?"

"Then we gather every cross-reference we can," Caleb said firmly. "We compile the missing lines from older texts. Or maybe more clues are buried in your grandmother's other journals." He glanced at the stack in her satchel. "We shouldn't leave any page unturned."

She felt a surge of gratitude for his calm determination. These private moments made her feel safe.

"Thank you," she whispered, meeting his eyes. "I was scared this might be a dead-end."

He reached across the table and gently squeezed her hand, sending little sparks of warmth through her veins. "No matter how messy it gets, we'll figure it out." He withdrew his hand with a subtle reluctance. "I'll help cross-reference. We can also ask a few discreet librarians for translation tips." His voice dropped. "We'll keep it quiet, though. These runes might be too valuable. If the Council learns we have them, they might demand we hand it over before we understand it ourselves."

Lila swallowed hard, imagining how easily the Council could confiscate her grandmother's legacy under the claim that it was necessary for the city's safety. Perhaps they wouldn't, but trust had grown thin in the last weeks. "Agreed. We'll proceed carefully." She pulled the bowl of yogurt closer and realized she hadn't even touched her breakfast. The berries glistened with colorful juices, and she took a quick spoonful, grateful for the jolt of sweetness. "We have more than illusions to worry about," she added, thinking of the infiltration attempts, a possible traitor in the Council's midst, and the swirl of rumors about Sebastian's next move. "But this might be the best lead we've found."

Caleb nodded, then reached for his coffee. Steam coiled around his face, intensifying the seriousness in his expression. "I propose we finalize a plan: you'll go through Evelyn's journals for additional references, I'll revisit the library's restricted sections with the notes. Then we meet again tonight to see how it all lines up."

She took a sip as well, letting the rich flavor ground her. "Tonight. That works. And after that..."

His eyes flicked to her face. "We likely try to map out exactly which corridors in the catacombs align with these runes. If the wards there are older than the Council's, they could be laced with illusions Sebastian is already using. We'll have to find the right vantage point to apply whatever incantation we piece together from your grandmother's text."

Her gaze dropped to the yellowed pages. A strange combination of fear and determination filled her ribs, as though she was bracing for a steep descent into darkness. "It's daunting," she admitted, her voice quiet. "But if it puts us a step closer to stopping illusions from overrunning the city, we can't stay idle."

Their eyes locked, and a current of understanding sparked. She let that solidarity wash over her. Yes, it was terrifying, but the alternative—letting illusions spread unchecked, condemning Manhattan to chaos—was worse.

Caleb folded the pages and handed them back to her carefully. "Keep these safe," he said. "I trust you more than any vault right now."

The weight of his trust made her throat tighten. She slipped them into the journal, then returned them to her satchel. The clink of porcelain cut through the sounds as she moved her coffee mug aside. Neither spoke for a stretch of moments, absorbing the gravity of what they had uncovered.

Finally, Caleb exhaled. "We should check the catacombs soon. We'll bring portable wards, maybe some detection spells. But I'm worried... the illusions might have grown more hostile."

"We'll be careful," she said gently. "One step at a time. For now, we keep investigating."

His shoulders eased a fraction. She recognized the slight slump as relief. "I know we keep repeating ourselves about caution, but it's worth repeating," he said with a small smile. "I'll look forward to tonight."

She finished off the last of her yogurt, stifling the swirl of warmth in her chest. Reluctantly, she folded her napkin and rose from the chair. "I should go before I lose this productive streak and get lazy."

He stood as well, following her to the door. "Text me if you find anything else in the journals. And try to fit in some rest. The illusions aren't going anywhere, and we can't help anyone if we burn out before we even begin."

She offered a shaky laugh, half jesting and half heart-felt. "I'll do my best."

She inhaled softly, noticing how a faint trace of his aftershave lingered in the air. Outside, the city roared with its usual vigor, but in here, for a moment, it felt like only the two of them existed. She glanced up at him. "Thank you for everything."

He touched her arm—a subtle, grounding gesture. "We can handle this, Lila," he whispered. "Whatever secrets those runes hold, we'll unlock them."

A faint tremor passed through her, part fear, part anticipation. She nodded, then let him open the door for her, then they took a moment to hug goodbye. He kissed her lightly and smiled. She stepped out, adjusting her bag's strap across her shoulder, and heard the door shut quietly behind her.

Exiting the building, she paused on the sidewalk. New York in early morning bustled around her, horns honking and pedestrians on their way to work. A slight breeze ruffled her hair, and she closed her eyes for a moment, letting the city's raw energy fill her. Part of her yearned to drop all of this and retreat to the normalcy of The Daily Grind. Yet illusions continued to churn across the boroughs, and the Council had pinned its hopes on any lead that could outmaneuver Sebastian.

She lifted her phone, sending a quick text to Maya: "I'll need more time off for the next few days. I'll help with the open shift soon, promise. Does that work for you?" Maya's earlier vow to cover for her still made guilt flicker in Lila's chest, but she pushed it aside. The stakes demanded she devote herself fully to the magical crisis.

She took a brisk step forward, heading home to lose herself in Evelyn's other volumes. Each would be thick with scrawled incantations, doodles, spells, maybe references to illusions from a different era. The day stretched out, hours of reading and note-taking. She wouldn't let weariness stop her. Resoluteness sharpened her steps.

By evening, she planned to cross-reference these new runes with the cryptic catacomb documents she brought home from the library. Tonight, she would meet Caleb again for a fuller study, combining knowledge gleaned from multiple eras. If all went well, they could piece together the incantation strong enough to sabotage Sebastian's illusions at their roots. The notion felt like a small flame in the darkness of her thoughts.

Night would come again soon, and illusions would swirl in the corners of Manhattan like restless ghosts. Sebastian might conjure new phantoms or strike at another unsuspecting Council outpost. Lila sensed time slipping between her fingers. But she also sensed the power of her grandmother's legacy, as though Evelyn's penmanship itself whispered that the Matthews line never surrendered to fear. Perhaps not every answer lay in the diaries, but it was more than she'd had yesterday.

She arrived back at her apartment and set the notebooks across her kitchen table, a determined glint in her eyes. The city's future felt bound up in these pages. She let her fingers trace the runic lines once more, recalling the firm reassurance in Caleb's voice.

Her heart fluttered. It was time to trust that their combined strength, plus Evelyn's carefully preserved knowledge, would be enough. Gently, she opened the first journal. When different factions in the Council wavered in doubt, she and Caleb would hold firm. They would keep these runes safe until they fully understood them.

With a final exhale, Lila settled in to read until her eyes blurred, determined to glean every snippet of knowledge she could. Tonight would bring the next step in their search for answers. After all, they had resolved to further explore the uncharted tunnels—ready or not.

CHAPTER

ELEVEN

By midday, Lila had a notebook filled with runics and incantations spells gleaned from Evelyn's note-books. But suddenly, she received a text that there would be a Council meeting in an hour, and all novices were required to attend. Shortly after she read that text, Caleb called saying to meet him at Council headquarters in an hour.

"What's this about?" asked Lila. "It seems like all we do is meet."

"I know, I feel the same way," but I'll see you there, right?"

"Of course. But this is cutting into my journal reading time and I was just getting to the juicy party," Lila laughed.

"See you in an hour," Caleb said curtly.

～

Bright afternoon light slanted through a row of high windows in the Council headquarters, illuminating the tense gathering of witches and warlocks. Lila could practically taste the unrest clogging the air. Whispers pinpointed her as one cause of the trouble, especially after rumors erupted that a new group of witches had broken away from the Council. That splinter faction questioned everything the elders stood for, and talk of negligence cast a dark shadow over the entire assembly.

Marcus stood at the far side of the dais, posture taut with impatience. His short-cropped hair and stern expression made him look every bit an enforcer of old laws. Several older witches ringed him, their stances echoing the same uncompromising posture. Lila lingered near the double doors, so aggravated she could hardly keep still. She sank her fingernails into her palms, forcing herself to focus on the arguments flying around the room.

A handful of novices sat rooted to their seats, silent or wide-eyed. Others, mostly older guardians, pointed at the main dais, shouting over each other. Words like "lack of leadership" and "Council secrecy" cut the air, each accusation more stinging than the last. Lila pressed her back against a marble column. The Council's main hall looked grand and imposing, but she could not ignore the swirl of tension that had already frayed every possible alliance.

At length, Marcus raised his hand. The crowd's ravings quieted, though no one looked at ease. "I realize," he began in his measured tone, "that trust is brittle right now. The splinter group forming in the city's underbelly does not trust our leadership, but we must take steps before illusions worsen. We discussed this before, but I think it's time to take offensive measures against anyone or any group that joins this rogue rebellion that's putting all of us at risk."

Murmurs rippled through the hall. Lila swallowed hard. Any heavy-handed measure could reduce their numbers and might even ramp up the other side.

She shoved off the column and stepped toward the center. "That's a fool's errand," she said, ignoring how her voice seemed to crack. "How exactly do you intend to ferret out others joining Sebastian? We already can't find them. Maybe a better approach would be to entice them to our side with a plan that actually shows results."

A few witches turned in their seats, eyes blazing with disapproval. One older guardian all but hissed. Another demanded, "She's barely out of training—why should we heed her opinion?" Several Council members stared at Lila with open animosity.

She should have held her tongue. Instead, frustration coursed through her like a flash flood. "Your approach might drive even more witches underground, or worse, into those splinter groups that say the Council doesn't care. If you listened to the city's novices, you'd see how reckless this is."

Voices rose in protest. Lila spotted Caleb standing near the tiered seating, shoulders tense. He offered her a quick glance, though his expression remained unreadable. She could sense the turmoil in him—he was nothing if not loyal to the Council's cause, but he also understood her arguments. Or so she believed. Right now, he kept his face impassive, as if wrestling with an invisible weight heavy enough to warp his usual composure.

Marcus put up both hands, summoning a purple warding glow that dampened the rising noise. "We will have order," he demanded. "This is precisely why we need firm measures. Sebastian's illusions slip further into the city each day, and we cannot have more of our members and especially novices joining his ranks."

"You mean you cannot have us messing up your reputation," Lila shot back, refusing to shrink from his hard stare. She was too angry, too fed up with endless talk of rules while illusions still lurked beyond these walls.

"Control yourself," spat an elder from the side, her braided silver hair quivering. "You stand before the Council as a mere novice. Show respect."

Icy fury raced across Lila's skin. The comment stung, but she angled her chin higher. Marcus looked ready to snap, and the tension in the hall had climbed to a suffocating pitch. Unable to help herself, Lila retorted, "If you had reacted faster when illusions first escalated, we might not be in this crisis. Now you want us to turn against each other at a time we should be pulling together to survive?"

An uproar exploded. Guardians leapt to their feet, hurling accusations that Lila had stepped out of line. Some novices shrank back, trying to avoid the storm entirely. A few voices hesitantly agreed with Lila, but they faded quickly beneath the ruckus. She caught sight of a witch near the dais rolling his eyes as if to say, That is enough from you, child.

Before Lila could speak again, Caleb's voice cut through the noise. "Lila, do you not realize what you're saying?" She heard the strain in his tone and turned. She expected him to defend her, or at least clarify her position. Instead, he spoke with the same sternness as the elders. "You're undermining the Council at a crucial time. Stand down."

Her stomach dropped. Of all people, she had not expected him to toss her under the wagon like that. She stared, unable to hide the disbelief blooming in her chest. "Undermining the Council?" she repeated, her voice trembling with confusion and hurt. "I'm only pointing out that as we sit here in these endless meetings we become more divided instead of actually coming up with a plan together to defeat this enemy."

Caleb's eyes flicked around the room. Something like guilt flashed across his face, vanishing as quickly as it came. "It isn't your place," he said, louder this time. "Arguing with senior guardians in the middle of an emergency meeting only feeds the chaos."

She inhaled sharply and tasted betrayal on her tongue. The hot flush in her cheeks matched the wave of murmurs racing around the hall. The elders, seeing she had been effectively shut down, launched into new complaints. A few demanded stronger punishment for novices who refused to heed the Council's established codes. Others slammed Lila's name specifically, insisting that her outburst proved novices might be more trouble than they were worth.

Marcus, apparently satisfied that the dispute had been

temporarily contained, struck the floor with his staff. "We will resume after a short recess," he announced coldly. "We have more pressing matters to finalize—especially if a splinter group is out there, recruiting witches who believe the Council has failed them."

The room emptied in a riled wave. Lila stood in the wake, numb with anger. A swirl of robed figures parted around her, leaving her alone beneath the tall arches. One older guardian—a man with a lined face—wore a grim expression, quietly remarking to a colleague that entire families had joined the new faction because they had "lost faith" in the Council's leadership. His tone suggested deep frustration. The swirl of magic in the air felt oppressive.

Lila clenched her fists until her nails bit into her palms. She noticed Caleb lingering by the wall. Rage flared anew as she saw him waiting, apparently wanting to say something. He caught her eye and nodded toward a side corridor. She stalked past him, chest tight. He followed, silent until they were out of earshot.

The corridor was narrow, with a row of muted lamps casting a dull glow on stone walls. Ancient tapestries of wards and symbols lined one side, their colors faded with time. Lila whirled on Caleb the moment they were alone. "You snapped at me like I was no better than a reckless child," she seethed. "In front of everyone."

He at least had the courtesy to look troubled. "I had to keep order," he said. "You saw them. They were ready to accuse you of treason. You're already under scrutiny because of your grandmother's role, your training with me—"

"Don't you twist this into some attempt to save me," she interrupted, voice shaking. "I don't need to be scolded like that to protect my reputation. You might have taken my side, or at least acknowledged my argument, but you just—" She pressed her lips together, furious tears burning at the corners of her eyes. She wanted to scream that the Council was ignoring the real problem: illusions creeping across the boroughs, novices locked in confusion, and a looming force that might splinter more families if they felt unprotected. Instead, this debate had become an exercise in finger-pointing.

Caleb exhaled slowly, the tension on his face unmasked. "Everything is spinning out of control. I can't hold it all," he said quietly. "I'm trying to fix what I failed to see months ago, with Sebastian, and it feels like my mistakes keep making the Council's job harder. Marcus thinks we need uniformity. He wants me to rein you in before any more novices riot against his leadership. So, I—"

She threw her arms in the air. "You sided with them to keep your own reputation clean." The words emerged sharper than she intended, but she did not regret them. Fury coiled in her gut, made worse by the sense of betrayal that she could not shake. Her chest felt tight, breath ragged. She wanted to fling all her pent-up frustration at him, at the entire Council who refused to hear reason.

His face hardened. "It's not about my reputation," he said, voice low. "It's about containing this crisis. The illusions have already driven some witches to Sebastian's cause. If you stir resentment against the Council in public, you boost Sebastian's hold on them."

She set a trembling hand on her hip. "So, I am a puppet? I should keep quiet because you and the Council fear losing face?"

For an instant, he looked ready to shout back. Instead, he raked a hand through his dark hair, eyes sparking with raw emotion. "This isn't the time to pick a fight with the entire Council," he murmured, though his voice shook with suppressed anger. "I'm doing everything I know how to do. If you're not careful, you'll wind up pressing the exact fear that Sebastian wants to exploit."

The corridor felt too narrow, every bit of air thick with tension. Lila's shoulders lifted in a mocking shrug as she lost the last shred of composure. "You talk like you're the only one with something at stake," she said bitterly. "I've got novices approaching me in secret, telling me they can't even cast a ward in their own apartments now. You think that's helpful? Do you?"

He moved closer, eyes blazing. "I never once said I agreed with everything the Council does. But storming into that assembly, insulting them outright, it accomplishes nothing." He paused. "I can't let you tear into them without thinking about the consequences. No matter how much I—" He cut himself off, chest heaving.

Her heart pounded, frustration boiling over. "No matter how much you what?" she demanded. She could not tell if she wanted him to finish the sentence or if she was simply spoiling for another argument. Anger overshadowed her better judgment, chasing out whatever warmth she normally found in his presence.

He pressed his lips together, then burst out, "No matter how much I care for you and want to defend you, or how infuriating it is to see you questioned. This entire crisis is bigger than us."

Silence pulsed between them, the tension crackling hotter. Lila threw up her hands, letting a ragged curse tear from her throat. "I can't do this," she said, voice unsteady. "I can't stand in that hall and pretend that these endless meetings and the ideas the Council is putting forward is going to help. But I also can't stand here and let you yell at me as if my perspective is worthless."

His jaw flexed. The anger and guilt in his expression mixed into something deeper: a strain that came from battling illusions and Council politics day after day. "You think it was easy?" he asked, stepping even closer. "You were about to tear the assembly in half, and half of them already blame me for Sebastian. They want an excuse to throw me out too."

She scoffed, the sound catching in her throat. "So, you risk me instead? That's a twisted way of protecting me, Caleb."

His eyes blazed as he gripped her arms, carefully but firmly. The corridor's torchlight glimmered, reflecting off the runes carved into the stone behind her. She stared at him, breath shallow, noticing how the fury in his gaze softened for a heartbeat. "I never meant to hurt you," he said, so quietly she almost missed it.

"But you did," she whispered.

He nodded, face etched with regret. For a slow, taut moment, neither of them spoke. The distant hum of angry voices drifted from the main hall, a reminder of the meeting that had ended with frustration and blame. Lila felt the full weight of the crisis pressing on them both—Sebastian's illusions, novices being cornered, the Council's prickly stance. All of it threatened to snap the fragile connection they shared.

A labored exhale left Caleb's lips. He pressed his forehead to hers, the brief contact sending a swirl of heat across her body. "I know how it sounded," he said. "Words came out wrong, or maybe they came out exactly how the elders wanted them. I—" He hesitated, shame in his eyes. "I can refute them in private, but in public, they... want absolute unity. It's suffocating. And I'm sorry."

His admission cut through her anger like a blade. Lila's lungs quivered as she tried to muster a retort, but all she managed was a frustrated breath. "We can't keep playing puppet, or stoic guardian, or naive novice. None of those roles help. We can't... trust half of them, not when Sebastian might have allies right here."

He tightened his hold on her arms, tension radiating from every muscle. "I know. I hate it too. But in their eyes, you and I are too close to the root of the problem. My past with Sebastian, your emerging power, your grandmother's knowledge—there's too much suspicion around us.

She let out a shuddering breath, tears threatening to spill. "I hate feeling powerless. I'm tired of fighting illusions and the Council at the same time."

His gaze softened, and he drew her closer, until her

anger and heartbreak twisted into raw need. She felt every breath as he pressed his forehead to hers. "I hate it too," he said, voice low. "And—" He exhaled, letting the rest remain unsaid: that they were together in this, no matter how many eyes watched or whispered.

An electric pulse of emotion flared between them. Days of stress, betrayal, and longing crashed into one single moment. Lila's heart thundered, and before she could second-guess herself, she leaned up, capturing his mouth in a fierce, desperate kiss. Her emotions spilled into him: frustration, lingering hurt, and a fierce bond that had grown despite everything.

He responded with equal urgency, each inhalation shuddering through their tangled tension. The stifling corridor melted away, replaced by the heat of his lips and the rasp of his breath. She tasted the salt of her own tears and felt the tremor in his body as he clutched the back of her shirt. For an instant, it seemed they might break from the dizziness of it all.

Caleb eased her backward until her shoulders brushed the corridor wall. They broke apart just long enough to stare at each other, as if each was checking for any last barrier. What she saw in his eyes shattered the remnants of her fury: sorrow, need, and the spark of hope that something stronger could exist between them, even when the Council threatened them both.

Her voice trembled with leftover anger and relief. "I hate you for doing that in there," she murmured, fisting her hands in his coat. "But I—" She lost the words when he cradled her face, brushing his thumb gently over her cheek. A broken laugh escaped her lips, colored by the absurd tension. "This entire situation is insane," she admitted with a quiver.

Caleb let out a soft, humorless chuckle. "It is," he agreed. Then he kissed her again, and the corridor's shadows felt less stifling. His mouth moved against hers in a firm, urgent press that spoke of regret and longing.

TWELVE

Twenty minutes later, Lila stood in a rubbish-strewn alley a few blocks away from a looming Art Deco theater, waiting for Caleb to finish the last of a whispered warding incantation. The old building's curved façade seemed to glow under the flicker of a nearby streetlamp. Chiseled faces decorated the theater's entrance, each visage cracked by decades of neglect. According to rumors, Sebastian's recruits were meeting beyond those doors tonight, plotting new ways to use illusions against a city on the brink.

She hugged her arms over her chest, keeping her breath even as she surveyed the small group of guardians huddled beside her. There were three: an older witch named Elysia, a muscled warlock named Rhys, and a quiet spellcaster whose name Lila had missed in the rush. They were loyal to the Council, or at least loyal to the city. At the close of the meeting Marcus had cornered Caleb and given him the assignment to investigate this building for signs of Sebastian and his followers. He had hastily recruited Lila and the other three to help.

Illusions crackled like phantom smoke along the theater's shattered marquee, showing partial letters that flickered in and out: L... A... T... bits of half-formed words that made no sense. It felt like Sebastian's calling card: illusions twisting even the smallest details. Lila glared at them, determined to prove she could hold her own.

"All set," Caleb said softly, stepping closer. A spell clung to him, wrapping their group in a faint silver shimmer that muted footsteps and prevented stray noises from escaping. She nodded, catching his gaze. Tension still sparked between them, but the mission demanded focus.

They slipped out of the alley without any further talk. Lila forced herself to stay calm, ignoring the gnawing ache in her belly. She positioned herself at Caleb's left, while Rhys peeled away to check if any wards protected the front door. Elysia and the quiet warlock circled to the side, scanning for illusions weaving across the tiled entryway. The spell kept them silent, but it did nothing for the clench of worry in Lila's chest. She tried to concentrate on each step, recalling how easily illusions could mask a trapdoor or conjure false floorboards. Sebastian's skill with illusions was unmatched, and if he had allies meeting inside, this infiltration could become disastrous with one misstep.

At a silent nod from Caleb, they slipped into the lobby through a side entrance. Dust and stale air enveloped them. Once, the high ceiling of this theater must have been a showstopper, with its gilded arches and exquisite murals. Now sharp cracks ran through the curved dome, and every wall wore a coat of grime. A faint bluish glow shimmered in the distance, spattering the marble floors with watery reflections. Lila sensed these lights weren't just low torchlights but illusions that flickered around empty sconces.

She and Caleb walked in tandem, glancing at each other whenever they tasted a surge of magic. Her left palm itched in that familiar way whenever illusions were close. She remembered the last time she had felt this creeping dread—her apartment had nearly been swallowed by illusions weeks ago. Now, with the possibility of Sebastian's recruits lurking in the wings, the risk was even higher.

They found a corridor leading backstage, where chipped posters lined the walls: old announcements of Broadway revues, comedic acts, and grand musicals. Each poster seemed on the verge of fluttering to life in the wavering illusions. Lila moved carefully, checking for wards. She heard the faint scuff of Elysia's boots behind them, though no true sound reached her ears due to the hush spell.

A faint bluish haze drifted around the corner. Caleb shot her a warning look, and she stilled, pressing her back against the wall. Ahead lay a narrow path ending in a half-broken door with a missing handle. Through a crack in that rotted wood, she saw a pale glow she recognized as conjured light. She gestured for the others to keep back.

Caleb crouched low, peering through the opening first, then half turned to wave Lila forward. Her heart pounded as she lowered herself to join him, her knees protesting at the awkward angle. The spell would keep them quiet, but if someone on the other side had placed wards, they might sense intruders anyway. She still had to risk it. She flattened her ear against the fragile wood.

Inside, voices rose and fell with tense frustration. One speaker's tone cut through the din, a man's voice. She couldn't place it for sure, but it carried that same quiet confidence she had heard among Sebastian's supporters in earlier run-ins. Another voice responded in a rasp, mentioning illusions that blanketed entire blocks. Lila caught fragments: "Prism resonance... alignment... powerful enough to warp wards." A prickle crept across her skin. They were talking about the Nexus Prism again, planning to harness it in just a matter of days. She thought of the Council's frantic warnings.

Caleb leaned closer, his body shielding Lila from the faint glow at the base of the door. She could feel him breathing steadily, though tension radiated from him. In the corridor behind them, Elysia and the others stood guard, eyes flicking toward the far end to ensure no illusions crept up on their flank.

The conversation inside continued, the voices sharper now that Lila was straining to listen. She picked out scattered phrases: "Sebastian wants it done by the night of..." and "the city's wards are thinner than ever." Another speaker laughed, a cold, humorless sound. Then they mentioned a date only a handful of days away, and Lila's blood ran cold. The Council had guessed that Sebastian hoped to exploit the alignment soon, but hearing it confirmed this directly was worse than she expected. A rebellion of fear coiled in her gut as she realized exactly how little time they had left.

She shifted her weight, trying to ease her cramped legs. That moment of movement made the floorboard under her sneaker creak. The tiny noise should have been muffled by the spell, but apparently the old wood's splintering was loud enough to translate through the barrier. Lila froze. She felt Caleb's grip on her elbow, urging her to stay still. Inside, the voices went quiet.

It felt as if she had swallowed a live wire. Her heart stampeded, and she imagined the shadowy figures inside turning to the door, illusions poised to strike. She sensed the spell flickering, as if some detection charm recognized they weren't alone.

They had the information they needed. That was the only thought that kept her from panicking. Lila carefully backed off, slipped out of Caleb's reach, and mouthed to him that they should leave. His eyes narrowed in agreement. The spell still clung to them enough to stifle footsteps, but every movement risked another squeak of old lumber.

A faint glow crept toward the base of the door, like someone inside had raised a witch light or shining orb. Her pulse hammered. She forced away the rising panic and pressed herself flush against the wall. She gestured at Elysia and the others to retreat.

One slender hand from Elysia tapped the line of runes etched in the air. She was reinforcing the spell as best she could. Caleb's lips formed silent words, layering another subtle incantation over Elysia's. It worked. When they stepped away, not even the faintest shuffle of shoes reached Lila's own ears. Yet her mind swarmed with tension, convinced that any second the door would swing open on a wave of illusions.

They crept back, hugging the crumbling plaster walls and the corridor's flickering gloom until they reached the wide lobby. Lila's eyes remained glued to the half-broken door behind them, expecting pursuit. She saw no one emerge. The spell shielded them like a bubble, a precarious gift that might fail if the watchers inside had sharper wards.

At last, they returned to the side entrance. Rhys opened it slowly, the faint squeak of metal hinges was the only sound. Cool night air washed in, a more honest darkness than the illusions within the theater. As soon as they slipped beyond the threshold, Lila felt her lungs expand with relief. The spell's boundary ended a few steps later, restoring the city's distant buzz. She could hear sirens in the distance, the hum of traffic punctuated by an occasional honk. Real noise. Real life.

Elysia exhaled, mouth pressed tight. "We got enough," she whispered, voice still soft with adrenaline. "We can meet you at the safehouse near Midtown."

Caleb nodded. "Go. Keep watch. If they suspect we were here, illusions might flood the area."

Rhys and the other warlock quickly slipped away, passing ghostlike into the darkness at the end of the alley. Elysia gave a brief salute and followed. Within seconds, Lila and Caleb were alone beside a dented dumpster, old newspapers plastered to the ground by spilled beverage. A neon sign in the distance flickered, throwing jagged colors onto the brick walls.

Lila tried to steady her breath, tried to rid herself of the memory of that creaking floorboard. Everything about this mission had been a gamble, and yet they pulled it off. She inhaled, chest tight with the knowledge that Sebastian's timeline was horrifyingly close. If they did not find a way to stop him, illusions would soon take over in ways the city might not survive.

Caleb subdued his warding aura with a quick flick of his fingers, then stepped closer. Neon light cut across his face, painting him in harsh red and green lines. She could see the concern etched in his eyes. The anger from earlier was still there but tempered now by shared resolve.

"We have a few days," she whispered, voice shaky. "Not weeks, not months. Days."

"We'll do what we must," he replied. His tone was quiet but fierce. She heard the same determination that laced his words whenever he vowed to protect her. Though her frustration with him lingered, she couldn't deny how safe she felt wrapped up in that unwavering dedication. The adrenaline throbbed inside her, making her fingertips tremble.

He reached for her hand, gently brushing his knuckles across her palm. She closed her fingers around his, uncertain if the pounding in her chest was fear or something closer to devotion. The memory of how he had thrown her under the wagon at the Council hurt, but this was a different moment. His eyes darted around, scanning the alley. When no illusions appeared, he finally let out a breath and turned back to her.

They stood together beneath the blue hum of a faulty streetlight, its flicker matching the beat of her heart. The night smelled of damp concrete and faint traces of garbage, harsh reminders of how far they stood from the Council's pristine marble halls. Yet in this moment, the rest of the city fell away. She only felt the warmth of his fingers.

"We'll warn Marcus," Lila said. "We have to do something big, and fast. "

Caleb gave a curt nod. "Yes. And no more of these half-measures from the Council. They need to listen this time."

The streetlight flickered. A scuttling sound echoed in the alley as a stray cat dashed for cover, startled by their presence. Lila pulled on Caleb's coat lapel, drawing him closer. She smelled the faint warmth of his aftershave, the comforting hint of old books that clung to him from countless hours in the Council archives. Maybe it was the mixture of fear and anger in her, or the closeness that felt more potent now that the spell had dropped, but every nerve in her body buzzed. She was sick of letting illusions or petty Council battles define them.

He said her name softly, as though a question. She didn't answer. Instead, she surged forward, pressing her mouth to his in a fierce, searching kiss. Every shard of tension erupted, fueling a desperate collision of lips. Their earlier argument, her sense of betrayal, his guilt at scolding her in front of the Council—none of it vanished, but it twisted into raw passion that demanded some release. She tasted the metallic tang of her own anticipation and felt him respond with equal fervor, his hand sliding around her waist. Their hearts thundered in sync, a feverish reminder that in a city overshadowed by illusions, their bond carried a spark of reality.

They pulled apart to inhale, her breaths ragged. He let his forehead rest against hers, eyes half-closed. She felt him shudder, as if absorbing the weight of everything that still lay ahead. She braced one hand on the worn brick behind him, searching for something stable to cling to. The slick humidity of the alley pressed in, reminding her that this stolen intimacy might last only a moment before the next wave of danger.

"Whatever happens," he murmured, voice rough with lingering adrenaline, "we face it together."

She nodded, letting the vow settle. "It was mentioned over and over in my grandmother's journals I've been reading all day that there is a Matthews amulet that has the power to dispel illusions. I think we have to figure out where it is and harness that power. It may be our only hope."

"I also read about an amulet with awesome power in the library archives but apparently it's been missing for generations. Many have searched for it, but all have reached dead ends," Caleb volunteered.

"Let's circle up with my grandmother and see if we can hit on something. I'll give her a call," Lila said as she punched in the numbers.

THIRTEEN

After conferring with Evelyn over dinner and asking her many questions about the amulet, and her magical lineage and who might have had the amulet last, Evelyn remembered her great-grandmother Rose, who had lived across from Riverdale Park in the upper Bronx. Evelyn remembered visiting a greenhouse there as a child and being enchanted by all the twisting vines and abundance of herbs and flowers. The house had been passed down through multiple generations of Matthews and was now owned by Evelyn since the death of her parents. She had rented it out for many years, but the property had now been vacant for years.

"I think I've gotten letters from the mayor wanting to condemn the property and exercise eminent domain, but I've thrown those letters in the trash," Eveyln laughed. "My attorney writes back that the property is a 'historical site.' They really don't know what to do with that."

A pale shaft of sunlight broke through the curtain of

low-hanging clouds as Lila, Caleb, and Evelyn stepped from the unpaved road onto an overgrown trail. Gravel crunched beneath their boots, and a damp chill clung to the air. Even so, a stubborn warmth pulsed at the base of Lila's spine—she suspected it was the same energy that surged whenever her budding earth magic awoke. The dog-eared letters rustled in her grip, each page brittle beneath her fingertips. They were her grandmother's, after all, left behind years ago to guard a secret no one had fully understood until now.

Lila glanced at Evelyn, who walked a few steps ahead with her shoulders set in quiet determination. A persistent guilt flashed across Lila's mind. She still wasn't entirely sure if she blamed her grandmother for keeping so many mysteries hidden, or if she felt only relief that Evelyn had finally shared them. Their time was short, and the city's illusions were spreading faster than anyone predicted. Each letter spelled out cryptic references to a greenhouse that once kept strange flora meant for relic cultivation— flora that Lila's great-great grandmother had nurtured, hoping to protect a powerful artifact. Evelyn's words in the letters had been vague, but the underlying message was clear enough: this place might hold a piece of the puzzle they needed.

Caleb walked on Lila's left side, silent and watchful. She could sense his tension pulsing underneath the calm exterior. He carried a faint blueprint of wards in his mind —she picked that up from the way he occasionally flicked his fingers against his coat pocket, as if preparing to cast a protective barrier on a moment's notice. His gaze drifted to the trees that framed the trail, half suspicious that illusions might lurk in every shadow. Before stepping over a mound of broken stones, he caught Lila's wrist gently, helping her over the uneven ground. Her heart kicked at the small contact.

They emerged into a clearing swallowed by wild grass and tangled vines. At the far edge stood the greenhouse, crumbling under the weight of time. Jagged shards of glass gaped from the rusted iron framework, and thick ivy cascaded from the roof. The metal skeleton groaned when a gust of wind rattled through. Lila swallowed hard. If she pressed her senses outward, she caught the faintest thread of old magic embedded in the place—a relic of spells once used to encourage plants to grow in unnatural ways. Or maybe that was just nerves, twisting her awareness into knots.

Evelyn paused in front of the entrance, where a pair of broken doors leaned off their hinges. Moss spread across the glass like a second skin. For a moment, no one spoke. A robin cawed somewhere beyond the briars, and a chill breeze rustled the vines overhead.

"Well," Evelyn said, her voice quiet. "This is clearly the right place, even if it looks about ready to collapse."

Lila tightened her fingers around the yellowed letters. "Guess we have no choice but to go in. If you sense anything odd—any illusions—please tell me right away." She directed that last part to Caleb, though in truth, she wasn't sure illusions from the city would reach them here. Then again, Sebastian's network of manipulated spells felt endless these days.

Caleb nodded. "I will. But watch your footing." He pressed a hand on the rotted door and gave it a firm push. The wood snapped, leaving a jagged opening into the greenhouse. He carefully stepped forward, scanning the gloom inside with narrowed eyes.

They entered single file, Lila in the middle. The smell of damp leaves and decomposing wood assaulted her senses. Strands of unidentifiable vines hung from the metal beams overhead. She glimpsed lumps of broken pottery, cracked wooden tables, and planters that had disintegrated into half-rotted rubble. A stale calm pressed in, as if nature had reclaimed every corner except for the faint aura of magic humming behind the scenes.

Evelyn walked along the edge of the nearest planter bed, gently nudging aside a cluster of dried weeds with her boot. "This used to be a place of healing," she said softly. "My great-great grandmother specialized in culti-vating plants with unusual resonances. Some for potions, others... for protective spells."

"And for relic enhancements," Lila added, recalling the references in her grandmother's journal. The idea that her bloodline had once played caretaker to bizarre, powerful objects still made her uneasy. She rubbed the back of her neck and tried to center herself. "Which side do we start with?"

Evelyn consulted the handwritten notes. "These pages mention a section near a fruiting vine. It apparently bore seeds crucial to grounding certain relics. It also says the chest would've been buried if the greenhouse was ever abandoned."

Caleb turned in a slow circle, scanning the long, rust-eaten rows. "We should look for an area that could have once housed that vine. Over by that far corner, maybe?" He nodded toward an arching line of twisted support beams. A wide chunk of glass was missing from the ceiling there, and thick tangles of brown vines dangled near the floor.

They approached, guided by the faint greenish light that filtered through the shattered roof. As they moved deeper into the greenhouse, Lila's pulse spiked. With each step, a subtle vibration flickered in her core—the same jittery rush she felt when illusions were near. Or perhaps it was the earth-based magic her grandmother always hinted resided in the Matthews lineage.

She crouched by a collapsed planter. Dirt spilled from the cracked edges, and the remains of a root system sat tangled in old netting. When she ran her palm over the soil, a stirring of warmth shot up her arm. Startled, she jerked back. "I think I found something," she said, voice shaky. She touched the soil again, this time more deliberately. Her head buzzed with the impression of something hidden, as if a whisper from the earth urged her to keep digging.

Evelyn sidled closer, features tight with curiosity. "The letters suggested your family line can sense relics... or at least sense places strengthened by ancestral magic." Her words were gentle but urgent, encouraging Lila to trust her instinct.

Lila exhaled a breath she hadn't realized she was holding and delved into the damp soil with her fingers.

The musty smell clung to her nails as she scooped out handfuls of dirt and dead foliage. The sensation in her chest magnified, a tug that felt like an invisible thread winding around her heart. Her pulse hammered. She tried to steady her breathing, scanning for illusions, but none flickered at the edges of her vision. This was pure earth magic, guiding her deeper.

A damp plank of wood emerged from the dirt. Caleb knelt beside her to ease it aside. Underneath was a battered corner of what looked like a small wooden chest. The metal clasp had rusted, fused into the wood with a mess of greenish corrosion. Lila and Caleb exchanged a charged look.

"This must be it," Caleb said, voice low. He pressed his hand carefully to the top of the chest, applying just enough force. The rotted wood creaked in protest but didn't break. "It's stuck."

Lila dug away more of the dirt until the entire lid was exposed. Prying her fingernails under the edge, she felt her magic flicker. The vibration in her chest turned into a steady rhythm. She took a slow breath, letting the magic flow through her limbs. Summoning just enough energy, she gave an upward push. The lid splintered with a crack, and a musty whoosh of trapped air escaped.

Evelyn leaned in, brushing aside stray leaves. "That's it," she murmured. "The chest mentioned in my notes. Stars above, I can't believe it's still intact." Her smile was a bittersweet curve, as if remembering all the years she could have told Lila about this place and chose not to.

Inside, a folded scrap of cloth lay dark with dirt and

decay. Lila lifted it gingerly, revealing a glint of silver beneath. Her heart thudded, and the sense of a slumbering power flared around them. She reached into the chest, fingers trembling, and touched what felt like carved metal. Pulling it free, she found a slender silver amulet etched with swirling runes.

The runes caught the weak light, shimmering with a faint luminescence. It looked like the amulet had been shaped from a single piece of silver, its design seemingly unbroken by any clasp or seam. Lila let her breath out in a rush. A warmth, gentle yet insistent, pulsed at her fingertips. She felt the amulet's energy stir, all but greeting her.

"This must be the key," Evelyn whispered. She hooked a hand over her mouth, tears welling in her eyes. "I hoped... but I didn't know if it was true. My grandmother used to speak of an artifact that could hold illusions at bay, something tied into the Matthews lineage. I only found real proof when I dug through the attic." Her voice wavered, heavy with the regrets of too many hidden stories.

Lila's own throat felt tight. The swirl of runes almost drew her in, as though they recognized her. She had touched magical items before, but this was different. It felt intimate, as if the amulet resonated with her heartbeat. She brushed a thumb over the nearest rune, and a delicate glow answered. She swallowed. "I can't believe this has been lying here all these years."

Caleb gently placed a hand over hers, pressing the amulet into her palm. His expression lit with a rare glimmer of excitement. "Feel that? It's matching your aura. There's a clear frequency humming between your magic and this silver. It could really be that missing piece we need."

Lila nodded, though part of her wanted to cry. Tension bled from her muscles, replaced by a surge of hope so strong it made her dizzy. "Do you think it can truly disrupt illusions?" she asked, looking from him to Evelyn. "Because if we're right, if this is the artifact that your notes described, we finally have something that might hold Sebastian's illusions in check."

Evelyn sniffed back a tear as she crouched by the open chest. "The writings say it's capable of neutralizing or weakening illusions when used properly—though it requires a Matthews bloodline signature." She placed a weathered hand on Lila's shoulder. "And that's you, dear. The bloodline is strong in you. This isn't a guarantee, but we know Sebastian's illusions are dangerously advanced. If anything can hamper his control, a relic keyed to your ancestry stands the best chance."

A swirl of conflicting emotions churned in Lila's stomach—relief, indignation at how long these secrets had been buried, and an unexpected surge of elation at the thought of finally fighting back. She lifted the amulet closer to her face, examining each swirling rune. The patterns reminded her of vines twisting up an iron trellis, gently curved yet unyielding. "I guess that means I'm the only one who can truly activate it," she said softly.

Caleb's voice steadied her. "Only you can use it at full power," he said. "But we'll be right beside you." Something in his gaze stirred warmth in her core, an intimate promise that she wasn't facing the city's crisis alone.

She nodded, heart pounding. The broken greenhouse seemed to close around them, the sweet, decaying scent of old foliage mingling with the metallic tang of magic. Glass shards sparkled on the floor, and the corners of the greenhouse groaned when the wind picked up again. She pressed the amulet tight to her chest, letting the echo of its energy ripple through her ribs.

Evelyn cleared her throat and reached into the chest one last time, rummaging beneath the tattered cloth. She pulled free a small scrap of paper with a flourish of runic script. Her wrinkled brow furrowed as she squinted at it. "Instructions of some kind, but half is missing... or rotted away."

Caleb moved to read over Evelyn's shoulder. "We can take it with us, see if the Council library or your old journals have the rest. Even partial clues might help."

The mention of the Council drew a flicker of unease across Lila's face. Their last confrontation with the elders had been fraught. But she swallowed the distaste and reminded herself that they did need the Council's resources. The illusions creeping through Manhattan were too vast for any one witch or warlock to fight alone. If the city was to be protected—and if Lila was going to stand any chance of facing Sebastian—she needed allies, no matter how tense the politics might be.

Evelyn slid the scrap into a pocket inside her coat. Then she sighed, a gentle exhalation that carried a kind of acceptance. "We'll sort that out back in the city. For now, we have what we need. Let's get this out of here safely."

Together, they rose, the rotted chest at their feet. Lila slipped the amulet onto the thin chain around her neck, still marveling at how it pulsed in time with her heartbeat. The last vestiges of the greenhouse's power coiled in the air, a silent witness to the dusty remains of planters and the legacy of Lila's ancestor. She let her gaze wander across the broken beams and glass, imagining how it might have looked in ages past—a tablet of thriving green, carefully cultivated spells, and magic used for growth instead of destruction.

Caleb motioned for them to head toward the exit. Evelyn trailed behind for a moment, casting one final, mournful look at the battered structure. Lila understood the sentiment. All around them, the city's illusions were warping everyday reality, and yet here, in the remnants of a facility designed to nurture life, they had discovered the relic that might finally allow them to turn the tables. The irony wasn't lost on her. She was both the reluctant barista who once spilled coffee under flickering café lights and, apparently, the heir to an earth-based enchantment line strong enough to challenge illusions that threatened everyone she knew.

At the threshold, boarding back into the wind outside, Caleb paused to place a gentle hand on Lila's arm. "We'll safeguard it together," he said, nodding to the amulet. "And I promise I'll do everything in my power to help you master what it can do." His voice was soft, full of that loyalty she found both comforting and terrifying, because it meant he believed in her—even if she sometimes doubted herself.

She tucked the amulet beneath her jacket, feeling the cool metal rest against the hollow of her throat. "We're so close," she whispered, and her conviction sounded stronger than it had a few hours ago. She could almost taste the sense of purpose surging behind her ribs.

Evelyn rejoined them, her boots clicking across a slab of fallen glass. A final gust of wind rattled the greenhouse frame, as if urging them to leave before the entire place decided to crumble. Setting her shoulders, Lila led the way, stepping back onto the overgrown path under the gray sky. No illusions flickered in sight, but she did not let herself relax. After a moment's silence, all three turned from the greenhouse. They had found what they came for.

Warm adrenaline still hummed through Lila's veins as they navigated the return path. She crinkled the letters in her hand, imagining how Evelyn must have felt all those years ago deciding when—or if—to reveal their family secrets. Yet at this moment, Lila didn't feel anger. She felt the tremor of possibility. This find changed everything.

At the end of the trail, she paused, letting both Evelyn and Caleb draw alongside her. She lifted the amulet out again, studying the runes that glimmered even in the cloudy afternoon light. The symbol at the center looked like a curling vine. It felt protective and alive. She closed her fingers around it, catching her breath when a warm pulse answered from inside the silver. Whatever came next, she had a real chance to stand against illusions that seemed unstoppable only days ago.

"This is our weapon," she said quietly, half to herself and half to them. "Our best shot at safeguarding the city."

Evelyn nodded, eyes glistening. "And you're the only one who can unlock it fully, my dear."

Caleb's hand brushed Lila's shoulder. "You're not alone," he answered, voice low but certain.

Lila exhaled, pressing her lips together in a faint, determined smile. Visions of swirling illusions danced at the corners of her imagination, reminders of everything at stake. But now she had a spark of hope to cling to. Carefully, she tucked the amulet beneath her jacket once more, letting it settle against her heart. A tremor of confidence rippled through her limbs, fueling her resolve.

Deep down, she knew they still faced many trials ahead. Bringing this relic back to the city would cause new ripples, political or otherwise. But for now, she let herself savor a quiet relief. She could do this. Holding on to that conviction, she turned and started down the path, Evelyn and Caleb flanking her. The greenhouse behind them groaned once more, as if whispering its last farewell.

As they reached the edge of the treeline, Lila paused. She wrapped her fingers firmly around the amulet, pressing the silver against her chest and feeling the surge of energy dance along her skin. She glanced at Caleb, feeling a bold flush at the intensity of his gaze, then at Evelyn, whose expression held both pride and regret. They all knew what a treasure this was. If it could help them stand against Sebastian's illusions, then the entire city might have a fighting chance.

Gripping the amulet, Lila raised her eyes. "This is it,"

she murmured. "We have our key." A fierce light burned in her gaze, fueled by the renewed hope sparking in her heart. The city could still descend into chaos, but at least now she had a weapon to protect it. She refused to let illusions swallow the place she loved.

And for the first time in weeks, she felt certain they had a real shot at victory.

FOURTEEN

Lila pressed her palm against the smooth silver amulet at her collar, the metal warmed by the lingering magic of the greenhouse. She sat in the front seat of the borrowed Council sedan, which hummed along a stretch of Manhattan's congested roads. Beside her, Caleb gripped the steering wheel tighter than usual, his knuckles faintly white with tension. Evelyn sat in the back, quietly re-reading the faded notes about the amulet's properties, the faint glow of her phone occasionally lighting the lines of worry on her face.

Outside the car window, the skyline was darkening despite the early hour. A coppery tint stained the horizon in an odd, sickly glow. Lila could not tell if the color was a trick of the dying sunlight or the result of mounting illusions in the sky. Her phone chimed for the tenth time in ten minutes.

She winced and picked it up. The screen was flooded with half-panicked messages from Council watchers: illusions thickening around Times Square, phantom silhouettes scaling the Empire State Building, and wave after wave of tampered traffic signals in Midtown. The newest notification read: "Requesting immediate response—dozens of illusions swirling near Columbus Circle. Unconfirmed sightings at the Public Library steps." Lila's heart thumped as she scrolled. Her previous training sessions had hinted that illusions were steadily expanding, but this sudden onslaught felt like a citywide meltdown.

Caleb frowned at her sideways glance. "Anything new?" he asked.

She nodded, throat tight. "They're popping up in every direction. We have illusions messing with traffic lights, with tourists in Times Square seeing shapes in all the billboards. It's a lot worse than two hours ago."

Evelyn lifted her gaze from the notes. "The Prism is stirring. The more active it becomes, the less stable the wards around the city will be."

A faint chill brushed Lila's arms. She recalled the greenhouse an hour earlier, how her newly claimed silver amulet had pulsed in tandem with her heartbeat. Even back there, she had felt a subtle tension coiling inside her bones. Now it radiated through her spine like a feverish wave, intensifying with each passing minute. It was the same feeling she usually associated with a storm building overhead, only this time, the storm throbbed from within.

"All these illusions can't just be random," Lila said, lowering her phone. "They must be tied to the Prism's... partial wake-up call, or whatever you want to call it. I've been getting these throbs and chills for days now. I felt them growing stronger this afternoon, right before we found the chest. It's like my body knows the Prism is... alive."

Caleb slowed the car to let an erratic taxi swerve around a corner. The streetlights flickered in odd patterns —one turned green, then instantly flashed red, confusing pedestrians. Some drivers honked in frustration. Others stared at the flickering signals, no doubt suspecting a city-wide power glitch, unaware illusions were weaving right through the flow of traffic.

"That sense in your body might be its resonance with you," Evelyn said. "Our family's lineage was always rumored to have a unique bond with relics, especially ones dealing with illusions. That bond may have grown stronger when you claimed the amulet."

The reminder made Lila's stomach roll with unease. She had only just begun to accept that this silver amulet was more than a trinket. Feeling an entire relic—one known to warp reality—call to her from across the city seemed too vast to comprehend. She forced a shaky breath.

Caleb turned onto a side street leading to Lila's neighborhood. "Let's regroup at your place," he said. "We can contact the Council from there, see if they want us at any specific location."

Evelyn did not speak as the car slowed to a stop near Lila's apartment building. Emerging onto the sidewalk, Lila immediately noticed something off about the air. It felt heavier. The neon sign of a nearby corner store flickered in swirling patterns that reminded her of a kaleidoscope's fractured image. A second later, the sign's letters rearranged into nonsense shapes before snapping back to normal, as if glitched by some invisible force.

Illusions, she realized.

A younger couple walked past the sign, oblivious, then paused in confusion. The man rubbed his eyes and shook his head, apparently deciding it was just a trick of the light. Lila's chest squeezed with apprehension, knowing that illusions had begun bleeding into everyday life in ways ordinary people might not ignore for much longer.

Evelyn, stepping around a puddle on the curb, clutched her purse close. "The entire city is humming with magic," she said softly. "This is what a partial activation of the Prism looks like. It hasn't fully awakened, but the waves it's releasing are already tearing at the wards. If Sebastian gains direct control of that power..."

Her voice trailed off. Lila exchanged a look with Caleb, who hovered an arm behind her shoulder as though he expected her to faint at any second. She lifted her chin, trying to muster confidence she did not feel.

Before she could take three steps further, her phone chimed again. She checked it to see frantic messages about illusions breaking out near the Brooklyn Bridge—some monstrous silhouette prowling along the cables.

"Another one. Brooklyn Bridge, apparently," she said in a thin voice. "We might only have hours before the illusions spread everywhere."

Caleb inhaled, then exhaled. "Let's get inside."

They hurried up the front steps to Lila's apartment building, shoving past a flickering overhead light in the hallway. On the second-floor landing, the bulbs winked in and out as if playing cat-and-mouse with their shadows. A wave of static electricity prickled across Lila's arms. Her amulet pulsed warm against her collarbone. She steadied herself, ignoring the creeping anxiety in her bloodstream, and unlocked her door.

Inside, Lila hit the switch—nothing. The overhead fixture remained dark. "Great," she muttered. "Power's out. Or illusions are messing with it."

She fumbled along the wall, found a spare lantern that Caleb had insisted she keep after the last infiltration, and flipped the switch. Its battery-powered glow bathed the cramped living room in a faint glow. She noticed the flicker in the corner of her vision—barely discernible wisps of illusions coiling near the ceiling. Were they drifting in through the vents?

Evelyn stepped forward. "Set this letter down," she told Lila, brandishing a folded page from the greenhouse notes. "Light wards might keep illusions from entrenching here, but it's going to be difficult with the Prism's partial activation feeding them."

Lila helped Evelyn spread the page on the coffee table. The sketched runes detailed a minor ward that supposedly repelled illusions, at least small-scale ones. Evelyn touched a finger to the swirling lines and began to murmur under her breath. A faint sheen coalesced in the air above the table, shimmering like morning dew. Some of the ephemeral shapes in the corners began to dissipate.

Caleb drew out a small piece of chalk from his coat

pocket. "I'll reinforce that," he said, dropping to one knee to trace a quick circle of runes on the floor. His voice was calm, but Lila detected stress in the subtle lines around his mouth.

As he worked, Lila found herself transfixed by a new wave of throbbing discomfort that rippled through her chest. It was not quite pain yet, but it made her knees quiver. She pressed her hand over her sternum, heart galloping. The amulet vibrated so fiercely that the whole chain trembled.

"Lila, are you all right?" Evelyn asked, glancing up from her warding.

Before she could reply, the sensation sharpened into a sudden jolt of searing pain. Lila gasped, doubling over. Her vision blurred white-hot, and she staggered, barely registering the way Caleb's strong arms caught her around the waist. For a split second, she felt like something was yanking her soul toward an unseen magnet.

"Stay with me," Caleb said. He tried to steady her, but his voice crackled. She thought she heard him mutter a ward meant to soothe pain, only for it to sputter in the charged air.

Evelyn hurried over, voice taut with concern. "This must be the Prism reaching out... drawing power from what it can. The amulet is part of that connection!"

Lila closed her eyes, panting. The pain ebbed slightly, though the phantom grip in her chest felt like it refused to let go. She could sense the city beyond her apartment walls, illusions pulsing in different corners of Manhattan, feeding off some monstrous source. Her blood practically buzzed with a need to move, as if the relic demanded she come closer.

Caleb pressed a hand to her forehead, brow creased. "Your wards are flickering," he said, nodding at the shimmering barrier that Evelyn had raised. "They aren't holding. The partial activation is too strong."

Lila forced herself upright, swallowing the taste of copper in her mouth. "I'll be fine. Help me get outside. I can't breathe in here."

Caleb guided her by the elbow. Evelyn led the way, chanting quietly to keep illusions from bombarding them in the hall. Once they stepped back onto the street, Lila gulped the cooler air, grateful for small mercies.

Night had settled, though not in the usual Manhattan fashion. Instead of bright marquee lights or tidy streetlamps, much of the neighborhood flickered as if caught in a psychedelic dream. Store signs flared with swirling patterns, flicking from normal letters to random shapes and back again. Traffic signals blinked in wild sequences, temporarily freezing cars in confusion. Shadows loomed at the corners of buildings, insubstantial shapes that drifted just out of sight whenever Lila tried to look straight at them.

"It's worse out here," Caleb observed under his breath. He released Lila, though he stayed close enough that his arm brushed hers.

A woman walked by, talking loudly on her phone about a snake-like figure she thought she saw near a streetlight. Another pedestrian raced past the group, muttering about city-wide blackouts and a sudden glitch at a local museum. The entire block buzzed with tension, as though a single spark could send everyone running for safety.

Evelyn's gaze flickered from a half-transparent silhouette drifting by a fire hydrant to a swirl of phantom letters dancing across the bakery window. "If the Prism fully awakens, illusions will swarm every structure in Manhattan," she said, her voice trembling with urgency. "This is already beyond anything usual. And if Sebastian gains complete control... there won't be any barrier between the mortal realm and magic. It will bleed together."

Lila gritted her teeth. She tried to quell the trembling in her stomach, focusing on the radiant weight of her amulet against her chest. Just an hour before, they had dared to hope that discovering the amulet could help them stop this madness. Now it felt more like a beacon leading her straight to the heart of the danger.

A swirl of intense magic flared in the subway grate at the base of the sidewalk. Colors splashed across the pavement, phantom beams that barely missed a group of teens with skateboards. Those teens stared wide-eyed, murmuring fast and pointing, presumably suspecting a trick of neon lighting. Lila cursed under her breath. She glanced at Caleb, whose posture was rigid and ready for an attack that could come from anywhere.

He caught her gaze, eyes full of worry. "You feel it too, right?" he asked. "That sense of being pulled?"

She nodded, pressing a hand to her chest again. Her voice came out low and unsure. "It's calling me like I'm part of it, or it's part of me. I don't know which."

Evelyn lowered her notes and pressed her free hand gently on Lila's shoulder, offering a trembling smile of solidarity. "If we let fear paralyze us, we lose. Sebastian's illusions thrive on our uncertainty. And the Council can't handle this alone without the amulet's help. We must stand together before the Prism crosses the tipping point."

A distant wail of sirens carried through the swirling magical haze. A police cruiser barreled along the avenue, lights flashing, likely responding to countless calls of unnatural occurrences. Lila felt her heart pound with an equal mix of dread and resolve. She thought of Maya, possibly still finishing a late shift at The Daily Grind, and prayed illusions were not wreaking havoc on the café's customers. She thought of the Council watchers, scattered across the city, desperately trying to contain illusions in tourist hotspots and quiet streets alike. Most of all, she thought of Sebastian, a man who had once walked these wards as a friend to Caleb, now harnessing unimaginable power for reasons she still struggled to fathom.

She curled her fingers around the amulet's chain, steadying herself on that small anchor. Beside her, Caleb drew in a slow breath, magic glimmering at the edges of his eyes. His wards rippled once more, staving off a swirl of illusions that floated near the curb. Evelyn stepped closer, forming a tight circle with them as they took stock of the shifting cityscape.

"This is only a taste of what the Prism can do," Evelyn said. "If it tips toward full activation, illusions will overwhelm everything. No boundary will remain between mortal and magical realms."

Exhausted but resolute, Lila clutched the amulet that she wore as a necklace and met Caleb's wide-eyed stare, both understanding they had no choice but to mount a stand before illusions tore reality apart. As the pulse of raw magic resonated throughout the half-lit streets, they braced themselves for the fight of their lives, steeling their courage and forging a united front against the breaking point they could no longer postpone.

FIFTEEN

Lila's eyelids felt grainy from too little sleep as she stood outside her apartment building, craning her neck to stare at a faint shimmer of color drifting across the sky. Morning light tinted Manhattan's skyline with a hazy gold, but the real spectacle was the ghostly glow dancing over rooftops. A bewildered passerby paused to snap photos, muttering that it must be some avant-garde aerial stunt. Lila knew better. The partial awakening of the Nexus Prism had begun spiraling out of anyone's control.

She inhaled a shaky breath and set off toward The Daily Grind, heart drumming faster with each step down the bustling sidewalk. Civilians were everywhere, clinging to routines—smartphones in hand, coffee cups balanced precariously. She clutched her amulet beneath her jacket, aware of its unfamiliar warmth pulsing in time with each swirl of magical distortion dancing in the sky.

Halfway to the café, she spotted a flicker of green aura around a nearby traffic light. It blinked red, then shimmered with an odd teal gleam, confusing the cars rolling through. She kept walking, resisting the urge to fling up a protective ward on the spot. The last time she had tried that in public, it drew curious onlookers and nearly set off a minor panic. Caleb would scold her if she risked that again.

At last, she slipped inside The Daily Grind's front doors, her pulse thumping at the prospect of another chaotic day. It took only seconds for new trouble to announce itself: an older woman in line gasped and nearly dropped her mug, which sprouted thin, wiggling vines like curling green fingers. The customer yelped, stumbling into the counter. She stared wide-eyed at her mug, jaw slack. Lila rushed over, plastering on a trembling smile.

"Apologies, the new supplies must be faulty," Lila offered in a low, urgent tone. She reached out and touched the vines, channeling a subtle thread of earth magic through her fingertips. The tiny green tendrils withered back into the ceramic almost immediately.

The woman glanced from Lila to her coffee, brow creased in confusion. Another two customers witnessed the bizarre sight, one of them already raising a phone to take video. Lila's breath caught. She prayed that none of them had recorded those vines.

Before the onlooker could focus, a gentle wave of distortion rippled through the café's air. Lila smelled ozone and realized too late that the espresso machine had begun sparking. Neon arcs zapped the metal spout, forcing a young man to jerk his hand away with a startled curse.

Murmurs escalated. Someone else aimed a phone at the sudden flickers. Lila felt tension build in her chest. She had to do something before half of Manhattan ended up streaming live illusions from the café. The overhead lights dimmed, then flared. She took a steadying breath, focusing on memories of her recent late-night drills with Caleb: each had taught her how to channel anxious energy into grounded spells. Her arms trembled as she let her thoughts center on the floor beneath her feet, feeling each tile and the heartbeat of city magic throbbing underneath.

The shot of calm settled enough for her to mutter a quick incantation under her breath. She channeled a small wave of soothing earth magic, pushing it through the café's worn tile. Instantly, she felt the chairs and tables come into sharp relief around her, as if the building itself tried to assist her. The air steadied. The flickering overhead bulbs normalized. The espresso machine stopped spitting sparks.

Yet the handful of customers who had witnessed the strange vines and arcs of light were gathering in a nervous cluster by the register. Lila's heart still pounded. Before she could think of a clever excuse, the bell over the front door jingled. She glanced up to see Caleb entering in a flurry of motion, blue eyes blazing with energy. He quickly took in the scattering of frightened patrons. In a swift move, he raised both hands and murmured something so low that the words seemed to slip from her hearing. It was a simple diversion spell, enough to obscure what they had seen and blur the memory into something easily dismissed as a faulty power surge.

Confusion crossed the customers' faces. A few blinked dazedly, shook their heads, and soon put away their phones or wandered out of line. Lila exhaled in relief, realizing how close they had come to being exposed. She hurried behind the counter to power down the espresso machine before it decided to spark again.

"Sorry if I'm late," Caleb muttered, joining her by the storage shelves. Despite his calm exterior, she perceived tight worry in the set of his jaw. "I barely slept."

She shot him a tired grin that felt more like a grimace. "No one is blaming you. Not after the night we had."

He nodded once, then let his gaze sweep over her. "You look as exhausted as I feel."

"I can manage," she replied, though her head still pounded. Even talking felt like a half-battle with the swirling energy that pressed at her consciousness. "That partial activation is really doing a number on the city, isn't it?"

His eyes flicked to the window, where a group of passersby had paused in the street. They stared skyward, gawking at bright arcs of color shimmering above tall buildings. Before the day was over, half of Manhattan might be turning its gaze upward, wondering if they should panic or treat it like a novelty light show.

A sizzle at Lila's elbow made her jump. The machine twitched again, nearly catching a spark in the drip tray. She scowled, tossing Caleb a look. He set a quick ward with a flick of his wrist, and the machine sputtered but finally went quiet.

"We could close the café," he said softly.

She hesitated. The rational part of her mind agreed, but she also knew the slight emptiness in her bank account. Ultimately, she couldn't risk a packed customer line if illusions kept intensifying. The best option, for now, was to minimize public exposure. "We'll do an early close," she said. "Better to limit how many people wander in here while the city's wards are spinning into chaos."

He touched her arm gently, letting the warmth from his hand assure her they were in this together. "Agreed."

Their conversation was cut short when the older woman who had nearly dropped her vine-sprouting mug ambled over, looking slightly confused. "Excuse me," she said with an uncertain laugh, "I was about to order a muffin, but am I losing my mind? I swear my coffee was acting up. Now I'm not so sure."

Lila pulled a relaxed smile onto her face she was far from feeling. "Oh, the machine's been on the fritz all morning. Might be something about the city's electrical grid. You're not losing it, I promise." She reached for a napkin and offered it to the woman, hoping her next words sounded convincing. "Caleb's about to do some repairs in the back. If you want a refund, I can get that for you."

The woman studied Lila, then nodded hesitantly as though not quite sure why everything felt so strange. "I'll take a refund, thanks."

Once that was handled, Lila exchanged a weary glance with Caleb, who took quick note of the last few patrons finishing up. They added small illusions to their explanations—flickers of confusion and easy acceptance—just enough to prompt those customers to leave without further questions.

Minutes later, Lila locked the doors, flipped the sign to Closed, and sank down on a stool behind the counter. She pressed her fingers to her temples. Tension radiated from the base of her skull, as if all the illusions across the borough were prodding inside her mind. The lingering hum from the Prism's partial awakening made her entire body feel wired and exhausted at the same time.

Caleb stood by her side, resting a hand lightly on her shoulder. "I can set a stronger ward around the entrance, but anyone who passed by earlier might ask questions."

She gave a short nod, swallowing her frustration. "Let's keep it subtle. We can't make the place vanish altogether. Too many mortals would wonder why their neighborhood coffee shop suddenly disappeared."

He huffed a small laugh, tired and humorless. "Subtle wards it is."

She watched him trace a few quiet sigils near the café entrance. The neon sign that advertised latte specials faded as if losing its power, ensuring no new foot traffic. She appreciated his skill and the calm that emanated from him, even when every muscle in his back seemed tense enough to snap.

When he was done, he returned to her side, worry etched into the lines around his eyes. "How bad are you feeling?"

She flexed her fingers, hugging her elbows close. "Like something is tugging at the edges of my brain. It's the

Prism, right? I've never felt so many illusions pressing from all sides."

He nodded. "The wards around Manhattan are bending, not breaking, but it's only a matter of time if we can't push back. Sebastian's illusions are feeding off any place where the city's magic is thin. That includes spots with half-formed wards, like old suburbs or corners of Midtown." His gaze flicked around the café. "Or small businesses run by witches still learning the ropes."

She grimaced. "I'm not the only novice with a job in the city. But I might be one of the only ones with an amulet that makes me feel every ripple in magic."

He reached out and lifted the silver amulet resting beneath the collar of her T-shirt. When his fingertips brushed hers, a rush of warmth passed through her. "I'm so happy we found that," he said softly. "It may be the thing that saves us all."

Before she could reply, a spike of pressure shot through her temples. She doubled over with a sharp gasp. The air smelled like ozone again; something scratched at the café windows. Out of the corner of her eye, she saw long, twisting shapes that weren't quite tangible. Her breath caught as she realized illusions tried to break inside, attracted by the pulse of her magical aura.

Caleb spun around, arms raised. He poured shimmering wards across the windows, golden shapes that flickered and sealed out the intrusions. Through the glass, Lila glimpsed swirling light patterns on the sidewalk, half-formed illusions that resembled dancing silhouettes. They reached for the door with hands that weren't solid.

Panting, she forced herself to stand, pressing her palm flat to the tile again. The soothing effect of her earth-based spell rooted the café's small territory in a heavier reality, repelling illusions from slipping through. Each breath burned, and her heartbeat thundered. She heard Caleb grunting with effort, his illusions countering the ones outside.

At length, the scratching subsided. The dancing shapes on the sidewalk dissolved into shimmering motes. An eerie calm replaced them, leaving only the afternoon sun glinting off the glass. Lila let herself breathe.

He offered a hand, and she allowed him to steady her. "You're sure you're okay?" Caleb's voice sounded ragged, as though they had fought for hours rather than minutes.

She nodded shakily. "There's nothing I would want more than to be nestled in your apartment, in your bed, more specifically."

He smiled at that and helped her gather her things from behind the counter, then guided her toward the locked doors. Together, they slipped onto the sidewalk. She caught a glimpse of the city as if seeing it through a fractured lens. Bright lights arced across rooftops in unnatural ribbons of color, a swirling tapestry that fanned out in slow motion. Near the traffic light at the intersection, a trickle of sparks ran down the pole before vanishing. A pair of tourists gawked at the phenomenon, rummaging for cameras.

Caleb slid an arm around her waist, half support, half reassurance. "We need to get to a vantage point. Somewhere we can see how widespread this is." His breath came in shallow gasps, betraying his own fatigue.

"Right," she whispered. The headache returned, a dull throb behind her eyes. She thought of the Prism, buried who-knew-where below the city's labyrinthine catacombs, its partial activation sending out wave after wave of distorted magic. Everything felt precarious, as if one more surge would topple the wards altogether.

Glancing at the storefront behind them, she noticed how the reflection in the glass shimmered like a loose thread threatening to unravel. "The illusions are everywhere," she murmured, watching how the passing cars wavered in and out of shape. Several pedestrians rubbed their eyes, uncertain if they were hallucinating. "If we can't stabilize Manhattan's defenses soon, it will be chaos."

Caleb's jaw twitched. "We'll call in additional watchers. Marcus must already be scrambling squads to every hotspot."

She believed that, but it offered little comfort. Her pulse fluttered angrily as she detected more static in the air—a sign illusions were still prowling at the fringes. Half-apologizing to each other for dozing off over the past few days, they stepped away from the café's meager safety, both locked on the view of rising magical curtains coating the skyline. The wards across the city were weakening. She saw it in the wavering outlines of tall buildings and in the flickering storms of color swirling overhead. It was like Manhattan's very bones trembled beneath Sebastian's creeping illusions.

As she and Caleb took in the sight, she felt the amulet beating against her chest. Warm adrenaline coursed through her veins, but she refused to let panic consume her. The two of them shared a single determined look. This was only the beginning; she could feel it in her bones. The city was buckling under relentless forces, and the illusions latched onto every stray pulse of magic they could find.

CHAPTER

SIXTEEN

Lila rushed down a side corridor of the Council headquarters, her sneakers squeaking on polished marble. She still wore her coffee-stained apron from the café and only now realized how out of place that looked amid the regal pillars and gilded sconces. Fresh from slipping out of The Daily Grind, she had responded to the Council's urgent summons without pausing to change clothes. Her heart thudded in her chest, fueled by too much caffeine and a creeping sense of unease over the illusions spreading throughout Manhattan.

A harried aide, gray-haired and wide-eyed, waved her toward the tall, double doors ahead. The heavy wood had etched runes glowing along the edges, a testament to the wards needed for high-level meetings. Beyond that threshold waited representatives from magical factions Lila had only heard about in Council briefings.

She reached the doors just as Caleb caught up to her. His breath was ragged, and a lock of dark hair clung to his forehead. "You ran off in such a hurry," he said softly, pressing a supportive hand to her back. His intense blue eyes shone with concern. "Are you alright?"

"As alright as I can be," she replied, trying to steady her voice. She noticed a faint scuff on his coat, likely from rushing through illusions earlier in the day. The city seemed to be fracturing under Sebastian's manipulations, and nobody had much time for niceties. "Let's just get in there."

Caleb nodded and pushed open the doors. A wave of thick tension marched out to greet them. The meeting hall was large, ringed by tall windows that had been magically darkened for secrecy. Rows of chairs stood in tight arcs around a central oval table. Faction representatives, each draped in distinctive attire, whispered in urgent tones. Lila picked out a group of witches wearing layered cloaks embroidered with stylized crescent moons—the Crescent Circle. Beside them, a tall woman with a shaved head and serpent tattoos stood with her arms folded. Her stance radiated annoyance; Lila guessed she was from the East River elemental witches. Toward the back, a man with broad shoulders and a hood half covering his face lounged near a small cluster of shapeshifters, all from Harlem if the discussion in earlier Council notes still held true. Every faction stared at one another the way territorial predators might regard a waterhole.

Marcus Steele stood at the head of the table, scanning the growing crowd. His posture was tense, jaw clenched. He looked every bit the authoritative Council elder, though subtle lines around his eyes betrayed exhaustion.

The moment he spotted Lila and Caleb, he motioned for them to join the gathered circle. She hurried forward, trying to ignore the suspicious glares aimed in her direction.

Only then did Lila realize how conspicuous her apron was. Coffee stains ran across the front like haphazard splotches. Whispered comments rippled among the faction leaders. Some recognized her from rumors: the untested novice the Council had to babysit. She felt her cheeks grow hot as she recognized one or two watchers from earlier training sessions. Their gaze held pity or, worse, impatience.

"We will come to order now," Marcus announced. The room quieted, though tension crackled in the air. Lila and Caleb slid into two empty seats near one end of the table. She rubbed her palms on the apron's fabric, wishing she could remove it, but that would only draw more attention. Within seconds, several voices clamored to speak.

An older man in a worn leather coat, presumably from the Crescent Circle, barked, "Is the Council truly so desperate that they call on us? We were cast out for dabbling in advanced alchemy, yet here we stand." He flicked his gaze at Lila. "And they let novices wander these halls wearing coffee stains?"

Lila's fists clenched under the table. She wanted to snap that illusions were ripping across the city while he fussed about appearances, but she held her tongue. Caleb must have noticed her anger brimming. He gently squeezed her shoulder in warning.

A woman dressed in dark robes with embroidered

wave patterns stepped forward next. "The East River witches want proof the Council is serious about cooperation. If illusions get any worse in the waterfront districts, my coven might not hold back. We can't give away our secrets unless we trust the watchers around us."

Several shapeshifters rumbled in agreement. One of them stepped clear of the shadows. His eyes gleamed with soft golden light, a telltale sign of his clan's partial shift. "We're not here to play second fiddle to the Council's old rules," he said. "Our people in Harlem have endured illusions creeping into daily life. We want real solutions."

Grumbles and suspicious glares passed around the table. Lila could sense the mistrust radiating in every corner. She wondered if these factions had ever gathered in the same room without bickering. Yet illusions across the boroughs had left them with little choice. She forced herself to take a calming breath.

Marcus cleared his throat, raising a hand for silence. "The Council summoned you because Sebastian Shell's illusions have begun systematically unraveling the wards we've placed across Manhattan. Those wards shield your territories as much as they shield ours. We must pool our information."

A tall alchemist let out a derisive scoff. "You want to share 'information' or do you mean you'll demand we reveal every magical trick we have?"

"At this point," Marcus continued, voice even, "we need each other. Every day, illusions twist everyday reality a bit more, and the city's wards are groaning under the strain. If we don't unite, Sebastian will succeed in warping the magical flows and endanger everything. Mortal authorities are already suspicious, though they call these phenomena 'tech glitches' or 'collective hallucinations.' If illusions continue unchecked, we will face widespread panic or worse."

A low wave of chatter circled the table. Lila studied the swirl of reactions: some wore fear as clearly as a badge, while others masked it behind scowls. She recognized that same fear in herself. Her entire body remained taut with the memory of illusions creeping inside the café. She breathed slowly, counting to five, the way Caleb had taught her.

A shapeshifter with braided hair raised her hand. "Imagine if these illusions bring about massive confusion in the subways or city highways. People could die. Are we in agreement that we must set grudges aside for now?"

Several witches nodded. The man from the Crescent Circle narrowed his eyes at her. "We agree in principle, but where does it leave us if the Council hoards all final decisions? We can't be pawns in your structure."

Marcus looked across the room. His gaze hung on Lila for a moment, who swallowed hard. "We propose that each faction chooses a liaison to coordinate with the Council day and night. In that sense, there will be joint decisions on how to curb illusions in your territories."

At first, the factions eyed one another with obvious distrust, twisting their mouths as though tasting something bitter. Lila's shoulders tightened, anticipating an explosion of argument. She couldn't blame them for hesitation. Sebastian's illusions had wreaked havoc for weeks, and the Council's resources were already stretched. She suspected every group in this room felt wronged or overlooked in the past. Mend those rifts or let illusions devour the city—it seemed the only choice.

The East River witch with the wave embroidery stood. Her voice was surprisingly soft but carried an air of authority. "We'll cooperate, on one condition. Our spells remain ours to use, and the Council does not micromanage them. We will share intel if it helps track illusions before they flood the waterfront."

A ripple of consensus spread through the shapeshifters and alchemists. A woman among the shapeshifters in a dark hoodie said, "Harlem's clan can do the same. But we're not bowing to every Council whim. We want real collaboration, not lip service."

Marcus exhaled. "Understood. We have no intention of forcibly taking your secrets." He inclined his head toward Lila next, clearing his throat as if to draw the room's attention to her. "I know some of you question the presence of novices here. But Lila Matthews and her amulet have proven essential in dispersing illusions in certain hotspots."

Murmurs erupted, some hostile, some merely skeptical. Lila's cheeks burned. She clenched her fists in her lap, trying to maintain composure. The memory of illusions swirling around the café that morning echoed in her mind, a reminder that she had more power than simply frothing milk and handing out cappuccinos.

An alchemist with salt-and-pepper hair pointed at her. "What are you going to do if your magic backfires, novice? Word has it you only recently stumbled onto your power. If you lose control around us, we might end up in worse shape than we started."

Lila opened her mouth to retort but felt Caleb's hand on her shoulder again. A subtle, calming pressure. She swallowed an outburst of outrage and forced herself to speak evenly. "I'm learning," she said. "But illusions are hitting everyday people out there, and I want to help stop this before it becomes a disaster none of us can hide. We can't keep ignoring each other."

A flicker of respect darted across the shapeshifter's eyes. The East River witch scanned Lila's apron as if noticing the coffee stains for the first time. No one laughed, though, and Lila appreciated that small mercy.

Marcus pushed a stack of hastily printed maps across the table, each one marked with red circles. "These are the reported high-activity illusion zones. We've seen repeated, targeted disruptions in these areas. If we share resources—talisman supplies, ward specialists, watchers on the ground—we might contain illusions quickly. We also propose rotating squads that can intervene before illusions spread to heavily populated areas."

A member of the Crescent Circle frowned. "Who leads these squads?"

Caleb cleared his throat and leaned forward. "We suggest each faction choose a field captain to coordinate with a Council warder. Communication lines will be shared, but we need watchers stationed in hot zones day and night. Illusions thrive on inattention. If we show a unified response, Sebastian's illusions might lose momentum."

Silence held for a tense moment. Lila lowered her gaze to the scuffed floor beneath her chair. Though her heart hammered, a spark of hope kindled at the idea of a truly combined effort. She remembered how illusions had nearly trapped her in a suffocating darkness outside her apartment weeks ago. Then she recalled the frantic phone calls from the café patrons who believed they saw monstrous shapes or swirling lights in broad daylight. If these factions could work together, maybe the city had a fighting chance.

Eventually, the East River witch spoke up. "We will assign one captain who understands aquatic wards. For illusions near the coastline, that might help."

"Same here," said a shapeshifter with a slight shrug. "I'll speak for our clan and coordinate in uptown neighborhoods."

"And we," said the alchemist with salt-and-pepper hair, "will handle Midtown, but we are expecting real time updates if illusions shift. No secrets, no locked doors."

Soft mutters of accord rippled around the room. Marcus exhaled, tension draining slightly from his squared shoulders. "Agreed. Let's finalize the details of these squads." He opened a thick ledger coated with a faint shimmering ward to record the names of the chosen liaisons. His quill scratched across the page, capturing every promise. Lila sensed that some part of him doubted these words would hold under stress, but for now, it was a start.

One by one, faction representatives stepped up to sign or provide tokens. Lila noted the subdued conversation among them: a shapeshifter handing a small carved charm to Marcus, an alchemist flipping a slender copper rod that apparently indicated trust. Small gestures, but they carried significant weight. She allowed herself a cautious smile.

When the signings paused, the East River witch turned to Lila. "You have the amulet that can disrupt illusions, yes?"

Lila's spine stiffened. "It helps. I still have a lot to learn about using it."

"Well," the witch said, quiet resignation in her tone, "don't be afraid to call on us for backup. The illusions near the East River have grown intense. We can share leads if we see anomalies that might connect to Sebastian's location."

Lila swallowed the knot in her throat. "I appreciate that."

A rustling motion at the table's head made everyone look up. Marcus set the ledger down and nodded curtly at the circle. "We have a working pact," he announced. "It isn't ideal, and I see skepticism in many faces. But illusions show no mercy. If we let distrust reign, we lose everything."

Murmured agreement, cautious but genuine, filled the hall. One shapeshifter patted the handle of a battered sword he wore, as though bracing for battle. The robed alchemist folded his arms, scanning the room with eyes that dared anyone to betray them. For a rare instant, they all shared an uneasy camaraderie.

Caleb rose, posture dignified, though Lila sensed the tension in his clasped hands. "We convene again in twenty-four hours," he said. "By then, each faction should have squads in place. Remain vigilant. Sebastian is cunning. Report illusions the moment you see them surge."

One by one, the factions trickled out. The shapeshifters drifted toward an exit near the hall's rear, quiet as shadows. The East River delegation withdrew through the main doors with a swirl of embroidered robes. The Crescent Circle group lingered awhile, as though they still debated the trustworthiness of a united plan, before filing out in silence.

Marcus, now alone except for a few Council watchers, exchanged a weary glance with Lila. "Thank you for holding back earlier," he said in a low voice. "I know it's hard to let them question you."

Lila, still conscious of the coffee stains on her apron, shrugged. "I'm just... tired of illusions upending every-thing. If these factions can help, I'm willing to deal with the attitude."

Marcus laid a hand on her shoulder in a fleeting gesture of respect. "You will be needed soon. Thanks to your bond with the amulet, you can disrupt illusions in ways none of us can replicate."

She offered him a tight nod. He walked off, muttering to a fellow guardian about next steps. Caleb approached, expression balanced between relief and lingering concern.

Outside, the corridor bustled with watchers preparing for new patrols. She inhaled deeply, letting the swirl of whispered spells and hurried footsteps ground her.

Caleb brushed her apron lightly, mouth quirking in a tired half-smile. "Does it help that I think you look charming, even in that stained apron?"

She snorted softly. "It's nice to know you approve of my fashion choices."

He lowered his voice. "We made progress here, but it feels precarious. The second illusions surge in unexpected places, some factions might suspect sabotage."

She gazed around the hall, where the lingering hum of wards mingled with the retreating footsteps of faction delegates. The battered city waited just beyond these enchanted walls, illusions simmering, ready to strike. Caleb's palm pressed lightly against her lower back, and she found herself leaning into his presence, grateful for his steady calm.

She closed her eyes and pictured the jumbled hotspots that dotted the Council's red-ink maps. Each location throbbed with illusions only half-contained. The notion that these alliances might fray at the slightest provocation twisted her stomach. Yet for the moment, they had agreed to work together.

She exhaled, letting the tension ease from her shoulders. "At least for tonight, we're on the same side."

Caleb's expression remained serious. "And we'll have to make the most of it."

He squeezed her shoulder one last time, a silent pledge of support. Then, with a mutual glance at the now-deserted center table, they turned to follow the others out. The acrid scent of old magic still clung to the air, and her mind buzzed with everything that had been said. If illusions spiked before their new squads took shape, this fragile pact might shatter. She felt the rhythmic pulse of the silver amulet under her shirt, stoking both her hope and her dread.

She paused under the high arch of the doors leading to the corridor. Though the hall's wards concealed the outside world, she pictured congested city streets swirling with half-seen phantoms. With all these factions gathered under one roof, the Council had bought them a sliver of unity. Whether it would last was another matter entirely.

Lila bit her lip, sensing that these forced alliances would not hold unless they produced results soon.

CHAPTER
SEVENTEEN

Night clung to the Council's chamber like a hunter. Lila smelled the residue of burnt sage and the sharp undertone of anxious sweat before she even crossed the threshold. Midnight had settled an hour ago, yet the vast marble hall was alive with tension that crackled in the lantern-lit air. Every seat around the circular table was filled: guardians, lead mentors, scribes, and high elders who had arrived in frantic waves. Their expressions matched the low sizzle of fear she sensed.

She slipped in quietly with Caleb at her side. Each step toward her seat made her heart pound harder, as if the echo of their footsteps might trigger a new argument before the meeting even started. Overhead, an aura of flickering orbs glowed with pale light, the usual perfect circle of illumination reduced to irregular pulses. The wards were unstable enough that even simple magic, like lighting the orbs, wavered tonight.

She and Caleb settled at the far end of the table. Their

usual seats—beyond the central dais where Marcus Steele held court—were only two chairs away from Zoe, who gave them a silent nod. Lila noticed how the usual serene confidence in Zoe's face had dimmed. Tonight, Zoe wore exhaustion as clearly as she wore her healer's cloak, the dark circles under her eyes evidence of how many illusions had battered the city recently. Nearby, two novices snapped to attention, exchanging anxious whispers. Lila recognized the exact brand of dread in their eyes: illusions had grown savage in just a few days, and entire sets of wards had buckled without warning.

Barely a minute passed before Marcus stepped to the raised platform at the center of the chamber, commanding immediate silence. He spread his hands wide, scanning the anxious crowd. His temples looked more silver than usual in the flickering lantern light, and from Lila's vantage point, it was clear the strain of the last few weeks had carved deeper lines into his face.

"This emergency session," Marcus began, voice gritty with tension, "has been called because illusions are warping public consciousness to a level we never believed possible. There is no reason to sugarcoat matters: if we lose control of the illusions, we risk all-out exposure. And once the veil is broken, there is no going back."

A ripple of uncomfortable murmuring swept across the table. Lila exhaled slowly, wishing for a moment that she were anywhere else. She had closed The Daily Grind early that afternoon, suspecting illusions might once again flicker across the café equipment if she grew agitated. Here, ironically, she felt her heart slam against her ribcage even harder.

Sensing her worry, Caleb slid his hand beneath the edge of the table and let his palm hover near hers. She closed the small space, fingers tangling in a silent gesture of comfort.

Marcus continued, "We have also received troubling reports that certain Council members—trusted guardians—might break ranks to join Sebastian if it serves their ambition."

The statement dropped like a boulder, hitting the assembly with enough force to elicit a chaotic burst of voices. One elder openly scoffed. Another pounded the table in protest. Lila could feel their unspoken terror: Sebastian, the rogue warlock, had proven cunning at recruiting disillusioned witches in the city. If he now had allies hidden among them, everything the Council built—flawed as it might be—was in danger of collapse.

"This is absolute bullshit," Lila whispered, the words leaving her before she could restrain herself. She leaned closer to Caleb, as though bracing for a reprimand. "They're turning on one another while illusions rage outside. It's so shortsighted."

Caleb responded with a faint nod. He kept his voice low, mindful of watchers nearby. "They're afraid. Fear makes people do... unpredictable things."

Along the table's arc, a stocky warlock with a white streak in his hair blurted out, "We can't keep splitting our forces over illusions and sabotage. If there's even a hint of betrayal, we must lock the city down. No movement, no open wards."

At once, three watchers on the opposite side erupted

into protests. One shook her head vehemently. "You'd destroy trust and push novices into Sebastian's hands. Those left out would think we no longer care for them. We should negotiate with these rumored defectors. Find out what they want."

Silence fell for half a breath, then voices rose again in heated debate. High elder traditions clashed with younger watchers who seemed more open to forging alliances with discontented witches. Lila's chest tightened at the sight of so much division. If the illusions feeding on the city's panic weren't enough, the Council's internal bitterness might fracture them from within.

Marcus raised his hand in a sharp, authoritative gesture. "Enough." He looked poised to say more when the chamber doors flew open, crashing back with a resounding thud.

An aide stumbled inside, eyes wide. "Couldn't wait," the young woman panted. "We've received fresh updates: wards are failing at an accelerated rate. The illusions are flaring in Midtown, then weaving downtown. Council watchers claim entire squares flicker with Sebastian's signature illusions, and passersby are starting to share videos in real time."

The mention of mortals capturing illusions on phones turned the room colder than winter wind. Lila could practically taste the jolt of panic. An older guardian slammed his fist on the table, cursing. Another demanded the Council double their infiltration squads and forcibly confiscate any recorded evidence. A third insisted illusions were ephemeral enough that humans would dismiss them as pranks.

Chaos built, voices overlapping one another. Lila's heart hammered. She hated the prickle of sweat at the back of her neck. The city felt close to meltdown. She swallowed hard. Caleb pressed his shoulder gently against hers, urging her to stay composed. She let out a long breath. Right. This was not the time to lose her temper.

Marcus's voice cut through the noise. "We will not let illusions run unchecked, no matter how many squads it takes. But we have a bigger concern." His tone burned with frustration he rarely revealed. "Rumors claim some in this chamber believe negotiating with Sebastian might be a better alternative than abiding by Council constraints."

More furious outbursts. Lila stiffened and whispered to Caleb, "They can't be serious. Sebastian's illusions nearly destroyed me a few times already. If he gets more allies, we're done."

Caleb's jaw tightened. He gave a subtle shrug that spoke volumes: desperation twisted reason. There was no guarantee the Council members in question truly wanted to join Sebastian. Some might be searching for a path they believed the Council was too rigid to consider, particularly after all the wards started collapsing. Still, it chilled her to imagine that people sworn to protect Manhattan might, by fear or greed, switch sides.

An older warlock in the far-left seat got to his feet. His shoulders squared, voice echoing against the marble. "Lock down the city. Shut it all down. Let illusions swirl outside while we fortify ourselves here. We can't risk letting novices or uncertain guardians roam free when we have suspect loyalty."

Immediately, another witch jumped up. "Your solution is to cower behind wards? Let illusions devour our neighborhoods while we hide? That's not why we joined this Council."

A third rose, eyes glistening with fury. "Better we protect ourselves, then rescue the city once the illusions subside."

Marcus tried to speak, but the arguments overlapped so swiftly that only a roar of voices broke over him. Lila's gut twisted. She recognized the escalation pattern—fear igniting blame, blame igniting anger, and anger fueling more fear. She found herself gripping Caleb's hand tighter, needing the anchor of his calm.

She felt a subtle shift as he cleared his throat, hoping to speak. But before he could, Marcus slammed his palm on the circular table with a resounding crack. The echo reverberated throughout the massive chamber, silencing the outcry.

"Enough!" Marcus shouted, chest heaving with barely contained rage. "We are guardians, not panicked children. We exist to protect, not to quake in corners. Are we truly so fractured that we'd consider turning on each other? If so, we are no better than the illusions wreaking havoc on our wards."

Marcus continued, voice raw. "Any who believe it wise to abandon this Council for the one who conjures illusions that injure innocents, step forward now." He scanned the hall. No one moved, yet the tension pressed around them all, unspoken accusations and doubts swirling in the stale air.

Standing near Zoe, a younger guardian holding a ledger quietly raised her hand. "Elder Marcus, if it helps, we've compiled a partial list of watchers complaining that the Council leadership is out of touch. Some blame the Council for not stopping illusions earlier. They feel neglected—"

"Neglected?" Marcus spat, an uncharacteristic anger roughening his words. "What do they expect? We've poured our resources into warding entire boroughs. How are we out of touch for trying to keep illusions from igniting mortal panic?"

He thumped the table again, making the ledger rattle in the guardian's grip. Lila watched the woman cringe, looking both embarrassed and fearful. Another delicate breath escaped Lila's lips. She respected Marcus, but in this moment, she feared his temper would be the match that lit a worse fire.

She closed her eyes momentarily, recalling illusions dancing across skyscrapers just a few days prior. The Council had tried everything—sleepless watchers, wards layered at major intersections, frantic attempts to squash social media rumors. Yet illusions fed on negativity. Sebastian must be smiling right now, sensing the swirl of conflict in this very room.

A red-haired witch along the perimeter raised her voice. "We're not calling you out, Elder Marcus. We're just saying that if we keep ignoring witches who feel used, someone like Sebastian can swoop in offering them power, or at least a voice."

A cold glance from Marcus pinned her. "You think I ignore them? We've been patching illusions in half the city. Meanwhile, infiltration squads vanish, illusions twist entire blocks. Our resources are thin, but that is not a license for treason."

Rumbling disagreement broke out. Lila bit her tongue before she snapped at the entire group. She agreed with Marcus in principle: turning to Sebastian was madness after witnessing his illusions in action. But the underlying grievances had roots that stretched deep. She had overheard novices complain about how the Council, with its endless protocols, left them feeling powerless.

Caleb gave her fingers a gentle squeeze under the table, glancing at her with a look that pleaded for patience. She tried to swallow her frustration, but her voice slipped out anyway, low and bitter. "Arguing about resources while illusions ravage the city is maddening. We're letting fear distract us from the real threat."

He nodded in silent approval, though she noticed the tension in his face. Whatever guilt or caution lived inside him weighed heavily tonight. He, better than most, understood how lost witches might see Sebastian as a rebellious path when the Council's help felt too slow.

Then an aide stepped forward, face pale as sculpted stone. "Marcus, the wards near West Village collapsed an hour ago. We're suspecting sabotage from inside. Another infiltration. This is the second infiltration in two days."

A wave of agitated mutters rippled through the assembly, sewing fresh chaos. Lila heard the word "traitor" hissed under more than one breath. Sebastian's infiltration. Possibly even watchers aiding him. She felt ill just imagining it.

Marcus's anger snapped like a drawn bowstring. "If betrayal sits in this very chamber, I will find it," he growled, pounding the table again. The ring of impact seemed to underscore his fury. "We will not stand idle while illusions creep in. Enough stalling. Enough of these petty politics. You think you can negotiate with a man who conjures illusions to devour novices' minds? You think he will show mercy once you yield him the city?"

Lila's gaze flicked around the room. Fear smoldered behind many eyes. A few watchers looked on the verge of tears, or perhaps on the verge of storming out. Tensions soared beyond anything she'd seen in these halls before. The strict composure, the quiet dignity, had shattered. Whispers turned to hissed accusations, fueling the notion that the midnight session might erupt into utter bedlam.

One guardian stood, silver hair gleaming under the lanterns. "So, what is your plan, Marcus? We're on the brink of losing wards. People out there call us incompetent while illusions swirl overhead. Should we not consider every possible approach?"

Lila bristled. She wanted to scream that "every possible approach" was code for letting Sebastian get a foothold. She dug her nails into her palm, remembering how illusions had nearly broken her in the catacombs. She pictured the twisted shapes clawing at her apartment door. Sebastian was merciless and cunning, not some outraged activist to be reasoned with.

Her frustration boiled over with a muttered, "This is absolute bullshit," loud enough that the novices on her left glanced at her. She clenched her teeth, forcing herself to keep quiet. Caleb traced his thumb across her knuckles, stilling her trembling. She wasn't sure if it was the closeness of him or the immediate quiet it invoked, but at least her throat loosened a fraction.

Before things could escalate further, Marcus exhaled a scathing breath and glared at the assembly. "We stand at an impasse. Very well." He pounded the table once more, a final motion that rattled papers and set tension over the watchers. "If all you want is to bicker, let us bicker outside these doors. I'm calling a recess."

The words thundered in the silence. No one moved for a full heartbeat. Then the tension erupted in whispered arguments and snatches of curses. Quickly, watchers began to break away from the seats, some grouping together in angry clusters, others stalking off alone. The novices looked lost, uncertain whether to request new instructions or simply vanish from this chaotic scene.

Lila pushed back her chair, aware that her pulse was so loud it roared in her ears. She rose alongside Caleb. She spotted Zoe addressing two novices, likely calming their frazzled nerves. A few elders cornered an aide for more details on failing wards. Everywhere, the swirl of parted cloaks and voices conjured an impression of a dam, fractured in countless places.

Caleb placed a steadying hand at the small of Lila's

back. "Let's get some air," he said softly. "You're trembling."

She exhaled shakily. "I know. It's... so pointless. If we can't unite, illusions will tear us apart anyway." The frustration left her on a drained sigh.

He guided her around the central dais, helping her navigate the bustle of council members. Marcus, still near the platform, stood seething in silence while two scribes tried to placate him. Over the clamor, Lila heard Marcus muttering something about traitors in their midst, how he wouldn't rest until they were rooted out.

The agitation in the chamber felt suffocating, so she let Caleb steer her toward the tall, ornate doors. One step at a time, they moved until they reached the corridor where the midnight chill met them like a vigilant guard. The corridor's lamps burned a dull gold, flickering as if the wards behind the walls were as shaken as everyone inside.

She and Caleb paused side by side, shoulders almost touching. Beyond them, muffled arguments spilled from the hall, voices snapping with alarm and suspicion. The weight of the session pressed on Lila's lungs. She wanted to vent her anger or fling spells into a training room just to get rid of the roiling tension. Instead, she stood, unable to do more than breathe.

Caleb exhaled slowly, the sound barely audible in the stone corridor. "You all right?" he asked, stepping close enough that she felt the warmth of him. "I don't blame you if you're furious."

She shook her head. "Furious doesn't begin to cover it.

They're more concerned about who might defect than the illusions themselves. We could lose everything."

His eyes flicked toward the still-cracked door. Inside, voices rose in more fractious debate. "Marcus is trying to hold them together, but these rumors about betrayal... it's tearing them apart from the inside."

Lila pressed her lips together, wishing she could shout sense into the entire Council. She had seen illusions in the streets, at her café, in subway tunnels. Arguing wouldn't save them. Action would. Yet the Council seemed tangled in its own fear. She realized, with a bitter pang, that Sebastian had orchestrated precisely this: illusions to sow enough fear that the Council would hasten its own collapse.

They took a few steps down the corridor, away from the immediate chaos of the doors. Guardians trickled out, some in silent groups, others with eyes blazing. Nobody spared Lila or Caleb more than a glance. Everyone was too lost in their own swirling frustration.

An uneasy silence settled over them both. Caleb finally slipped his arm around her waist, a gesture that might have drawn scowls from the more traditional elders, had they been watching. But no one was paying attention, and the quiet comfort in his touch calmed her fraying nerves.

"We will figure out a path," he said softly. "Even if the Council tears itself to pieces, we won't let illusions have free rein."

A tiny spark of gratitude glowed in her chest. She nodded. "We just have to hang on. Marcus can salvage this if they stop shouting long enough to listen."

His smile was weary but sincere. "Agreed."

They lingered for one final moment, letting the corridor's calmer air ease the clamor in their heads. Somewhere behind those great doors, an entire Council was unraveling. Beyond the building's wards, illusions prowled through Manhattan's streets. Their next steps would decide if the wards fell completely or if they found a way to stand firm together.

Side by side, they turned toward the hallway that branched away from the chamber doors. Lila's heartbeat still hammered, but at least she no longer felt alone. As they walked, that comforting sense of partnership balanced the anger roiling at the back of her mind. Whispers of betrayal, illusions tearing wards, the city's rising panic—none could be ignored. She just wished they had more time to plan.

She caught Caleb's gaze, and though neither of them spoke, they reached a mutual understanding as the noise from the chamber rose again. Marcus's furious exclamation drifted through the open door, flanked by a fresh wave of indignant protests. The illusions lurking outside felt less dangerous than the distrust raging in that circular hall.

Lila swallowed, turning her back on the noise. They would regroup after the recess, but for now, the Council was in disarray. Their unity felt like a delicate tapestry just waiting to be ripped.

She and Caleb cast one last look over their shoulders, confirming the break in the session. Then, wordlessly, they exited the Council's chamber into the corridor, shoulders set in grim resolve. A fresh tide of angry voices burst from the hall as more guardians stormed out to huddle in whispered clusters. Lila's pulse thrummed with dread. She and Caleb followed the line of watchers seeking a brief reprieve from the suffocating tension, neither knowing what the next meeting would bring.

Shoulder to shoulder, they could practically feel the Council's unity shredding behind them like paper poised to be torn apart.

CHAPTER

EIGHTEEN

Lila slumped on the worn wooden bench in a far corner of The Daily Grind, heart thudding with exhaustion from another fitful night. The café was between rushes, so the clamor of espresso machines and hissing steam wands had subsided, leaving only the low hum of background chatter. She rubbed her eyes, remembering how the Council meeting yesterday devolved into a shouting match that left her frayed and hopeless. Even her fingertips felt sore, as if the tension of controlling her magic had burrowed into her bones.

She glanced around the shop. Most customers sat at tables near the front windows, oblivious to any mention of illusions or wards. Meanwhile, Maya was punching orders into the register, wearing a bright floral blouse that clashed with the subdued energy Lila felt. After one more peaked glance around, Lila beckoned Maya over.

"Girl, you look like a ghost," Maya muttered once she approached. Concern lined her features, softening the lively spark usually dancing in her eyes. "Are you gonna crash in the back if I turn my head for five minutes?"

Lila forced a weak laugh. "Sorry. I'll be fine." She patted the seat next to her with a trembling hand. "Can we talk? And I mean really talk. No customers, no interruptions."

Maya raised a brow. The serious tone must have struck her because her gaze flicked toward the café entrance, assessing if they could spare the time. Finally, she let out a resigned sigh, gestured to the young barista at the counter, and slid into the seat across from Lila.

"Okay, spill," she said, voice quiet yet firm. "I can't keep watching you stumble around like a zombie. Something's up."

Lila inhaled, her stomach twisting into knots. She had sworn an oath to keep magical matters within the Council and never reveal their secrets to unsuspecting mortals. But the strain of hiding the truth from Maya had left her unraveling. She needed her best friend's support more than she feared the Council's wrath.

She stared at the half-empty latte in front of her. The spiral of foam had gone cold. "You remember all those weird things happening lately?" she began in a whisper. "Like the flickering lights, the green sparks near the espresso machine, the fact I've been working irregular hours...?"

Maya nodded. "I thought you'd gotten yourself tangled up with some shady landlord scam or joined a weird yoga cult. The landlord thing made more sense." Her small attempt at humor made Lila smile briefly. Then

Maya's voice dropped lower. "But something else is going on, right?"

"More than you can guess," Lila said, swallowing hard. The words lodged in her throat, as if her oath tried to choke them off. She clenched her hands, forcing the confession out. "Magic is real, Maya. I'm not talking about cheap parlor tricks or illusions from a stage show. It's real. And I'm part of it."

For a beat, Maya just stared. Her brown eyes widened in skepticism, then flicked toward the café, as though expecting hidden cameras or a prank. "Come on," she said in a forced laugh. "If this is a joke, it's not funny."

"It's not a joke," Lila insisted, voice trembling. "I... I've been training with a secret group—a Council of witches and warlocks who protect the city from things you won't believe." She noted how ridiculous it sounded, but she pushed on. "There's a threat—someone who can conjure illusions that affect everyone in town. I can't keep pretending everything is normal. It's tearing me apart."

Maya opened her mouth, closed it, then stared at Lila with a mix of astonishment and concern. "You—I can't believe you actually—" She exhaled in a rush. "Are you saying you're a witch now? For real? That this isn't just exhaustion and nightmares messing with your mind?"

Lila tried to keep her voice level, even as a tremor ran through her. "I have powers I never asked for. I've seen illusions so real they could make us question our entire reality. And a rogue warlock is using these illusions to tear the city apart if the Council can't stop him."

Maya's shock gave way to a string of curses. Her hand

shot out, grabbing Lila's wrist. "You're serious." It wasn't a question.

"Dead serious." Lila looked around, making sure no one hovered too close. A surge of guilt rippled through her as she thought of the Council's vow, how furious Marcus would be if he found out she was telling a mortal about illusions and wards. But a bigger part of her needed Maya's help. She needed a friend who would stand by her side without demanding magical loyalty.

Maya's eyes flickered with newfound worry. "Is that why you keep vanishing at weird times? Missing half your shifts or calling me last minute to cover? Because of... spells?"

"Partly." Lila snatched a quick breath. "I'm sorry for always making excuses. It's been the Council forcing me to do training, attend emergency meetings. This warlock—Sebastian—he's creating illusions all over Manhattan, messing with everyone's heads. The city's in danger if we can't contain him."

"Holy—" Maya flopped against the back of her seat, scanning the café as if it might transform at any moment. "I thought I was the best friend who knew everything, but you've been caught up in... in this entire magical war? Do you realize how messed up that sounds?"

"I do." Lila's voice cracked. "But it's real. I've seen illusions that nearly destroyed my shop. I've watched the Council tear itself apart arguing over how to handle all this. I didn't want to drag you into it, but I'm losing it, Maya. I'm losing myself, and I can't keep lying."

A long silence held between them. Maya covered her

mouth with one hand. Then a fierce light took over her expression, and she reached across the table to grip Lila's hand. "Are you okay? Is anyone hurting you? Are you safe?"

Lila let out a shaky laugh that verged on tears. "I'm safe. Sort of. The Council's complicated, but I have an ally there who's been helping me learn my magic. It's not perfect, but it's something. At least now I know I'm not insane."

Maya stared, still grappling with the idea. "Okay," she breathed. "I can't promise I understand everything, but if magic is real, and there's some psycho warlock trying to blow up the city—" She paused, pressing her lips together. "Then you bet I'm not letting you walk into that by yourself, best friend oath or not."

The wave of relief washing over Lila nearly broke her composure. "You... you're not mad?"

"Mad?" Maya snorted. "Oh, I'm furious you kept this secret so long, but I'm more worried than mad. The minute you say 'magical illusions' and 'danger,' all I can think is how I want to protect you." Her voice caught, and Lila realized just how deeply Maya cared. "So, you tell me what to watch for. Weird customers. Flickering lights. Random green sparks or illusions. If anything seems off, I'll let you know."

"That's perfect," Lila said softly. She squeezed Maya's hand back, tears prickling her eyes. "I don't know what the Council will do if they find out I told you. They have these rules about secrecy, and I just... I can't carry it alone."

Maya set her jaw. "I won't go shouting it from the rooftops. But if they try to threaten you, I swear, I'll— I'll figure something out. I'm not letting you walk into shady meetings blind."

A shaky laugh escaped Lila. Maya's readiness to fight for her sparked renewed resolve. "Thank you."

Before they could say more, the door swung open, and a small flood of new customers trickled in, looking for early afternoon caffeine fixes. Maya glanced at them, annoyance flickering across her face. "Duty calls. But you, me—this conversation isn't over." She leaned closer. "And if you need me to do anything more than watch the café, just say the word. I'd rather risk the Council's anger than let you get hurt."

Lila nodded, a silent promise in her chest. The feeling of dread hadn't disappeared, but it felt less crushing now that Maya's unwavering support was out in the open. At least one piece of her life felt less lonely, though the Council's reaction loomed like a storm cloud on the horizon.

She rose from the table, stepping back to her usual station to help with the sudden wave of orders. All the while, tension coiled inside her. She could practically see Marcus's furious glare if he learned she'd spilled everything to a mortal. But she couldn't regret it. Not if it meant Maya was at her side in this fight.

Late afternoon brought a haze of sunlight that barely reached the café windows. Lila claimed she had errands and slipped away half an hour before closing time, leaving Maya to finish out the shift. They parted with a charged glance, Maya's lips tight with solemn understanding. Out on the sidewalk, Lila tugged her jacket tighter around herself. The city's noise pressed in from all sides, and her heartbeat matched the frantic pace of passing cabs.

She darted onto a side street, stepping through the illusions that overlay a hidden Council entrance. The old metal door hummed under her touch, wards scanning her presence before clicking open. A claustrophobic hallway stretched ahead, lit by a single flickering torch that cast elongated shadows.

Lila pressed onward. She suspected another fractious Council assembly might be in progress, or at least a smaller meeting of watchers trying to regroup after all the fighting. But her immediate priority was to check in with Caleb. Her conversation with Maya still rattled inside her, leaving her uncertain if she'd just saved herself or doomed them all. She needed reassurance that telling Maya wasn't an irreversible disaster.

Her footsteps echoed off the corridor's stone walls, and she slowed near a twisting corner. The air felt denser here, as if illusions lingered from the previous day's arguments. She paused, hugging the wall. Then, a faint silhouette slid into view—a tall figure with broad shoulders and dark, unruly hair. His presence was so familiar that her pulse twitched.

"Caleb."

He turned, eyes narrowing. In the dim overhead light, the sharp lines of his face gave him a wary, haunted appearance. He looked exhausted, as if he'd been pacing these halls for hours. "You finally made it," he said quietly, stepping forward.

She exhaled, relieved to see him. "Were you waiting for me?"

He hesitated, letting his gaze trail over her face. "I sensed you approaching through the wards. I knew you'd come." His eyes glinted with concern. "You disappeared after the Council fiasco. I was worried."

She managed a brittle laugh, stepping closer until they nearly touched. "I had to talk to Maya. She's my best friend, and she's been seeing all the weirdness at the café. She wouldn't let it go. I... I told her the truth, Caleb." The words came out in a rush, tinged with guilt.

He went still. "You told her?" A tangle of emotions flickered in his features—surprise, concern, and a trace of alarm. "Do you know what that means? The Council—"

"I know what it means," she snapped, hands balling into fists. "But I can't keep living a double life without any real support. I trust Maya more than any Council elder. I'm drowning here." Her voice was sharper than she intended, weighted by sleepless nights and the fear that everything could fall apart because she'd broken the vow.

Caleb raked a hand through his hair, agitation evident in the tension of his shoulders. "Lila, the Council's entire enforcement hinges on keeping our existence hidden. If they find out—"

"Let them find out," she blurted, her frustration boiling over. "What else was I supposed to do? My life is descending into illusions and secret missions, and they expect me to handle the café and my finances while fending off Sebastian's infiltration all alone?"

He said nothing, jaw clenched. The corridor's torch crackled overhead, illuminating the subtle swirl of magic around them. She shoved her hand through her hair, fighting tears.

"Look, I'm grateful for your help," she continued, voice quivering with anger and raw relief. "But I can't hold up the whole damn world by myself. Telling Maya was the only way to stay sane."

For a moment, Caleb's eyes flashed with conflict. Then he closed the distance between them, grasping her shoulders with firm, warm hands. The tension in the hall felt electric, a reminder of how easily illusions could spark if either of them lost control. She saw the anguish in the lines creasing his forehead.

"You weren't supposed to carry it alone," he said, voice softer. "I'm so sorry it felt like you had to choose between isolation and risking Council punishment."

A spike of emotion tore through her, a mix of relief and frustration at how complicated this had become. "I can't do it by myself," she whispered. "I won't."

He drew her into a fierce hug, arms folding around her with surprising strength. Her cheek pressed against his chest, and he smelled faintly of ritual incense mingled with soap. For several seconds, neither of them spoke. She closed her eyes, letting his heartbeat pound in her ear. That steady drum quelled the trembling in her limbs.

"Just... promise me you'll be careful," he murmured against her hair. "If word gets out, Marcus will question your loyalty, and I don't know how that will end. But we'll face it together. You hear?"

She felt tears burn the back of her eyes. Her arms crept around his waist, clutching him in return, afraid to let go. She sensed his genuine worry and realized it mirrored her own. "I hear you."

He held her like that for a moment longer. Then, in a rush of pent-up desperation, he tipped her chin up and kissed her. The motion was abrupt and unplanned—like lightning striking in an already simmering storm. She rose onto the balls of her feet, returning his kiss despite the swirl of conflicting emotions. It tasted like shared panic and a flicker of hungry relief all at once, her breath mingling with his in the dim hallway.

When they finally broke apart, she clung to his jacket, heart pounding. They stared at each other, breathless, the remnants of that kiss leaving her lips tingling.

"You have no idea how worried I've been," he whispered, voice low. "Every time illusions flare, I think you might be in the crossfire. And now, the Council's infighting is making it worse. I don't want to lose you to their rules or Sebastian's illusions."

She swallowed. Part of her wanted to bury her face against him and just breathe. Another part reminded her they stood in a corridor where anyone could pass by. "We'll handle it," she said. "We have to. Right now, I just... need you."

His expression softened. "I'm here."

They stood entwined in that muted corridor for another trembling heartbeat. Then Lila pulled back, wiping the corner of her eye. She drew a shaky breath, remembering Maya's vow from earlier that day. Maya had promised to spot any suspicious activity in the café and warn her the moment illusions crept in. The thought made Lila's heart ease slightly. She wasn't alone in the mortal world either.

Still, the cost weighed on her: telling a mortal friend about the Council was no small betrayal. If Marcus discovered the breach, there could be serious consequences. Yet she couldn't regret it. Not when the alternative was facing nightmares by herself.

Caleb's gaze flicked across her face. "Let's go. We can't stay here in the open. I'll escort you inside. Maybe we can find a quieter space to talk next steps." He paused, carefully tucking a stray lock of hair behind her ear. "I'm sorry if I sounded harsh about your decision to tell Maya. It just... caught me off guard."

"It's okay," she replied in a tired murmur. "I'm just not sure which will be worse—fighting illusions or explaining to the Council how a mortal knows half their secrets. But we'll see." She forced a small, wry smile. "Thanks for not letting me break down alone."

He slipped his hand into hers, giving it a reassuring squeeze.

They walked deeper into the hallway, footsteps echoing against stone. Lila's nerves still frayed with every step, anticipating the possibility of crossing paths with another Council member. Yet beneath the dread, a kernel of hope flickered. Maya was now half in the loop, determined to help from outside the Council's labyrinth of spells. And here, in the dim passage where illusions could twist reality at any moment, Lila had Caleb's unwavering presence.

It might still end in disaster, but for the first time in weeks, she felt a stubborn assurance that she hadn't made the wrong choice. With Maya aware of her magical ties and Caleb standing by her side, Lila felt a strange sense of unity building around her. If the Council demanded answers or illusions escalated again, at least she wouldn't be staggering along by herself. She had allies—one inside these walls, and one in the café she called home.

That knowledge rested in her chest like a steady beat, guiding her forward even as her pulse quickened. She didn't know how the Council might retaliate or whether Sebastian's illusions would strike next, but she had shared the burden, and for a single breath, that was enough.

They reached the next turn in the corridor, and Lila inhaled, preparing for whatever came next. The day had begun with dread. Now, it brimmed with fragile hope. She wasn't sure if that hope would shatter under the Council's rules, but the sound of Maya's fierce promise rang in her ears, and the memory of Caleb's desperate kiss warmed her mouth. No matter how treacherous the path ahead, she was no longer alone.

CHAPTER

NINETEEN

Lila slumped onto the old couch in her apartment, letting her shoulders sink into the worn cushions. She had returned from yet another punishing round of Council briefings less than an hour ago. There had been endless discussions—new illusions reported downtown, fresh ward anomalies near the waterfront, and suspicious magical signatures that no one seemed able to pinpoint exactly. The meetings left her mind knotted with worry. Her body ached as though she had run a marathon, though she hadn't set foot outside the Council corridors for most of the day.

Night pressed heavily against her windows, drowning the tiny living room that felt too thick to be comforting. She pulled a throw blanket over her legs and exhaled a trembling breath. The overhead lamp flickered slightly, hinting at her unfocused magic that always pulsed with her emotions. She tried to calm the restless energy beneath her skin. Too many spells cast in too few hours had frayed her control more than usual. All she wanted was a moment's rest—a chance to feel like the ordinary barista she used to be, if only for one fleeting second.

She closed her eyes. The apartment was quiet, aside from the distant hum of traffic below and the faint, uneven buzz of wards that layered her walls. Exhaustion finally weighed her eyelids shut, and she drifted into a shallow doze.

She wasn't sure how many minutes passed before the dream descended like a trapdoor swinging open beneath her feet. One moment she was in the dim memory of a normal life—frothing milk at The Daily Grind or teasing Maya about a complicated coffee order—and the next she found herself standing in an unearthly space that made her heart stutter.

It was an immense cavern lined with dark, jagged walls. Ghostly torches flickered along each side, casting greenish light across a polished stone floor. The air felt laden with magic so thick her lungs struggled to draw breath. At the center of the chamber hovered the Nexus Prism—an unsettling crystal mass suspended in midair without chains or pedestals. Multicolored light churned inside its facets, swirling blues and purples pulsing like a heartbeat gone wrong. Each throb created a resonant boom that rattled Lila's bones. It felt alive.

Her throat went dry. She tried to move closer, but her feet refused to obey. A murky shape slipped into the corner of her vision. Sebastian. Tall and lean, wearing sleek black robes that shimmered in the Prism's glow, he surveyed the artifact with a greedy intensity. Even from the side, she could see the cruel twist of his lips. Then he lifted a hand, illusions rippling off his outstretched fingers in smoky trails. The Prism's colors flared, cycling faster as if feeding on his power.

A flicker of light arced outward, revealing illusions that took shape as monstrous silhouettes crowding the chamber's edges. They writhed and clawed at the air, hungry for more energy. Sebastian turned enough for Lila to see his face, and a sharp bolt of horror gripped her. He was smirking, an almost triumphant satisfaction etched into his features. The illusions leaped and twisted, bending to his command. In a sudden flash, she saw their possible targets: Manhattan's skyline warping under colossal illusions, streets falling into chaos, everyday people unable to distinguish real from unreal. Her pulse thundered in her ears.

She tried to shout, to warn someone—anyone. But the dream gave her no voice. The cavern floor trembled. The Prism pulsed again in a rapid staccato, as if caught between worlds. Sebastian pivoted, his piercing eyes locking on hers. A malevolent grin curled his mouth, illuminating the cruel satisfaction he took in harnessing the Prism's raw might.

Then it all collapsed in on her. She jerked awake with a ragged gasp, drenched in sweat as she practically tumbled off the couch. The overhead lamp flared for a moment, sputtered, then steadied. Adrenaline shot through her limbs as she frantically looked around, trying to recall where she was. Her living room lamp. Her battered coffee table. A half-eaten muffin on a plate, abandoned from earlier. She was home, but her heart was racing as if she'd run a mile.

She pressed a clammy palm to her forehead, breathing in quick, shallow gulps. A nasty tang of stale magic clung to her mouth, as though the dream had spilled residue through her wards. Just then, her phone rang, the vibration rattling the clutter on her coffee table. She almost dropped it when she saw Caleb's name light up the screen.

Lila fumbled to answer. "Caleb?"

He sounded breathless. "You're awake. Are you all right?"

"I—yes," she croaked, though her voice betrayed the quiver in her chest. "What happened?"

"I felt a spike across our ward link," he said, his tone tight with concern. "It flared like an alarm. I could sense your magic surging. Tell me exactly what you saw."

She swallowed, still dizzy from the remnants of the vision, but forced the words out. "I had a dream—or maybe it was more than a dream. The Nexus Prism was there, suspended in some underground chamber. And Sebastian was using it to conjure illusions, bigger than anything I've seen. He looked so... in control. I don't know how to describe it other than terrifying."

Caleb's silence crackled over the line. Finally, he murmured, "Your aura spiked so hard I felt it blocks away." He paused. "I'm coming over. We can't ignore what you've experienced, especially if it involves the Prism."

Before she could protest that he should rest—he'd had an even longer day than she had—he ended the call. The phone dropped from her fingers onto the couch cushion.

Lila exhaled shakily and tried not to shiver. The dream's imagery clung to her eyes: the Prism's swirling lights and Sebastian's triumphant glare. Rubbing her arms, she pushed herself off the couch and stepped into the small kitchen, eager for a glass of water—anything to ground her.

She flipped on the overhead light, illuminating peeling linoleum and a few stray coffee cups stacked by the sink. As she sipped, she noted her reflection in the window. Her hair was plastered to her temples, and her cheeks burned with residual embarrassment, as if she'd been caught doing something wrong rather than rattled out of sleep by a nightmare.

But it was more than a nightmare. She'd sensed magic in that vision, felt the Prism's pulse thrumming against her rib cage. That was not how ordinary dreams worked. Heart pounding, she willed herself to keep calm. The residue of that dream was an itch beneath her skin, like static looking for a release.

Her front door wards flickered in her awareness about ten minutes later, announcing Caleb's approach. She set down her water, rolled her stiff neck, and tried to appear collected when she opened the door. He greeted her with eyes that held more worry than greeting. His hair was windblown, suggesting he'd rushed here without his usual composure.

She stood aside to let him in. He stepped into her dimly lit apartment, scanning it quickly for any sign of illusions. The wards must have looked stable enough to him because he turned to face her, studying her expression.

"You're pale," he said softly.

She half-laughed—a brittle noise that stuck in her throat. "I might have just had the scariest dream of my life. Can't blame me for looking a little off."

Without waiting, he stepped closer, lifting one hand to rest lightly on her shoulder. Relief warred with a strange sense of vulnerability. She had never grown fully used to how his presence could calm her nerves, even when her magic was in disarray. Tonight, though, his face was knotted with unease, and his usual stoic facade held an undercurrent of alarm.

"Start at the beginning," he said. "Let's piece this together."

She guided him to the couch, settling onto the cushion where she'd dozed earlier. He joined her, leaving perhaps a hand's breadth of space between them. The soft overhead lamp cast shapes across the walls. Lila inhaled, ignoring the slight tremble in her hands.

"I saw an enormous underground chamber—bigger than the usual catacombs or corridors we've explored. The Prism hung in the air. It was... alive, somehow, each color swirling like it was breathing. And Sebastian was there. He was channeling illusions off it. The power I felt—" She paused, shuddering at the memory. "It wasn't normal. It was as if the Prism was fueling everything he did, letting him reshape illusions into something monstrous."

Caleb frowned. "And he saw you?"

"It felt like he did. Near the end, he looked right at

me... almost like an invitation." She closed her eyes, recalling that smug glint. "That grin on his face... I hate it."

Caleb studied her features, eyes narrow with concern. Suddenly, a faint ripple of magic brushed Lila's consciousness. She stiffened but realized it was coming from him, a gentle probing that read her aura. The wards around them glimmered in her peripheral vision. She sensed him quietly verifying that no hidden illusions had followed her out of the dream. At his slight nod, she released a breath she hadn't known she was holding.

"It's not just a random nightmare," Caleb said, his voice carefully controlled. "I can sense your family's signature magic flickering around you. It feels as though you stepped halfway into a real magical space and then snapped out of it."

She dropped her gaze. "I know it must be weird, but the Prism was so real. It kept throbbing in my ears like my heart was tethered to it."

He exhaled slowly, turning his gaze to the window. "The Council has spent months trying to locate the Prism before Sebastian fully harnessed it. Now it seems he's close—too close. Your vision might indicate he's found a hidden stronghold big enough to anchor illusions on a massive scale."

Her stomach twisted at the thought. "Marcus and the others need to hear about this."

"They do," Caleb agreed. He shifted closer, his knee brushing hers. "But I wanted to see you first, make sure you were safe and not still caught in some residual illusion. I felt that surge, Lila. It almost knocked me off my feet."

She let out a ragged sigh. "Crashing from it left me in a cold sweat. I'm still shaking." She forced a small, wry grin. "Am I going to get used to the city's illusions constantly attacking my mind?"

He offered a somber tilt of his head. "I don't want you to get used to it, because it shouldn't be happening in the first place. Sebastian's illusions are off the charts lately. If your dream is any hint, he's pushing the Prism's power beyond anything we've accounted for."

She reached out, her fingers curling around his hand on the couch. In the silence that stretched between them, she felt the rapid beat of his pulse. He looked at her with an intensity that made warmth surge in her chest, a promise she couldn't quite put into words.

"It feels like the Prism is calling me," she said quietly, staring at their joined hands. "In the dream, I sensed it was trying to... link with me somehow, or maybe it was just Sebastian's illusions. But I can't shake the feeling that something huge is about to break."

His thumb traced slow circles over her knuckles. "Then we find it. We don't wait for another unhinged vision to strike you. We'll talk to Marcus, gather every bit of intel we can. We track down the Prism's location before Sebastian can warp reality any further. And we do it fast."

TWENTY

Lila walked briskly along the torchlit corridor, the Council's latest briefing still echoing in her ears. Her mind buzzed with the same worries she had been nursing for days: illusions seeping into city streets, the Council's stagnant bureaucracy, and Sebastian's cryptic name always hovering in the background. Tonight had offered little in terms of tangible progress. Most of the Council elders rehashed old procedures, and she could practically taste their tension each time a new rumor about Sebastian's spreading influence surfaced. The corridors reeked of candle wax and lingering ozone—the hallmarks of too many spells cast in haste.

She paused at an intersection where two side passages branched away into gloom. The air felt thick, clinging to her skin in a way that made her stomach clench. She drew a slow breath, tucking her hair behind her ear. She tried to steady her thoughts by pressing a hand against the silver amulet beneath her coat. Its metal felt reassuringly warm, the faint pulse in its chain reminding her that her lineage carried at least some promise of defense against illusions.

"Lila," a voice whispered from somewhere to her left. She whipped around, eyes narrowed, half expecting a trick of the gloom. But she saw two hooded silhouettes lurking by a tall braided column. One figure took a cautious step forward, palms raised in a gesture of peace. The flicker from the corridor's torchlight slid across faces partially shadowed by the fold of their hoods.

Goose bumps prickled across Lila's arms. She glanced over her shoulder, seeing no one else passing by. This corridor sometimes served as a private route to an antechamber, where minor Council tasks got handled. It was deserted now except for the magic swirling in the lantern flames. The two strangers looked nervous.

"Who are you?" Lila asked, shifting her weight to a defensive stance. She found herself wishing Caleb were at her side. Instead, the only reassurance she had was the amulet thrumming against her collarbone.

The first witch lowered her hood slightly, revealing a narrow, freckled face and dark, watchful eyes. "We mean no harm," she offered in a soft voice. "We knew you'd come this way after the briefing." Her gaze flicked to the corridor behind Lila, as if checking who might overhear. Then she raised her eyes again. "Please. We need to talk to you."

Lila eyed them both warily. Beneath the second hood, she saw a younger, broad-shouldered figure, glancing uneasily around. "The Council won't listen to us," that second witch muttered, voice taut with frustration.

A dryness settled in Lila's throat. She was far from naive about infiltration attempts, and it was possible these two were illusions themselves. Yet something about the first witch's trembling hands seemed too real, too raw to be a simple trick. Lila felt her curiosity tug, alongside a flicker of sympathy. She tightened her grip on the corridor's stone wall, letting her earth-based magic nudge the surface. No illusions shimmered in response, at least none she could detect.

"All right," she said, heart banging in her chest, "I'll hear you out. But keep it quick."

The first witch exhaled shakily and motioned for Lila to step a couple paces closer, away from the main hallway. The torch nearest them sputtered, casting shifting shadows across the polished floors. "We followed Sebastian for a time. We believed he wanted real freedom for witches and warlocks—an end to the Council's secrecy and a chance to use illusions without shame. That's how he drew so many of us in with all his grand talk about liberation."

The second witch swallowed and continued, voice tinged with regret. "But we saw the cost. He began twisting illusions into something cruel, using them to force lesser casters to obey, locking them in illusions that felt all too real. Then rumors of missing novices started surfacing—some conscripted, others just... vanished. We had to get out. We've been hiding ever since."

Lila's stomach clenched. She had suspected Sebastian's tactics were brutal, though hearing direct accounts struck a deeper nerve. She thought of the illusions at her café, the creeping vines, and the neon sparks that rattled unsuspecting patrons. Everything so far seemed small-scale compared to what these witches were describing. She squared her shoulders, keeping her voice low. "So why approach me?"

"Because we've seen how the Council operates," the first witch said. She folded her arms across her chest, as though the memory of old conflicts weighed her down. "They're too bureaucratic. They spend more time arguing about regulations than actually rooting out Sebastian's expansions. But you—they say you're different. We heard whispers about a Matthews witch with a special amulet, an artifact that Sebastian fears might counter illusions."

The mention of her family name sent a jolt through Lila. She pressed her lips together. "People sure know how to spread gossip."

She expected them to push further, to demand she prove the amulet's potency, but the two witches simply exchanged anxious glances. After a beat, the second witch dug out a small candle stub from a pouch and swept it through the air, igniting a gentle glow around them. The light revealed the etched lines of exhaustion on both witches' faces.

"You probably sense we're not illusions," the first witch said quietly, "or you'd have run by now. We're hoping you'll trust us just enough to listen." She shot a frantic look over her shoulder, as if expecting a Council guard to burst in on them at any moment.

Lila pursed her lips. She didn't see any immediate trap,

and the sincerity in their eyes made her chest tighten with empathy. "Go on," she managed.

The second witch leaned closer, gripping the candle stub with knuckles blanched white. "We've found a derelict church near the Lower East Side. It's barely standing, crumbling walls, broken pews. Beneath it is a chamber where Sebastian or his followers have been conducting test runs of illusions, amplifying them with partial wards so they can lash out at people who stray inside. Some novices he's managed to recruit escape with wild stories of living nightmares that felt too real—animate shadows, flickering monsters. He's binding them to him through fear."

Lila inhaled sharply, forcing herself not to flinch. She imagined novices like she once was—terrified, half educated on controlling their gifts, suddenly cornered by illusions too potent to dismiss. The memory of her own early illusions, though less malevolent, made her shiver. "Does the Council know about this place?"

The witches shook their heads in unison. The first witch stepped forward, voice trembling with urgency. "Telling the Council would mean risking blowback if Sebastian has a mole still lurking here. We're not sure if it's safe to trust these halls. Some factions remain loyal to him, or at least sympathetic to his claims about tearing down the old system. We all witnessed how a traitor nearly fed him inside information before. But you—" She paused, eyes drifting to Lila's neckline. The silver amulet was partially hidden, but evidently its subtle glow drew her attention. "We heard you're the one he's after most. He brags about controlling the 'Matthews key' once he gets the chance. So we thought you'd want to know the truth. If Sebastian is building a bigger stronghold, that church could be at the center."

Heat flushed under Lila's skin. She felt a surge of indignation at how casually Sebastian bandied her name among his twisted circles. A fleeting memory flared: illusions attacking her in the street, a mocking laugh that still made her chest tighten at night. She swallowed and whispered, "If I want to investigate this hidden chamber, how do I know you two won't lure me into a trap?"

"We have nothing to gain by betraying you," the second witch insisted. "We're done with Sebastian. All we want is to see him stopped before he sinks the entire city into chaos."

Silence clung to the corridor, broken only by a sputtering hiss from the nearest torch. Lila scanned the two witches' faces. They seemed earnest—haunted by a regret that oozed from every corner of their posture. She recalled how the Council had thus far struggled to keep illusions off the streets. Perhaps an inside perspective was exactly what they needed. Still, caution tugged at her, a reminder that illusions could mask manipulative truths with a single flick of magic.

She exhaled. "Fine. I'll do what I can." The uncertainty in her voice rang loud in her ears. "But if you come to me with a fabricated story—"

They both shook their heads quickly. The first witch took another step. "We'll prove our honesty. Here." She tapped the air, conjuring a faint blue spark that crackled upward, forming a hovering sigil. It swirled, then coalesced into a tiny charm that dropped into her waiting palm. She offered it to Lila, eyes earnest. "An old contact charm. You can sense if illusions tamper with it. Keep it, and use it to reach us. If we sense you casting the spell, we'll come."

The second witch opened her hand as well, producing an identical charm. "In return, we'd like to have something from you—something to confirm you're the real Lila Matthews. Not the Council's entire ward code, obviously. Just... a small token linking you to the amulet's aura or your personal signature, so we know if an imposter tries to approach us."

Lila glanced down at the amulet. She knew better than to hand off anything vital to suspicious parties, but a subtle protective twist of her aura might suffice. Closing her eyes, she drew on a sliver of her earth magic. A faint emerald glow spread along her fingertips. She pressed her hand to a spare scrap of parchment folded in her pocket, whispering a mild anchoring incantation. The paper glowed and cooled in her palm, bearing a faint trace of her magical imprint.

She held it out, feeling a twinge of hesitation. "This is a minor imprint of my magical signature. It'll let you confirm it's me. Just promise me you won't do anything reckless."

The witches pressed the imprint between them. "No more recklessness. We want to see Sebastian's illusions snuffed out, not unleashed."

Relief and unease tangled inside Lila. She tucked the

newly earned contact charm beneath her coat, ensuring it touched the amulet's chain so any illusions would register against her family's magic. Her hands still shook, adrenaline coursing through her at the thought that Sebastian was testing illusions in a half-ruined church, forging an army from the ranks of the desperate. The witches murmured thanks, then melted back into the shadows, footsteps soundless against the stone.

For a moment, Lila remained rooted, heart pounding. She stared after them until the corridor's seemed to envelop her. The torch's flame guttered, casting spastic, dancing shapes against the wall. She sucked in a breath, trying to steady the pulse roaring in her ears. If these defectors spoke the truth, the city's illusions were on the verge of something bigger—something even the Council's wards might not handle.

She forced herself to keep walking, turning down the corridor until she emerged by the main staircase that spiraled toward the Council hall's exit. She found herself longing for fresh air or at least one of Caleb's chilled illusions to cut the stuffy warmth. She needed to share this news and see if there was a path beyond the endless Council debates.

Cracking open a small side door, she slipped outside into a narrow courtyard where the night breeze brushed at her hair. Stars glinted behind a haze of city lights, only partially obscured by the Council's wards overhead. Lila drew in a steadying breath before stepping onto the street, merging with the late evening flow of pedestrians. A passing car horn jarred her, and she blinked, readjusting to the mundane bustle after the oppressive quiet of Council corridors.

Back at The Daily Grind, now closed for the night, she found Caleb leaning against a tall lamppost by the entrance, his arms folded. Relief spread across his face the instant he spotted her. He had likely felt her tension across the wards they sometimes shared—those subtle links that flared whenever one of them was uneasy.

"You look rattled," he said softly, locking eyes with her. Even in the buzzing light of a flickering streetlamp, his gaze held warmth. He stepped closer, voice lowered. "Council meeting was that bad?"

She snorted softly. "They spent hours rehashing the same arguments. But that's not it." She glanced around, confirming they were alone. "I was cornered in the corridor by two witches who claim they used to follow Sebastian."

CHAPTER

TWENTY-ONE

Lila rubbed the heel of her palm against her temple, trying to banish the lingering headache that had hounded her since daybreak. Outside the wide glass windows of The Daily Grind, the street bustled with commuters in rumpled coats and half-buttoned shirts. She felt their tension in the air, a shared unease that crackled like static over the sidewalk. Scooters zipped by in erratic arcs, horns blared in staccato bursts, and overhead a trio of pigeons flapped in jittery formation, as if the entire city was on edge.

She wiped the counter clean for the third time in ten minutes, unable to shake a feeling of dread. Customers trickled in, some yawning and impatient, others snapping quick greetings before burying their noses in phones. But a few, she noticed, behaved oddly—eyes darting sideways at flickers in the corner of their vision. One man halted by the pastry case, stepping backward with a hissed oath when he glimpsed something swirling near a table of empty chairs. Lila followed his gaze, skin prickling as she caught a faint shimmer reminiscent of illusions she had dispelled only days ago.

She clenched her jaw. Ordinarily, illusions kept to the shadows, the hidden corners of Manhattan that the Council preferred remain unobserved. Yet here they were, drifting into a daylight café. The man shook his head hard, then hurried to the register to order a croissant, muttering that he must be sleep-deprived. His eyes held fear, though he forced a stiff smile for politeness. Lila's chest tightened with sympathy as she rang him up, wishing she could whisper: Yes, you did see something strange. No, it is not a mere trick of light.

"Hey, kiddo." Maya's voice cut in softly from behind. Her friend leaned beside the counter, face grim with uncharacteristic worry. "You sure you're all right? You've been cleaning that same spot so hard you'll rub a hole in the counter."

"I'm fine," Lila replied automatically, but the disquiet in her chest betrayed her. She set aside the rag and forced a smile for the next customer, a woman who asked about gluten-free muffins. Lila guided the woman to the pastry display, mustering all her usual friendliness while her heart pounded.

The morning passed in fits and starts, a frantic rush softened by lulls that felt eerily silent. Then the door would clang open again, letting in a fresh wave of rumors about bizarre apparitions or neon bursts at random street corners. Whispers drifted through the line of customers: flickering lights near Times Square, taxi windows that reflected half-translucent figures, flowerbeds that glimmered in Manhattan's parks. More people ventured inside to find a semblance of comfort in a latte or cappuccino, but tension laced every conversation.

By noon, the café bristled with so many edgy patrons that Maya had to open the second register to keep the line moving. Lila slid cappuccinos and Americanos across the counter to frantic office workers, who kept glancing at their phones for the latest news. She heard the words mass hysteria and tech glitch repeated over and over. One woman insisted it was a new marketing stunt by some streaming service. Another man cursed about incompetent city officials letting new "hologram technology" spin out of control.

The entire time, Lila felt magic stir in her breast, as if the illusions beyond the café's threshold were rapping at the windows. She tried to quell the buzz in her limbs, focusing on repetitive tasks instead: grind, tamp, brew, serve. Yet now and then, faint sparks danced over the café's neon sign, drawing startled yelps from passersby.

"This is bad," Maya murmured during a lull, voice pitched low. She placed a hand on Lila's shoulder. "They're calling it a citywide malfunction, but half the people in line think New York's cursed. You're trembling, hon. Don't tell me you feel nothing."

"It's just nerves, Maya," Lila said, though there was no conviction in her words. Her apron strings twitched under her restless fingers. "So many rumors are floating around, it's making me anxious."

Maya nodded but watched her too keenly for Lila's

comfort. On another day, she might have tried distracting her friend with jokes about new coffee flavors, but the haunted set to Maya's gaze said she understood this was more serious than idle chatter. The last time illusions appeared this openly, Lila had found herself in the thick of magical trouble.

Maya opened her mouth to speak, but a man at the far table let out a startled shout. Lila's head snapped up. The café's neon sign outside had just crackled in a burst of emerald sparks, bright enough that the flicker reflected against the inside windows. A handful of customers turned and stared, wide-eyed. Most of them had no clue illusions existed, but they all saw the flash of something green. Lila felt her stomach clench, the sensation of swirling magic too close for comfort.

She hurried around the counter to check the sign from inside. Glowing motes of faint energy still danced against the glass, but they faded the moment she concentrated, as if sensing the presence of her own magic. It left behind a hum in the café, broken only by the spitting sounds of the espresso machine. Desperate to salvage calm, she forced a bright laugh.

"Wow, guess that old sign's on its last legs," she said, projecting a steady tone. "Must be messing with the wiring. Nothing to worry about, folks."

The man who had shouted cleared his throat, looking sheepish. He mumbled an apology to the table and resumed typing on a laptop between jittery glances at the window. Bit by bit, patrons settled in again, though an uneasy feeling clung to the space.

Maya found Lila by the pastry display, her voice low enough that no one else would hear. "You sure you can handle another few hours of this? The city's, like, going crazy."

Lila swallowed. "I'll be fine. But... maybe keep an eye out for more weird bursts. If it happens again, I'll say we're closing early."

Maya pressed her lips together. "I can do that."

Once the lull ended, more customers poured in with wild stories: a faint glow in the East River last night, swirling lights near the Public Library, and something about ghostly shapes in a subway car. Each rumor gnawed at Lila's nerves, but she plastered on a polite smile and handed over change, cursing internally every time the spells thrummed in her bloodstream.

The day finally wheezed to a close around six, the café's busy hum tapering to a few scattered customers finishing their drinks. Lila took off her apron, the fabric heavy with coffee stains and sweat. She kept glancing at her phone, half expecting a Council summons. Indeed, a single text from Marcus had arrived: "We have teams on active watch. Minimal illusions in your area. Remain vigilant." She scoffed. Minimal illusions, sure. It felt like illusions were crawling into every shadow.

"Go on," Maya urged softly, noticing Lila's frantic gaze. "I'll handle the last few stragglers. You look like you need fresh air, or maybe a stiff drink."

Lila mustered gratitude in the form of a weak smile. "Thanks. I owe you."

Without another word, she slipped outside, letting the

brisk early-evening wind envelop her. Over the city's skyline, she spotted shimmering clusters of colored motes dancing—barely visible, but enough to spark alarm if anyone stared long enough. A pang of worry tugged at her chest. The illusions had never been so widespread at once. The Council was already stretched thin quelling illusions in remote corners of the city, and the more they scrambled, the more alarmed mortals grew.

She was halfway down the block, mind racing, when she spotted a familiar figure leaning against a lamppost. Caleb's dark coat caught the fading light, and a swirl of tension in the pit of her stomach eased at the sight of him. He lifted his hand in greeting, features set in a grim line.

"It's getting worse," he said in greeting, voice low. A gust of wind brushed his hair over his forehead. "We've had watchers in Times Square putting up illusions of city maintenance crews to keep people from panicking, but it's messy. No one's fool enough to ignore those bursts of phantom shapes floating around."

"How bad is it?" she asked, ignoring her own tight breath.

"Council teams say illusions are cropping up like weeds," Caleb replied. "So far, no mass hysteria, but folks are spooked. Marcus told me we're short-staffed for direct cover-ups. The illusions are easier to explain away as 'glitches' in smaller pockets, but they're spreading fast."

Her heart sank. "I saw some in the café. Sparks on the sign, little flickers inside. People are already throwing out theories about citywide sabotage or new VR technology gone rogue."

Caleb's gaze flicked to the sky, where faint glimmers pulsed in the gathering twilight. "Every illusion that the Council doesn't neutralize in time draws more suspicion. We can't hide everything, not at this rate."

Lila shuddered, the memory of customers darting anxious looks behind them still fresh. "So, what do we do?" she asked softly.

He exhaled. "Council watchers are dispatching teams to answer concerned citizen groups. Just a quick handshake, a few illusions that 'prove' it's some city experiment or municipal test, enough to keep the masses calm. It's damage control."

She read the tension in his posture, the same frustration she felt. "And that's where we come in?"

Caleb nodded. "Marcus wants us to go check on a neighborhood board meeting near the East Side. A handful of locals have started demanding official answers. They're rallying outside an old building, calling for city representatives to show up and explain the weird lights. We're the closest watchers, apparently."

A hollow laugh escaped her. "Great. So, we spin them a story, hope illusions don't pop up mid-sentence, and then vanish before they ask more questions?"

Caleb's mouth quirked in a humorless smile. "That's the idea."

They set off together, weaving through side streets to avoid potential illusions overhead. The wind carried the echo of sirens and the hum of anxious conversation from every corner. By the time they reached the East Side, darkness had fallen, casting the old stone buildings in murky shadows.

They found a small group—maybe a dozen mortals—gathered on the sidewalk outside a poorly lit community center. Their voices rose in frustrated unison over the swirling wind.

"This can't just be a glitch!" a man in a red beanie shouted. "I saw something in my apartment mirror. It looked at me!"

A woman standing beside him added, "My kid woke up crying about shapes dancing by the window. How is that a tech glitch?"

Several others chimed in with similar complaints, brandishing phones where they claimed to have recorded videos. Lila's stomach twisted imagining what might show up on those screens—grainy illusions flickering in and out of focus.

Caleb cleared his throat and stepped forward. "Evening, folks," he said, voice steady and reassuring. "We heard you're worried about the lights. I'm... part of a local community outreach program looking into these phenomena." He flashed a forged city ID the Council had crafted for such cover-ups.

Lila nodded in affirmation, though her insides prickled. One woman stared at them suspiciously. "Never seen you before. Which city department are you from?"

"Experimental Tech and Infrastructure," Caleb offered without blinking. "We're here to gather data and reassure you that no one is in danger. Sometimes new lighting systems get tested at night, and—"

"Testing in apartments?" demanded another voice in the crowd. "I got an electric shock when I switched on my bathroom light. Felt like something was in there with me!"

Murmurs of agreement rippled through the group. Lila's heart thumped. She reached into her jacket pocket for the small notepad the Council insisted watchers carry, planning to scribble some official-looking notes. "We'll compile these reports," she said. "We appreciate your patience, and we can pass this along to the appropriate departments."

Most eyed them warily but fell quiet as Caleb gently steered the conversation, pressing each person for details about where and when they saw the lights. His manner was calm but firm, offering half-truths about flickering wiring and potential expansions of municipal tech. Lila backed him up with nods and the occasional mention of new pilot programs. It was a flimsy charade, but hopefully enough to calm these folks for now.

Then the wind picked up, carrying a sudden chill that rippled across the cracked pavement. Lila felt the prickle of magic under her skin, and she noticed a shimmer above the community center's roof. A swirl of faint ghosts flickered into existence, half-formed illusions drifting down. One figure seemed to unfurl from the night sky, shape dissolving and re-forming like a living shadow.

Several in the group turned and gasped. "Look!" shrieked a younger woman, pointing skyward. Her phone flew up to capture it on video.

Caleb cursed softly under his breath. He lifted a hand, letting a discreet warding spell ripple from his palm, but the illusions were strong, likely powered by the city's overall surge. Translucent apparitions danced like wind-blown scraps of cloth.

In seconds, panicked cries rang out across the sidewalk, and people pressed backward, colliding into one another. A man stumbled off the curb, nearly toppling, until Lila grabbed his arm and pulled him upright. Fear spiked in the air, feeding the illusions. She felt the energy flicker like a living thing, twisting overhead.

"Everybody move back," Caleb said, voice raised but steady. "We have a safety protocol for this. Maybe... maybe stand over there." He gestured lamely toward a strip of benches near the fence.

A few obeyed him, but panic was too strong to calm with mere words. One woman fumbled with her phone, trying to dial what might have been the police. The illusions roamed higher, forming something akin to phantom arms stretching across the sky. Lila's spine tensed. If they unleashed any serious manifestation, it would become impossible to explain away.

"Caleb," she whispered through clenched teeth. "We can't keep them here."

He nodded. "We need to retreat before we lose control." Then more loudly, he turned to the crowd. "We'll call in specialists. Please, everyone head home for the night. This meeting is adjourned until further notice." Most of them still stared, reluctant to leave.

Realizing time was short, Lila mustered a subtle coax of her magic, nudging a wave of gentle compulsion. She hated resorting to it, but illusions were swirling overhead, forming ghostly phantoms that pulsed with each heart-beat. The crowd's fear only fed those shapes further. Softly, she spoke, "It's dangerous to stay outside in these conditions. For your safety, please go indoors. We'll handle the rest."

Whether from her plea, the ward's nudge, or their own building panic, the group slowly dispersed, some muttering that the city better reimburse them for damaged property. Others stared once more at the phantoms, then hurried away, phones clutched tight. Lila's pulse hammered at the knowledge that at least a few had likely recorded something they shouldn't.

TWENTY-TWO

Lila Matthews leaned back against the cold marble pillar in the Council's briefing chamber, trying to steady her breath as murmurs swirled through the crowd of assembled guardians. The rhythmic thump of her pulse echoed in her ears, making it hard to process the nervous chatter that filled the vaulted room. Her gaze flickered across the circle of robed figures, each wearing the pinched expressions of worried individuals stretched thin by the city's relentless illusions.

Caleb Blackwood stood beside her, arms folded over his chest, posture rigid. The flicker in his eyes betrayed his tension, though he kept his face carefully schooled into a calm mask. Only Lila, perhaps, could read the frustration lurking beneath that composure. She felt it too. Things had gone from bad to downright horrifying over the past couple of days. Illusions kept intruding into everyday life, nearly exposing magic to mortals. More worryingly, the very guardians tasked with protecting the Council had started pointing fingers at each other.

She exhaled slowly. They were supposed to finalize a new plan tonight after the Council's latest scouting mission. Rumors circulated that illusions had broken through wards in key spots near the old vault corridors, the same vault that once safeguarded the Nexus Prism. Just remembering that relic made Lila's skin prickle; the city might have been spared a catastrophe when it disappeared from that vault, but it had never truly been safe since.

A door on the far side of the chamber creaked open, catching everyone's attention. Zoe Blackwood, Caleb's sister, strode in, grey cloak swirling around her ankles. Her pace was brisk. She held a thick bundle of parchments tucked under one arm, while the other remained curled in a fist at her side. Even from across the room, Lila noticed how tight Zoe's knuckles looked beneath the lantern light.

Marcus Steele, stood at the center of the briefing table and gestured for silence. His tall, austere frame loomed beneath a single orb of enchanted light that bobbed overhead. "We have urgent matters," he said stiffly, his deep voice carrying easily in the cavernous hall. "Zoe Blackwood brings information that cannot wait. Everyone, take your seats."

Lila and Caleb exchanged a glance. The faint warmth of his arm brushing against hers eased her nerves, reminding her they faced this crisis together. They moved toward two free chairs near the table's edge. The carved wooden seat pressed uncomfortably against Lila's spine, but she kept her posture firm.

Zoe cleared her throat, stepping into the ring of guardians. She spread the parchments across the table's surface. Several watchers peered closer, eyebrows furrowed. Others exchanged uneasy whispers. Zoe didn't speak right away. Instead, she carefully laid out each sheet, pressing her palm over them one by one as if ensuring the illusions hiding within wouldn't vanish prematurely.

Then her voice rang out, clear and resonant. "I discovered discrepancies in the daily security rosters and night-watch logs," she said. A few Council members, including an older warlock in the corner, stiffened at her words. "At first, I assumed it might be a clerical error. But the deeper I dug, the more I found illusions layered over the official records."

Lila tensed. Illusions. The word carried new weight these days, conjuring images of flickering phantoms and twisted shapes that had plagued the city. But illusions woven into record-keeping? A fresh kind of deviousness. She caught the slight crease in Caleb's brow—he'd clearly realized it too.

Intrigue sparked in the circle of watchers, distrust coloring the air. Marcus nodded for Zoe to continue.

She traced her fingertip across the topmost parchment. Though it appeared ordinary, a faint shimmer pulsed under her touch. "There are forged entries listing nonexistent guardians. Portions of the real roster are hidden beneath a glamour. Whoever did this made it look like certain watchers were on duty at times they weren't. Meanwhile, others who truly were on duty have been wiped from the logs altogether."

A ripple of gasps coursed through the group. Lila leaned forward, curiosity prickling. The Council used these rosters to maintain order, ensuring watchers guarded key strongholds—like the vault that once contained the Nexus Prism. If illusions corrupted the rosters, it meant traitors could sneak around undetected. The thought made Lila's stomach roil.

At the table's center, Marcus's jaw went rigid. He skewered Zoe with a hard stare, though his anger was clearly not directed at her. "Are you certain about these illusions, Miss Blackwood?"

Zoe lifted her chin. "I tested them thoroughly. Stripping away the first layer revealed only half the truth. Whoever worked this deceit layered illusions multiple times to mislead even our standard detection spells." She slid one parchment aside to expose the underside, where faint scrawls shimmered in runic script. "See? The real text lurks here, overshadowed by illusions."

A chorus of low curses slipped from several watchers. The sense of betrayal rippled through the room like a cold draft. Lila folded her arms against her chest, her heart pounding. They had worried about infiltration for weeks, but never guessed illusions had wormed their way into core Council logistics.

Zoe's tone hardened. "What's worse, wards near the vault corridor have been partially undone from inside. I suspect the same individual or group behind these illusions tampered with the protective runes. This is no small offense. They're covering their tracks and framing watchers to deflect suspicion."

Caleb cursed under his breath. Lila reached out discreetly beneath the table, brushing her fingers to his. His return squeeze was fleeting but comforting. The last time sabotage compromised wards, illusions flared across the city with terrifying strength. And the memory of the Nexus Prism's theft still hovered like a ghost in everyone's mind.

Marcus braced his palms on the table, his voice low with controlled fury. "You mean someone purposely allowed illusions to run rampant around the vault? So we would suspect the wrong guardians?"

Zoe nodded grimly. "Yes. And if not for stumbling over contradictory rosters, I might never have seen the underlying illusions. Conflicting schedules and phantom watchers gave them away."

One of the Council elders—a woman with silver braids coiled at her nape—stepped forward, her voice shaky. "That corridor was sealed after the Prism vanished. Why compromise it now?"

Lila thought of the illusions creeping through the city, intensifying day by day. Sebastian's name flickered at the back of her mind. She hadn't forgotten how he once threatened to reacquire the Prism's powers if it surfaced again. Could he still be orchestrating this infiltration, or had he left it to allies within the Council?

At that question, Zoe's gaze flicked across the assembled guardians. "We don't have definitive proof it's about regaining the relic. But suspicious footsteps were heard echoing in that corridor last night. A guard posted near the west catacomb entrance swore he sensed slight magical pulses, as if illusions were being tested in short bursts. When he tried to investigate, the pulses vanished."

"Vanished?" repeated Marcus, hostility edging his tone. He rapped the table once for emphasis, making the parchments rustle. "This is unacceptable. We have an insider capable of weaving illusions to manipulate our official records, sabotage wards, and apparently roam freely where no one should be."

Beside Lila, Caleb's breathing grew heavier. She pictured him replaying memories of Sebastian's infiltration months earlier, the guilt he carried for not foreseeing his old friend's turn. Lila's frustration rose too—no one should have to revisit that nightmare. Worry gnawed at her. The city was already fragile from illusions lurking in public spaces. Now they faced infiltration at the highest level.

One of the watchers tried to speak, but Marcus cut him off with a glare. "Whoever this traitor is, they have skill. The illusions hidden here are advanced, enough to fool standard wards." He clenched his fists on the table. "How many times must we be undermined from within? Do these collusions never end?"

Then he slammed his fist onto the wood so hard that an echo reverberated through the chamber. Lila flinched, and a few watchers gasped. "I have had enough!" Marcus roared, letting slip a harsh curse that charged the air. "I will not stand by while illusions swirl unchecked in our own halls."

The communal tension thickened. Lila swallowed back her own fear, capturing Caleb's gaze. Despite his calm mask, she read the alarm in his eyes. They had both suspected a traitor might linger in the Council, but it stung to realize how deeply illusions had become entangled in official affairs.

Zoe's voice wavered, though she kept it steady as she continued. "I propose immediate screening of all guardians with advanced anti-illusion spells. Anyone showing suspicious magical signatures or contradictory schedules must be interrogated. We might catch the manipulator before they do worse damage."

A heated debate erupted among the watchers. Some nodded vigorously at Zoe's suggestion, while others talked about the violation of personal privacy. The question of secrecy loomed large: if illusions had been used to scapegoat certain guardians, how could they trust a blanket screening?

Marcus raised a hand, silencing the clamor. "I regret it has come to this, but we have no choice. We cannot allow illusions to trick us into turning on our own. We must isolate the infiltration."

He looked around, eyes blazing. "We lock down the corridors near the vault. Restrict access to the advanced library. All watchers, senior or junior, undergo a thorough check for illusions. If you have nothing to hide, you have nothing to fear."

TWENTY-THREE

Lila fumbled with her apartment keys, arms trembling from another punishing day of unraveling illusions and grappling with mounting Council tensions. Her exhaustion ached in every limb. She could still taste the stale coffee she had used to keep herself awake on the ride home, a bitter tang clinging to her tongue. The corridor lights flickered overhead, reminding her that Sebastian's magic was likely circling the building. Whispers of illusions clung to the corners of her vision.

She finally managed to unlock the door and stepped inside, nearly slamming the door shut behind her. The tension seeped from her shoulders for only a moment before she realized the lights were already on. Evelyn and Caleb sat at her tiny kitchen table, faces etched with concern as they sifted through a scattering of family letters and half-translated notes.

Lila let out a startled breath. "I could have sworn I locked this door," she said, dropping her keys on the nearest shelf. "Don't either of you have anything better to do than wait around my apartment?"

Evelyn glanced up, eyes warm but clouded with worry. She was in the middle of a sentence, pointing a slender finger at one line of text, before turning to Lila. "You didn't call me back," she said. "I was worried about you."

Caleb stood, offering Lila a supportive nod as he approached. His presence steadied the swirl of tension inside her, though his gaze flickered with caution. "We just arrived," he said. "We knew you were out handling Council business, but... we needed to talk with you as soon as possible."

Evelyn rose from her seat, tucking a few sheets of paper under one arm. "I discovered something in the old journals. I had to bring it here immediately." There was a hint of reproach in her voice, the gentle scolding that Lila remembered from childhood whenever she forgot to return a phone call or vanished without explaining herself. "You must let us know if your illusions worsen, dear."

Lila swallowed against the dryness in her throat. She had spent the afternoon trying to help quell illusions drifting along a few city blocks, illusions that flickered over sidewalks. Every step home had weighed on her thoughts. Now, seeing her grandmother and Caleb huddled together, she wished she had told them she was all right. Instead, she had charged off alone, as usual.

"I'm... sorry for leaving you to guess," she managed. "There was no real time to breathe today, let alone text."

Evelyn nodded stiffly and smoothed the top letter on

the table. "It is all right, child. You are here now." With that, she gestured for Lila to join her, pointing to a line of text underlined in heavy ink. "Read that," she said. "I found it just last night in one of my older diaries. This is a new translation of a family incantation, clues that I once overlooked."

Lila shrugged off her coat, letting the battered fabric slump over the back of a chair. She stepped closer to scan the passage. The letters were faint, likely remnants of older script translated across multiple pages. Her name—no, her family's name—seemed embedded in runic form. She had grown used to seeing archaic references to "Matthews lineage," but this was more explicit than before.

Caleb joined her, standing close. She caught the subtle scent of his cologne whenever he shifted. Although she felt her cheeks warm slightly, she kept her focus on the text. The cramped, looping handwriting spelled out something about earth-based harmonization. Phrases like "ground your spirit" and "align the silver heartbeat" jumped off the page.

Evelyn tapped her finger. "It references the amulet you carry... and a chant that can synchronize its frequency. According to this, you can dampen illusions—at least temporarily—if you match the amulet's core to the resonance in your own magic."

Lila's pulse kicked in her chest. She touched the silver amulet resting against her collarbone. Days ago, she had found it in that old greenhouse. The memory of muddy hands and an overgrown chest still sent a shiver along her spine. Since then, she had sensed an odd pull in the amulet, as though it responded to her moods.

"Wait," she said, lifting the amulet gently. It twinkled in the overhead light. "So now you think we can... quiet illusions? Just like that?"

Caleb's hand brushed lightly at her shoulder, a comforting gesture. "Not exactly just like that," he said. "But your grandmother discovered a fresh translation that references earthen magic. It is similar to what we have been trying in certain wards, but far more specialized."

Evelyn nodded. "Exactly. I believe your family's line has a unique attunement to this artifact. If you chant the correct words, you might be able to subdue illusions around you. Or at least clear them from your immediate surroundings." She paused, her eyes flicking to the front door. "Given how illusions keep gathering whenever you are exhausted, this discovery is timely."

Lila blinked, a whirlwind of excitement and nerves building in her chest. "We should try it. Right now."

Evelyn's brows arched. "Are you certain you have the energy?"

She was beyond certain. After the day's frustrations—Council watchers complaining that illusions spread too easily, her best friend Maya worrying over her fraying nerves, and the entire city feeling on the edge of a meltdown—Lila needed proof that she could push back. She longed for a moment where Sebastian's illusions did not pin her chest so tightly.

"I'm fine," she insisted. "Tell me what to do. I have to try."

Evelyn pursed her lips, then set the papers down. "The incantation is in fragments. I will read it slowly, so you can repeat it in your own words. The important thing is to focus on your connection to the earth, the same magic that has guided you until now."

Caleb cleared his throat. "If this backfires, I will step in. Don't worry about losing control. I have some wards prepared if the energy surges too high." He lifted one hand as if checking the invisible lines of magic in the air.

Lila swallowed hard. She remembered how her power sometimes flared in uncontrollable bursts when illusions pressed close. She drew in a breath to settle her heart, then nodded at her grandmother.

Evelyn lifted the page and began reading a string of syllables. Lila translated them in her head, forming sense out of the rhythmic structure. She closed her eyes. Her palm settled over the amulet, the metal cool under her touch. The space felt charged with anticipation. The hum of the worn refrigerator mingled with the faint street noise outside. Everything else seemed to fade.

She started chanting, voice low at first, stumbling over the unfamiliar vowels. The words felt both foreign and strangely familiar in her mouth. She pictured roots curling through the floor, anchoring her. She pictured the swirl of illusions that kept haunting her walk down the hall. Then, slowly, she let the chant flow fuller.

The amulet began to pulse. One heartbeat, then two, then a swift rhythm in her hand. A warmth coursed up her arm. Lila's eyes snapped open. At the edges of her apartment, the paint seemed to shimmer as if illusions were trying to seep inside. A faint greenish light radiated from the amulet, flaring brighter with each syllable.

Caleb stood at her right, posture tense, magic coiled in his fingers in case he needed to shield her. Evelyn watched from the other side, expression a mix of concern and pride. The swirling illusions at the threshold took shape, half-formed shadows flickering in the entryway. They looked like vaporous phantoms clinging to the doorknob, waiting for a crack in the wards.

Lila inhaled sharply. The chant resonated in her bones, creating an odd vibration that shook her entire chest. She directed her focus at the illusions. She imagined them as smoke caught in a sudden breeze. The amulet's glow flared so hot that her fingertips burned, but she held on.

A sudden surge of energy pulsed outward from her body. Green light rippled across the walls, casting wild shadows. She gasped. It felt as though the city had dropped out from under her feet. Something inside her mind twisted, and for one terrifying instant, she saw illusions flicker away—only to slam back again with doubled force.

Caleb exhaled a steadying chant of his own, a calm ward that merged with her pulse. Evelyn whispered encouragement, telling Lila to keep going. Lila's voice quavered, but she found the next line in the incantation, letting it ring through the air.

Then, like a silk sheet being pulled away, the illusions peeled from the apartment threshold. The phantoms near the door dissolved in a swirl of silver motes. The flickering at the corners disappeared as though it had never been there at all. The entire apartment brightened, free of that eerie half-light. Lila's heart thundered. She tasted salt on her lips, realizing she was drenched in sweat from holding the magic so tightly.

She let the chant fade on a final syllable. The glow around her amulet died down to a faint hum. Outside, the corridor light clinked, but no illusions shimmered beneath it. Even the thick tension she had felt upon arriving seemed to have lifted.

For a long moment, no one spoke. Then Caleb lowered his arms, an awed relief in his eyes. Evelyn rushed to Lila's side and pressed cool fingertips to her forehead.

"You did it," Evelyn said. "Are you dizzy? Can you breathe?"

Lila nodded, chest hitching as she steadied herself. "I'm fine," she whispered. "It just... burned a lot hotter than I expected."

Her grandmother's expression softened. "Equipment for illusions can be so varied, but our family's artifacts often draw heavily on your core. You will need practice to make sure you do not overextend. But you saw how quickly it worked."

Caleb stepped away from the table, crossing to stand just behind Lila. His voice was gentle. "That was incredible. You cleared those illusions as if they were only shadows."

His closeness made her heart spin faster than any leftover magic. She remembered the day's chaos: illusions in the city center, the Council's frantic calls, her exhaustion that had threatened to swallow her. Now, for at least a glimmer of a moment, she felt a sense of control.

She turned to face him fully. She found a hint of admiration on his face even though caution still lingered behind his eyes. "It will take more than one chant to fix everything," she said softly, "but this is a start, right?"

Caleb nodded. He leaned in, but just enough to catch her eye, as if testing whether she needed support. "An important start," he said. "Imagine if we can replicate this in other areas. The illusions might back off, long enough for us to reinforce wards." The worry lines around his mouth eased a little.

Evelyn cleared her throat, stepping aside to give them space. "We must not rush you," she said, spreading the notes across the table once more. "I only discovered this piece of the chant last night, so we still do not know the full extent of its power. However, we do know the amulet responded strongly, which confirms your direct lineage connection is key to channeling the magic."

Lila untangled the chain from her neck to examine the amulet in her palm. The silver disc still glowed faintly with leftover energy, warm to the touch. Her thoughts spun in rapid circles. If this little test of the incantation could clear illusions in her cramped apartment, could she do the same on a larger scale? Could she silence the illusions that threatened entire city blocks?

She raised her gaze to Evelyn. "Is it safe to try a higher-level incantation, or should I just practice this one spell?"

Evelyn's lips pursed. "For now, stick with this. There are advanced verses, but I have not deciphered them. The notes mention backlash, plus the potential for illusions to rebound if you lose focus. I would rather you master the basics than risk a citywide surge."

Lila nodded, a knot of unease tightening in her stomach. She recalled how quickly illusions had tried to creep back during her chanting. The price of untrained spells might be higher than she liked to imagine.

Caleb took the amulet from her hand, briefly tracing the runic markings with his thumb. "You feel how it vibrates?" he asked. "It is like it has its own heartbeat, connected to yours."

She met his gaze. "I felt it." Part of her wanted to sink into his arms, let the reassurance of a quiet moment replace the day's terror. Instead, she squared her shoulders, determined to stand tall. "This means we might actually have a shot at stopping Sebastian's illusions, doesn't it?"

Caleb's expression turned grim. "Sebastian's illusions are fueled by more than a single artifact, but if your amulet can nullify illusions in your immediate range, we have a new advantage. We can act before illusions anchor themselves." He handed the amulet back to her with unmistakable reverence.

Evelyn reached for a fresh sheet of paper. "I plan to translate the rest of these runes tonight." She exhaled softly, as though each breath carried centuries of remembered spells. "If we can piece together the complete chant, you could theoretically dampen illusions on a broader scale. Just promise me you will not attempt advanced spells unless I am by your side."

A thousand thoughts whirled in Lila's head. Visions of city streets flickering with illusions. The Council struggling to maintain secrecy. Maya pacing in the café, worried about weird lights. She swallowed the thickness in her throat. "I promise I'll be careful."

Her grandmother's mouth curved into a half-smile. "You do not always need to be so brave alone, child. Take help where it is offered."

Lila shifted her gaze toward Caleb. Their eyes met in silent acknowledgment of everything that lay ahead: illusions, Council politics, and the personal threads of longing that drew them closer. He touched her arm gently, a firm but comforting grip.

His next words came in a low murmur. "You are not alone."

She squeezed the amulet in her fist, letting the warmth of his proximity settle through her. She ran her free hand across her brow, still trying to anchor herself in the aftershock of the magic. "That incantation took more out of me than I expected. I feel... drained but hopeful?"

Caleb's lips curved in a faint smile. "Hopeful is good."

Evelyn nodded. "Hopeful is vital. Remember, illusions feed on fear and chaos. If you can bring clarity, we might limit Sebastian's reach."

A faint tremor ran up Lila's spine. A flicker of doubt pricked at the edge of her mind: what if the illusions were stronger next time? What if Sebastian attempted some new twist?

She inhaled slowly, determined not to yield to that worry. Meeting her grandmother's gaze, she placed the amulet around her neck again. The chain glided over her skin like a promise. "I'll keep practicing," she said. "Let me catch my breath, and then maybe we can look over those notes again."

Evelyn inclined her head. "All right. Why don't you rest a moment. Caleb and I will gather the relevant passages."

Dazed but flooded with fresh determination, Lila nodded. She stepped toward the window at the far side of her apartment, where the lights of Manhattan glowed beyond the glass. The city looked deceptively calm. Somewhere out there, illusions drifted. Beneath the surface, Sebastian's magic still pulsed. She imagined them swirling along rooftops, searching for cracks in the wards. But in her living room, for the first time in days, she felt aligned with her own power. She closed her eyes and let that comfort wash over her.

Behind her, she heard Caleb and Evelyn exchanging quiet words, shuffling pages, discussing the next steps. She could almost sense Evelyn's excitement. The apartment no longer contained any whiff of illusions. Her warded space stood cleansed, at least for now.

With a deep breath, she turned away from the window. She crossed back to the table, meeting her grandmother's watchful eyes and Caleb's steady gaze. Her heart beat loud in her ears. She remembered that moment of bright clarity when the illusions tore away, as though the amulet had severed their hold on reality.

She pressed her hand over the silver disk against her chest, tracing a small spiral with her thumb. "I never guessed it would react so strongly," she said, voice tight with awe. "I was afraid it might do nothing."

Evelyn slid a final open notebook across the table. "There is far more to discover. But tonight gave us proof that you are on the right path." Her voice softened. "Trust the amulet, yes, but trust yourself more."

A surge of gratitude, terror, and excitement clashed inside Lila. She recalled the green flash, the sensation of raw power coursing through her veins, and how it had banished that throng of illusions in seconds. She forced herself to breathe, adrenaline still buzzing in her limbs.

Caleb's hand found the small of her back, gentle pressure guiding her to relax. "The glow you unleashed... I have never seen illusions vanish so cleanly."

Lila met his gaze, a soft flush warming her cheeks again. "It was terrifying," she admitted, "but it felt... right. Like I was actually using my magic for a purpose."

He nodded, understanding shining in his eyes. "Exactly."

Evelyn gathered up the notes and gave Lila a knowing glance. "The immediate danger here seems contained. You should rest, or at least eat something. I promise to refine these translations by morning. Then you can practice again under safer conditions."

Lila nodded, though her chest felt too light to rest. The knowledge that she had finally discovered a tangible weapon against Sebastian's illusions filled her with nervous energy. She held the amulet in trembling fingers and studied its runes once more, seeing them in a new light that made them shimmer faintly, almost as if they pulsed with her own blood.

Her head was spinning, but she smiled. "Thank you, Grandma. Thank you, Caleb."

Evelyn set her notes aside. "We have always known your lineage was special. I only wish I had discovered those written passages sooner."

Lila closed her eyes for a second. An ache lingered in her muscles, and she felt the lingering strain from the earthen chant. Yet beneath the weariness, a thrilling spark urged her forward. The city was trembling under illusions, but she had a new shield.

She touched the amulet one final time. Then she exhaled, letting a soft laugh escape her lips. "I guess I know what I'll be doing for the next few days."

Caleb rested a reassuring hand on her shoulder. "We will all be working on this," he said. "Starting with perfecting that chant."

Lila opened her mouth to reply, but an unexpected wave of dizziness struck, no doubt from the wave of magic she had spent. She gripped the edge of the table, heart fluttering. Caleb shifted closer to catch her if she fell. She managed to stand upright, drawn by the concern on his face and the steady warmth of his presence.

She took a shaky breath, forcing a smile to reassure both him and Evelyn. "It was worth it. At least we know the chant works."

Caleb's quiet voice resonated close to her ear. "Please, promise you will sit down before we leave."

"I promise." She pressed a hand against her forehead.

Her grandmother hovered at her elbow, ready to help, and for once, Lila welcomed that fussing. She sank onto the chair, letting the tension ebb from her legs.

Evelyn placed a hand on her shoulder. "You have done more than enough for one day, child."

The overhead light shuddered for an instant, and Lila cast a wary glance at the front door. No illusions flickered there now. The sight jolted a wave of relief through her. She had cut through the illusions, if only in a small pocket of her life. It was a start.

The amulet pulsed gently, a reminder that she had tapped into a deeper well of power than she had ever known. She tucked a stray strand of hair behind her ear, breath unsteady. Then she allowed her eyes to drift to the pages scattered across the table, details of runes yet untranslated. Each line might hold new secrets. A single fresh chant had made illusions vanish in an instant. What would the full incantation do?

Lila rubbed her palms against her thighs, torn between excitement and a sudden rush of anxiety. If she could hone this skill, Sebastian's illusions could finally be undone for good. But if she channeled her power incorrectly, would the city pay the price?

She looked to Caleb, who still hovered protectively near. His quiet confidence steadied her jumbled mind. She looked to Evelyn, who wore a proud but worried smile. They had faith in her, even if the next steps loomed large.

Her pulse pounded, echoing through the amulet in steady throbs. She inhaled, searching for any leftover illusions, but the threshold remained clear. A sharp certainty sliced through the lingering haze of fatigue. The amulet was more powerful than she had ever guessed. She caught a glimpse of her reflection in the windowpane, eyes lit with a spark she had never seen in herself before. This magic felt like it had always been meant for her to wield.

She gasped, delirious with both triumph and bone-deep worry: if she could harness it properly, maybe Sebastian's illusions could be undone. But if she failed, the shockwaves might unravel everything she loves.

TWENTY-FOUR

Lila stood in the Council's mirror chamber, heart pounding as her gaze scanned the circle of ornate frames gleaming against the polished walls. The chamber felt colder than usual, all quiet except for the occasional hiss of magic that pulsed across the reflective surfaces. Faint runes glinted around the edges of each mirror, reminiscent of delicate frost patterns in midwinter. She tried to calm her shallow breathing, but an unsettling tension pressed on her like a physical weight.

Marcus had summoned her and Caleb here moments ago, citing signs of unusual activity in the Ethereal Mirrors. Other guardians stretched along the perimeter of the circular chamber, each perched on edge, their soft whispers rising and falling in waves of apprehension. Dim orb-lights hung overhead, flickering with every stray ward in the air.

She settled her focus on the largest mirror in the center—taller than the others and framed in twisting silver vines. A faint swirl of violet tinted its surface, a reminder that illusions were sometimes known to slip through these channels. She could feel Caleb's presence a step behind her, watchful and alert. When she stole a glance his way, his expression reflected the same unsettled mix of caution and anticipation. He gave her a small, firm nod, as if to reassure her that no matter what lurked on the other side of the glass, they would face it together.

Tightening her grip on the silver amulet that hung against her collarbone, Lila tried to steady the racing tempo of her heartbeat. She had tested the amulet's power only recently, learning how it responded to her incantations, but she had never seen illusions appear with such menace in this mirror chamber. The runes etched along the mirror's edge seemed to pulse in time with her own growing dread.

"Are we sure it's Sebastian behind this?" she whispered, directing the question toward Marcus, who stood on her left. She remembered the rumors circling through the Council about illusions hijacking communications. But illusions were intangible. They slipped in through fractures in the wards, leaving only faint echoes behind. The possibility that Sebastian would dare to appear so openly unsettled her.

Marcus's tall frame bristled, tension locked tight in his shoulders. "We have evidence of illusions creeping through these mirrors," he said in a low voice. "If Sebastian means to taunt us, he could do it here. We're preparing wards to trace his location, but illusions have gotten more advanced. That is why I demanded that you and Caleb arrive immediately." His gaze flicked to her amulet, as if silently conceding that she was now part of the Council's best chance at countering Sebastian's illusions.

Caleb edged closer, the subtle scent of his cologne somehow reassuring. "We need to be ready," he affirmed. "If Sebastian does appear, capturing any trace of his location is our priority."

Faint ribbons of color glimmered across the biggest mirror. At first, it looked like a reflection of dancing torchlight, but it quickly sharpened into something more deliberate. A swirl of ghostly shapes flickered across the glass, then resolved abruptly into Sebastian's face—smooth, angular features and dark hair framing his sharp silver eyes. Even through the mirror, his gaze radiated self-assured confidence.

A ripple of murmurs passed through the onlooking guardians. Lila's throat went dry. This was the first time she had ever seen Sebastian's face so clearly, rather than glimpsing illusions or hearing rumors. He looked almost pleased to be here, as though stepping into a conversation he had orchestrated from the start.

"Finally," Sebastian said with a low, mocking laugh. "It is about time I received a proper audience."

Caleb shifted, bristling at Sebastian's smug tone. Lila could practically taste the tension rising around them. The runic lights in the mirror chamber flickered, casting elongated shadows behind every guardian. She drew in a breath, trying to quell the knot in her stomach, and steeled herself to speak.

"This isn't your audience," she said, fighting to keep her voice level. "You're trespassing in Council space."

"And yet here I am," Sebastian replied, spreading his arms in a theatrical gesture. His image rippled slightly, as if the reflection were barely containing his presence. "You should know I am far beyond the Council's reach now."

Marcus stepped forward, hands clenched at his sides. "Name your purpose," he demanded, each word laced with authority. Some guardians behind him murmured agreement. Others merely watched, grim-faced, prepared to cast spells at any second.

Sebastian's gaze lingered on Lila. An unnerving light danced in his eyes. "I only wish to speak," he said, voice soft as satin. "I hear that Lila Matthews has become quite invaluable. New magic surging within her, fresh blood from a lineage that once held keys to unimaginable power."

A chill slid across Lila's skin, and she involuntarily pressed one hand to her amulet. She refused to show fear in front of him. "Your illusions have done enough damage. If you have a message, deliver it. Otherwise, we have nothing more to say."

He offered a slow, amused smile. "Direct and bold. I like that. Then I'll be succinct—your Council is hopelessly stuck in the past. They fear progress, cling to stale rules, and keep novices caged. I propose a new order, a chance to reshape our realm in ways the Council cannot imagine. And you, Miss Matthews, stand at the heart of it. Your paternal line carried a certain gift—raw earthen power strong enough to anchor illusions or break them.

The relic you now possess can help me open new frontiers."

Caleb cut in, voice vibrating with anger. "You will not drag her into your schemes." He stepped near enough to the mirror that Lila could sense his pulse pounding. "We know what you've done, Sebastian. Stealing relics, corrupting guardians—did you honestly think we would bow to you once we saw your illusions tear through our wards?"

Sebastian's face twisted in a brief flash of scorn. "You, of all people, should know the Council's limitations. They condemn methods they do not understand. I merely harness illusions to free us from stifling secrecy. Look around—how many novices tremble in these halls, terrified of spells that might harm mortals if they slip? How many more witches hide in squalor, denied the knowledge to protect themselves? This primal fear-laced system must end."

He turned his chin, addressing Lila directly, ignoring Caleb's glower. "With your heritage, you could help forge a more transparent, more equitable society. Why chain your power to this broken Council? They will only use you when convenient and discard you the moment it suits their agenda."

She braced both hands against her hips, grappling with a surge of fury that rose in her like a wave. Sebastian's words clawed at her lingering insecurities. But she clenched her jaw. "Anyone who has witnessed the chaos your illusions sow should know you aren't freeing people," she said. "You're controlling them. Warping their minds so they think your illusions are real."

Crackling energy accompanied Sebastian's short laugh. "So naive. Progress always demands upheaval." His eyes flicked to Caleb. "Caleb, old friend, you know I speak the truth. When we studied illusions together, you saw how the Council suppressed breakthroughs they deemed disruptive. But you never had the courage to challenge them."

Caleb erupted in a half-step toward the mirror, fists tight at his sides. "Shut your mouth," he snapped, voice trembling. "You gave up any right to lecture me. You're the one endangering everyone in this city."

Sebastian's reflection shimmered, then magnified as though leaning closer. "Come now, do not let guilt over-shadow your reason. I offer Lila a partnership—nothing more. She harnesses the power of her lineage. I lend the illusions that have advanced beyond the Council's stifling wards. Together, we usher in a new world."

Lila felt a roiling in her stomach, half disgust, half fury. She stepped in front of Caleb, blocking Sebastian's unwavering focus. "I won't be your pawn," she hissed. "Let me guess—you wave illusions around, and I anchor them with the amulet? The city burns while your so-called 'equitable realm' crumbles under your thirst for control." Her voice hardened. "No."

Sebastian's mouth curved into a sneer. "Tracing illusions to me, refusing to see the bigger picture—you parrot the Council's dogma well. But you will discover soon enough that there is no sealing illusions once they grow beyond your wards. Ask dear Marcus if he truly believes in your potential or if he just sees another novice to exploit."

Ignoring the spike of temper flaring in Marcus's eyes, Sebastian twisted his gaze back to Lila. "You have a choice: stand with the Council or break free. If you raise that amulet against me, you will regret the day you turned away from an ally who could help you master it. The Council is not the only source of knowledge. They fear what you might become."

Lila's muscles tightened. Considering all she had recently learned about how illusions seeped into the city, she refused to let his taunts rattle her further. Sebastian's illusions thrived on sowing doubt. Her spine straightened as she affirmed, "I stand by those who protect innocent people. That is not you."

A flicker of anger crossed his features. He stared at her, illusions dancing like faint shadows around his reflection, then twisted his lips into a half-smile. "Such resolve. I admire courage, even misguided courage." His head tilted toward Caleb. "But do not blame me when the entire city collapses under illusions the Council can't contain."

In that tense silence, Caleb glared back with unspoken fury. The other guardians stood clutching wands, staff heads glimmering, or half-formed incantations buzzing on their lips. Lila's heart hammered, half expecting Sebastian to strike with illusions that would fling them all into chaos. Instead, Sebastian gave a final, mocking inclination of his head.

"Until next time," he drawled.

Before anyone could blink, runes flared along the edges of the mirror. Fiery lines flitted across the silver frame, coalescing into a single charred rune that pulsed once and then blackened into place. Sebastian's face twisted in a parting smirk, and the reflection dissolved into dark smoke.

Caleb exhaled a shocked breath. "He's gone." The air in the chamber felt electrified, coats of warding spells trembling like they had just been struck by a physical force. Lila strained to slow her mind, to process that abrupt exit.

"Look," she gasped, pointing to the rune still glowing in faint embers on the mirror's frame. She recognized a partial symbol connected to her family's amulet. The mark reeked of Sebastian's illusions. It hovered like a brand, mocking all of them.

Marcus lunged forward, chanting a swift locator glyph that flashed gold under his fingertips. "We can still trace him," he barked.

For an instant, the mirror's surface shimmered with promise. Then it sparked, crackled, and spat out a web of purple illusions that extinguished the glyph. A jolt of energy surged through the entire room, forcing one watcher off balance and causing gasps among the others.

"No," Marcus muttered through gritted teeth. "He blocked us." His expression turned thunderous, the lines around his mouth deepening. "Clever parasite. He contorted the runes specifically to deflect tracing spells."

A ripple of accusatory murmurs broke out among the guardians at the edge of the chamber. One warlock in a heavy cloak glared in Lila's direction. "He singled her out," he hissed. "She's the reason these illusions keep targeting us."

A witch next to him crossed her arms, knuckles bone-white. "As if we needed more proof—he basically asked her to join him. The more he fixates on her, the more vulnerable we become."

Anger twisted inside Lila, mingled with a rush of anxiety. She refused to let their suspicions undermine her or the vow she had made to help protect the city. Marcus's gaze flicked to her, measuring her composure. On the other side, Caleb made a low sound of protest, stepping immediately into the shallow gap between Lila and the accusing warlock.

"She isn't to blame," Caleb snapped. "Sebastian is the one invading these mirrors. The Council has known from the start that Lila's lineage is significant—and that we might need her power to halt illusions. Don't you dare point fingers at her."

Murmuring churned the air, uncertain guardians weighing accusations against their real need to hold the fractured Council together. The tension felt suffocating to Lila. She tugged at the chain of her amulet, swallowing the impulse to yell. Instead, she faced them, voice as firm as she could manage, hoping to slice through their distrust.

"Sebastian attacked all of us tonight," she said, scanning the room. "He wants us divided, so we're too busy fighting each other to defend the city. I won't let him succeed."

Several watchers exchanged glances, uneasy but less openly hostile. Marcus remained near the mirror, scowling at the charred rune. Finally, he turned back to the group, drawing a deep breath. "We cannot lose these channels. The Ethereal Mirrors are crucial for our watchers patrolling outside. Disabling them would blind us to illusions spreading across Manhattan." His voice dropped a notch. "But we risk letting Sebastian slip illusions through them. We have to be strategic."

A rumble of agreement rose from those present. Caleb sighed, letting tension drain from his shoulders. Lila tuned her focus to the single charred symbol. A faint claw of worry tapped the back of her mind: Sebastian was growing bolder. How many illusions might flicker through the city if he could hijack Council mirrors so easily?

One of the elders across the chamber spoke in a wavering voice. "Perhaps we can temporarily seal the main mirror and keep the peripheral ones open. Or place watchers on every reflection. At least that way—"

Marcus cut him off. "We will consider any step necessary, but we can't give Sebastian free reign. I am assigning watchers to monitor these reflections in shifts. We also need improvements to the wards at once."

Many guardians nodded, though a few continued to throw wary looks Lila's way. She forced her chin up, ignoring the faint tremor in her hands. Sebastian's mocking invitation still echoed in her ears. Another sliver of magic seemed to pulse through the amulet at her throat, reminding her that the city's fate might hinge on her ability to push back illusions—and the burden weighed heavily.

Caleb stepped beside her, voice low. "Are you alright?"

She glanced at him, relieved to sense his concern. "I'm fine," she lied. A swirl of anger, fear, and defiance collided inside her, forming a tight knot in her chest. "Just furious that he got away again."

His hand hovered just short of touching her shoulder in front of the others. "We'll stop him. The next time he appears, we'll be ready." But worry lingered in his eyes, matching the unspoken urgency in her own.

Marcus lifted his hands, calling the chamber to order once more. "Enough. Tonight's incursion proves that Sebastian can still manipulate illusions from afar. We either improve our security now or risk him turning these mirrors into a permanent gateway. We will not allow him an easy path. Lila, you will continue your training. Caleb, I expect you to assist in fortifying the wards around every mirror until we have a better solution."

Lila managed a short nod. Her heart twitched with an odd mix of pride and frustration, wishing she had the perfect spell to track Sebastian instantly. But illusions never yielded easily to direct pursuit.

Quiet stretched over the chamber, the guardians eyeing the extinguished glyph and the mirrored surfaces that no longer displayed Sebastian's mocking face. One by one, they drifted away from the center mirror, whispering about fresh defensive measures. Some broke into smaller clusters, discussing runic sequences or advanced illusions intended to cloak the Council's presence. Others stared accusingly at the charred rune, as though it continued to taunt them. Caleb stayed close to Lila, silent yet supportive, while Marcus stepped away to confer with an older warlock about layering wards.

A wave of exhaustion crashed over Lila. She pressed a shaky hand to her forehead, recalling Sebastian's smug invitation: a "partnership." He clearly believed her powers and her amulet could help him push illusions further than ever before. The notion made her chest hollow with dread. No matter how convincing or persuasive he tried to be, she refused to let him drag her into his twisted dream. The city deserved better. Every mortal—and every magical soul—deserved more than illusions capable of rending reality.

Tightening her grip around the silver amulet, she set her jaw. Perhaps Sebastian was right about one thing: life under the Council could be stifling, and old rules sometimes left novices adrift. But unleashing illusions over unsuspecting neighborhoods, distorting truth itself, was not the answer. Even if the Council had flaws, Sebastian was using those flaws as an excuse for destruction. He would do far worse if no one stood in his way.

An almost electric hum settled as a small group of watchers returned to the largest mirror and began chanting a protective incantation. The reflection shimmered faintly, though the new wards only partially coated the runes. Caleb observed them, crossing his arms in a vigilant posture. Soft green light pulsed along the frames, forming a net of containment spells.

Drawing a breath, Lila locked eyes with Marcus, who

finished speaking to the others and turned to face her. "You understand Sebastian's words carry honeyed poison," Marcus said quietly. "He singled you out hoping to prey on your uncertainties, to weaken your resolve."

She lifted her chin. "He'll fail."

TWENTY-FIVE

Lila hovered by one of the tall shelves in the Council's private library, tapping her fingernails lightly against the spine of a worn tome. Sleep had been elusive; she kept feeling phantom pulses of magic in her veins, as if the entire city breathed in broken rhythms beneath her feet. She tried not to stare at the papers spread across the library's reading table—reports from the Council and frantic letters from watchers stationed at key locations around Manhattan. Each stack hummed with escalating worry.

She risked a glance at Caleb, who stood on the opposite side of the oak table. A soft pool of morning light fell across his lean frame, highlighting the faint circles under his eyes. They had each spent half the night reading not only ancient texts and more recent diaries but also through messages about illusions blooming in unexpected places: rooftops warping into twisted silhouettes, rows of shop windows shimmering with false reflections. People were starting to panic. The official news networks called it some elaborate hoax, but no hoax would have guardians reeling in disarray.

She inhaled a shaky breath, remembering the line of text from one of the watchers' messages: illusions have grown so tangible that ordinary wards vanish in bursts of green sparks. The idea alone made her palms itch with the memory of poorly contained magic.

Caleb looked up from a scrawled report. "Zoe just messaged," he said in a low voice. "One of our guards downtown tried dispelling an illusion near a corner store. The illusion retaliated. It trapped him in a dreamlike maze, then left him catatonic." He shook his head, frustration tightening his jaw. "She's on her way to help him now."

Lila's stomach twisted. She focused on the sense of calm she usually drew from him, but now even he seemed wound tight, bracing against an onslaught. She stepped closer, letting her fingertips brush his arm. "I hate all this waiting."

He nodded, though worry clouded his intense blue eyes. "The illusions are accelerating. Sebastian is forcing us to move faster than the Council can coordinate. Teams keep trying to seal entire blocks, but every attempt gets sabotaged by illusions morphing in ways we've never seen before. If we don't get ahead of this, the wards across the city might collapse."

Lila tightened her grip on the side of the table, scanning the mesmerizing swirl of half-legible spells transcribed by watchers overnight. The swirl of fear and frustration woke her own magic, a faint hum along her arms. She wanted to push it down, if only so she could think clearly.

The library door suddenly clicked open, and Marcus Steele stepped in with determined strides. He wore a dark coat, and the lines etched into his face looked deeper than ever. His gaze flickered over them, then settled on Lila. She felt his tension immediately—he radiated that Council authority that made her want to stand at attention, though she also carried a simmering anger that matched his.

"Marcus," she greeted quietly, mustering the calm she wished she felt.

He wasted no time. "I assume you've heard the news by now," he said, voice edged with impatience. He dropped a small folder onto the table, scattering a few of the papers Caleb had been organizing. "Sebastian is not just making illusions in hidden pockets anymore. He's flaunting them across the boroughs, sowing fear among mortals and guardians alike."

Lila exchanged a glance with Caleb, then looked back to Marcus, forcing herself to hold his gaze. "What happened on the ground?"

Marcus's frown deepened. "A team of watchers on the Upper West Side reported entire swaths of illusions draping over streets. Passersby actually thought the buildings were somehow growing out of shape. Some illusions roamed the rooftops like living silhouettes. And each time watchers raised wards, the illusions detonated them in green sparks that left watchers reeling. It's as if Sebastian's illusions adapt the moment they sense a barrier forming."

Lila felt a flicker of heat in her core. A few weeks ago, illusions were an unsettling but manageable threat. Now they were sophisticated enough to push watchers to their limits. The old tension rose inside her, reminding her of the first few times she'd lost control of her magic. She inhaled slowly, trying to ground herself before her anxiety could spark.

Marcus's expression turned grim as he lifted his gaze to the library's high ceiling. "We can't keep letting him move freely. This city is on the verge of a situation that normal mortals will no longer accept as a bizarre prank. He wants them to see magic as a force that cannot be contained. A herald of darkness, imposing illusions that might eventually reshape reality itself if left unchecked."

She heard the anger lacing his words. Herald of darkness, she thought. It was a dramatic phrase, but Sebastian's illusions had earned it by now, warping Manhattan and the other boroughs step by step.

Caleb's voice had a steel edge when he spoke. "We need a coordinated plan, something that goes beyond scurrying from one meltdown to the next. Right now, we're forever behind Sebastian's illusions." He touched the stack of watchers' reports with a careful hand. "We can't let fear freeze us."

Lila straightened and cleared her throat, ignoring the slight tremor in her arms. "So, let's not wait. Let's push first. Sebastian is feeding his illusions with every location that's lightly warded or insufficiently guarded. If we figure out which wards he's likely to compromise next, we can go to him before he can fully anchor his illusions."

She felt Marcus's sharp gaze flick over her, assessing whether she was stepping out of line. But instead of scolding her, he nodded thoughtfully. "The illusions are clustering around nexus points. If we could identify where the next wave of illusions will manifest, we might corner him or at least disrupt his conjurations in real time."

Caleb let out a slow breath. "You're suggesting infiltration teams, then. Smaller squads, each posted near rumored hotspots. We trace any illusions back to their primary source."

"Yes," Marcus affirmed. "We have partial leads on certain pockets—abandoned areas in Midtown, some infiltration attempts near the catacombs, even rumors about illusions creeping into old defunct tunnels. None of it is confirmed, but we must act on what we have."

Lila felt relief and apprehension twist together. Acting first sounded far better than letting illusions chase them around the city. But the idea of confronting illusions that sprang out of nowhere also churned her stomach.

Marcus pressed his hands against the back of a chair, leaning in. "If we do this, we need every piece of intelligence we can gather. Isabel Ramirez has found references to illusions that can feed upon ambient magic, effectively swallowing wards from within. We can't risk watchers stepping into those traps without the right counter-spells."

Lila thought of the battered pages in her grandmother's journals, the cryptic runes that had helped them piece together older illusions. Maybe that knowledge could help her and Caleb. But she doubted the Council would want novices on the most dangerous infiltration.

She swallowed, glancing at Caleb. "We should at least consolidate data from the watchers on each side of town. My friend Maya—" She cut herself off, realizing she probably should not mention the mortal friend who had been let in on some secrets. "I mean, we've all heard the rumors. People see illusions near random corners, under certain neon signs, along battered alleyways. We need a mapping approach to link the anomalies. If we can see the pattern, maybe we predict the next big cluster."

Caleb inclined his head. "We can do that. We gather info, chart the illusions' progression, and move squads into place before the illusions spread further."

Marcus exhaled. "It's our best lead for now. We must do more than patch holes and watch illusions slip away. If Sebastian is bold enough to broadcast illusions in broad daylight, we cannot let him hold control of the city's magical nexus for much longer. A single slip of secrecy and we could be exposed to the entire mortal population."

The edges of Lila's vision prickled with tension, but she forced herself to keep calm. She could recall the swirling illusions that once tormented her apartment, or those that nearly caused accidents on busy streets. If Sebastian's illusions had grown that stable, it meant real danger for anyone who got ensnared.

She steeled her shoulders, raising her chin to meet Marcus's gaze. "We can't let fear keep us pinned. If these illusions can truly become tangible, we need to be just as bold. Gather watchers who are willing to push back, not just run for cover. We should coordinate with healers like Zoe too, because illusions are leaving mental scars."

Marcus's mouth twitched, and for a moment she thought he might lecture her on Council hierarchy again. Instead, he inclined his head as if acknowledging that her suggestion made sense.

"All right," he said. "I will speak with the Council's senior circle. Caleb, you and Lila gather any updated sightings from watchers and cross-reference them with those older illusions we uncovered last week." He paused. "Once we have the full picture, we move. No more dithering."

She glanced at Caleb, reading the flicker of concern in his eyes. She knew he worried about her throwing herself into the fray too hard or letting her magic flare out of control. But she also knew that if the city faced illusions strong enough to trap minds, none of them could afford hesitations.

Marcus looked down at his phone, presumably checking messages from other Council watchers. When he looked up again, his gaze flicked between Lila and Caleb. "We should finalize the infiltration plan soon. Notify me as soon as you have something concrete."

"Yes, sir," Caleb said quietly, though his formal tone had a calm strength.

Marcus snapped shut the folder of scattered reports on the table. He turned to leave, halting at the door. "Sebastian has always been cunning," he muttered, voice low. "He's a herald of darkness, intent on proving illusions can overshadow reality itself. Do not underestimate him."

"Never again," Lila replied, jaw tightening.

Nodding curtly, Marcus stepped toward the threshold. Then he stopped. Lila waited, heart beating a slow, unsteady rhythm as she watched the older warlock rub a hand over his temple. He cast a glance back at them, as though verifying they were truly alone.

Before he walked out, he turned toward Caleb, motioning for him to draw close. Marcus lowered his voice to a near whisper. Lila caught only the faint rustle of words, but she could see the faint lines across Caleb's brow deepen, and a flicker of alarm flashed in his eyes.

Lila's pulse quickened. She caught the final echo of Marcus's low murmur, but not enough to parse meaning. Whatever it was, it ended on a grave note that made Caleb's lips part in a startled intake of breath.

Caleb took a step back as though reeling from the weight of it. Marcus nodded once, meeting Caleb's gaze. Then, with a stern set to his jaw, he pulled the library door open and disappeared into the hallway.

TWENTY-SIX

Lila exhaled a shaky breath the moment Marcus's footsteps vanished down the hallway. A peculiar stillness settled in the small antechamber, broken only by the distant hum of magical wards shifting in the Council's main corridors. She glanced at the man beside her. Caleb's shoulders were rigid beneath his jacket, and the usual calm in his face had darkened into something else—anger or worry, she could not quite tell.

She reached out and let her fingertips brush the back of his hand. "Marcus looked upset when he left. You do too," she said. "What did he say to get under your skin like that?"

Caleb turned toward her slowly, the ghost of tension still flickering beneath his eyes. "Not just under my skin," he said in a quiet voice. "Marcus shared news that could weaken our entire defense against Sebastian."

Her breath caught on Sebastian's name, that swirl of dread rising at the memory of illusions flickering across the city. She steadied herself by taking a small step closer to Caleb. "Tell me."

He hesitated a moment, as though choosing words carefully. His gaze swept across the door Marcus had used. "He said the Ethereal Mirrors have been compromised."

Lila blinked. She had only heard passing mentions of these devices, usually in remarks from older guardians. "The big scrying mirrors, right? I thought they were well protected."

"They are." Caleb raked a hand through his dark hair. "Or should have been. The Ethereal Mirrors act like a magical communication network, letting guardians stay connected and coordinate stealth missions around the city. Each mirror is hidden in a Council outpost or warded stronghold. They do not rely on mortal technology and are nearly invisible to people outside the Council's circles."

She frowned. "And now they are compromised?"

"Marcus received reports of bizarre reflections twisting across the mirrors' surfaces," Caleb explained. "Someone sees a corridor from miles away, but it looks abandoned or flickers with cryptic runes. Other times, they glimpse a wild grin—a grin that looks a lot like Sebastian's. Then the mirror flickers back to normal. Marcus believes Sebastian or someone aligned with him is probing for vulnerabilities. By tainting the Ethereal Mirrors, he is essentially eavesdropping on Council communications."

A chill crawled across the back of her neck. She remembered the last time illusions seeped into the Council's interior wards. If Sebastian could manipulate one mirror, he might glean enough intelligence to sabotage entire squads attempting to root out illusions across Manhattan. "So shutting them down is not an option?"

"He told me that some guardians advised exactly that," Caleb said. "They wanted to disable the entire mirror network. No reflection, no infiltration. But if we do that, we lose real-time coordination. Essential wards would be left blind. We would not be able to warn squads in time if illusions flare up in some distant part of the city."

"Which plays right into Sebastian's hands." Her voice sounded sharper than she intended, but fear tightened her chest. "He wants chaos."

Caleb gave a solemn nod. "Marcus proposed a compromise. He wants to keep a handful of safe channels active through backup mirrors. They have to be painstakingly secured with advanced wards, code phrases only a small circle of trusted guardians knows. It is not foolproof, but it might keep communication alive while limiting how much Sebastian can spy on us."

Quietly, Lila let the information settle. The corridor's glow orb flickered overhead, making her aware of every scuff on the stone walls and the faint hum of magic in the floors. She glanced at Caleb. "If Sebastian can do this, do you think he—"

She stopped as footsteps approached from behind. A younger Council page stepped into the antechamber, scanned them, and bowed stiffly. "Sir, Ma'am. Marcus requested you both join him at Council Chambers. The setup for the safe channels has begun."

Caleb glanced at Lila. "We will be right there." The page nodded and left.

Lila swallowed the dryness in her throat. "Marcus does not mess around with warnings. If he is in crisis mode, it means this infiltration could help Sebastian launch illusions anywhere."

Caleb's voice quieted. "Which means we need to see these mirrors ourselves and decide how to guard them."

They left the antechamber side by side, walking deeper into the Council's labyrinth of marble corridors. Tension followed them like a wary phantom. Lila tried to quell a swirl of anxious thoughts: illusions targeting their only means of communication, more threat to an already fractured Council, and a looming sense that every step they took was under Sebastian's watchful eye.

When they arrived at the Council Chambers, they found the main hall crowded with guardians murmuring in urgent tones. Many wore sleepless shadows beneath their eyes, and several novices stood clustered near the far column, exchanging frightened looks. Lila recognized one from a recent training session—a wide-eyed warlock whose illusions had accidentally triggered while reading a dusty tome. He met her gaze, then turned away, as if too unnerved to speak.

Marcus motioned them over, posture rigid as he conversed with a small circle of senior warlocks. The light overhead made the streaks of gray in his hair more prominent. He nodded at Lila and Caleb's approach.

"We are designating fallback mirrors," he said by way of greeting. "You realize how precarious this is. If there is infiltration at any step, squads in the field will be stranded, or worse, lured into illusions."

Caleb folded his arms. "I assume you have chosen only the most secure mirror sites. Which ones remain active?"

Marcus extended a sheet of paper scrawled with runes and columns of location codes. He pointed to several lines. "Only these. The rest we have shut down. If this infiltration turns out more severe than we thought, we will close them all."

Lila scanned the paper's neat columns. She recognized a few site names: a hidden station near the Manhattan Catacombs, a warded basement in Central Park's old boathouse, and a backup mirror in the Council library's restricted section. Each site was an entry that squads relied upon to share urgent illusions news. She bit her lip. "If Sebastian knows about the fallback mirrors, will he not just target those too?"

TWENTY-SEVEN

Lila stood outside The Daily Grind with only a thin hoodie against the frigid night air. The city vibrated with more than just winter's chill. Every streetlamp, every corner store window, seemed to carry the echo of a phantom presence that set her teeth on edge. She rubbed her arms, inhaling the smell of coffee beans drifting from the café's closed doors behind her. The usual comfort it gave her felt distant tonight, overshadowed by the electric unease sparking across Manhattan.

Days had passed since she last enjoyed a moment of calm. Illusions in the city had spiraled from bizarre curiosities to outright chaos. She had seen streetlights flicker with unsettling glows, their bulbs pulsing in bright purples and oranges. Some nights, entire blocks appeared to shift, as if the concrete itself was alive under Sebastian's manipulations. And the worst part: pockets of witches who felt used or ignored by the Council had begun openly voicing praise for Sebastian, calling him a visionary who would upend the old structures.

Lila had heard them just that morning, not far from an abandoned station entrance near Midtown. They chanted phrases like "freedom from secrecy" and "join Sebastian for a liberated magical world," while illusions crackled overhead, shaping ephemeral green flames in the sky. She shuddered remembering the fervor in their voices. It was the tone of desperation, of witches who had lost faith in a system that was slow to protect them and a Council that, despite heroic efforts, still felt distant and bureaucratic.

She zipped up her hoodie and started toward the sidewalk. Caleb had asked to meet her at the Council's gathering place in Greenwich Village, where a crucial assembly would soon begin. She only had a few minutes to get there. Holding her phone, she keyed in a quick message to Maya, letting her friend know she would be out again. Maya's worried texts had nearly doubled in frequency the past week. Between illusions threatening the city and Lila's extended absences, Maya's concern was justified. But Lila needed to handle this. She had chosen this path the moment her magic awakened.

She hailed a taxi and spent the ride anxiously tapping her foot against the floor. Outside the smudged window, she spotted ghostly silhouettes drifting along the sides of towering skyscrapers, illusions that shimmered like living art. Tourists on the sidewalk gawked, phones raised to document what they likely assumed was some elaborate art installation. Lila knew better. She recognized the eerie tang of Sebastian's illusions, the same power that had threatened to devour her in the narrower tunnels beneath the city weeks ago.

The taxi rattled to a stop outside a secluded courtyard in Greenwich Village. Lila paid the fare and slipped through a weathered iron gate that led to the Council's hidden entrance. The wards parted at her tentative touch, granting her passage. She stepped inside, finding the courtyard lit by floating orbs that glowed with nervous energy. Dark vines clung to the high stone walls. At one part of the interior, she could see a swirl of illusions flickering in and out, like something that never fully settled.

Marcus Steele had summoned them all for a late-night assembly in the open air, an unusual choice for the Council. Lila understood: illusions had pummeled the official chambers. The Council needed space wide enough to accommodate watchers, novices, and their uneasy alliances without the risk of illusions cornering them in cramped hallways.

Farther in, she spotted rows of tense figures. Some were watchers wearing simple black coats over their Council uniforms. Others were witches, hoods drawn low, eyes darting at every flicker of magic around them. The crowd spanned from novices younger than Lila to graying warlocks who looked ready to snap at the slightest provocation. She swallowed hard, scanning for a familiar face. That was when she found Caleb.

He stood off to the side, arms folded, gaze sharp. Though he wore a plain dark jacket, his posture carried the authority of someone who had fought illusions, trained novices, and survived too many near-misses to count. She could see tension etched into his face, a faint scruff lining his cheeks. He looked exhausted but resolute. When he spotted her, the concern in his blue eyes mixed with relief.

She made her way through the throng. Mutted conversations surrounded her:

"Have you seen the illusions in Midtown? Three watchers hurt—like physically clawed."

"I heard some witches switched sides. They claim Sebastian offers them a seat of power once the city is his."

"Marcus says we have to coordinate or we lose it all. He might not be wrong."

Each whisper sent a chill up Lila's spine. She reached Caleb at last. He exhaled a quiet breath, as though relieved merely by her presence.

"Hey," she said softly. She touched his sleeve. "Any new updates?"

He nodded grimly. "The illusions have gotten worse downtown. And we had another infiltration in the old catacombs. Marcus wants to address everyone before squads deploy."

"If we can keep illusions at bay until we corner Sebastian, maybe people will stop... joining him," Lila said. She swallowed the doubt lurking in her mind. She hated how easily Sebastian's twisted vision had seduced some witches who felt neglected by the Council.

Together, they moved closer to the central clearing, where a small platform of aged stone served as a makeshift stage. Marcus paced at the edge, conferring quietly with Zoe Blackwood, Caleb's sister, and Keira

Costa. Zoe offered Lila a brief nod of acknowledgment, while Keira's dark eyes flashed with worry behind her calm facade.

Lila took a settling breath. The courtyard's large wrought-iron torches cast wavering light across the gathered watchers. She counted at least fifty guardians assembled, some sporting fresh bruises or bandaged arms from illusions that had become dangerously tangible. Their faces reflected a single shared anxiety: none of them could predict what Sebastian might do next if left unchecked.

Marcus lifted a hand to quiet the murmuring crowd. Brent, a stocky warlock from an earlier infiltration team, stepped aside to let him pass. Silence fell over them, punctuated only by the crackle of illusions dancing above the courtyard's perimeter. Lila's gut tightened. She knew the illusions were pressing close, perhaps feeding off the tension.

Marcus's voice cut through the night. "Thank you all for coming at this late hour. Our city is on the brink of losing what precious unity remains. You have seen illusions warping every corner of Manhattan. Some of you have faced witches proclaiming Sebastian as the rightful leader of magic in these times. Let me be clear: if we do not stand together, we stand no chance. Sebastian will spread illusions faster than we can contain them, and the mortal world will be forced to see what we have long kept hidden."

A ripple of uneasy agreement ran through the group.

Marcus continued, "I have called you here to assemble squads. We will secure vantage points around the city, seal off known catacomb entrances, and intercept any loyalists who attempt to anchor illusions further. Our efforts will not be easy, and we must trust one another—no matter our past differences."

Marcus gestured for several watchers to come forward, one by one assigning them areas: Times Square, Central Park, the catacombs near Harriet's Gate, the old subway tunnels beneath Midtown. The watchers nodded grimly, stepping aside to await final instructions. Then Marcus summoned a scribe to note different squads. Names were murmured, pens scratched over runic papers.

Finally, the Council elder turned his attention to Lila, Caleb, Zoe, and Keira. Many in the courtyard watched the four of them with guarded expectation.

"Lila Matthews," Marcus said, voice carrying authority, "your unique abilities have proven vital in disrupting illusions. You will lead one of our infiltration squads alongside Zoe Blackwood and Keira Costa. You will secure the southwestern quadrant, focusing on the catacombs rumored to harbor Sebastian's loyalists."

Lila breathed in slowly to keep her voice steady. "Yes, sir." Part of her bristled at his formal manner, but she sensed no hostility in it tonight. His eyes held only exhaustion and a desperate hope that this plan might hold.

She glanced at Zoe. The healer's brow furrowed, but she quickly offered Lila an encouraging little smile. Then Keira stepped closer, the embroidered crescent on her robe reflecting the torchlight.

"I will anchor illusions if they become too dense,"

Keira said softly. "We will keep them contained so they do not spread above ground."

Zoe gave a determined nod. "And I will handle any physical or mental injuries. We cannot afford more watchers fainting from illusions that claw at their minds."

Lila squared her shoulders. She had never imagined leading anything, much less a squad that included two of the most competent witches she knew. Yet the city was unraveling, and if her presence could stabilize illusions, she would do whatever it took.

Marcus shifted his gaze to Caleb. The older warlock's expression softened, acknowledging in his stiff way that Caleb's expertise was needed. "Caleb," he said, "you know Sebastian's illusions better than most. You will coordinate with the main strike team. We plan to corner Sebastian's loyalists if they gather in enough force to attempt something reckless."

"Thank you, Marcus," Caleb said. His voice held quiet restraint. "I will do my part to keep illusions from overtaking these vantage points. If we can isolate Sebastian's loyalists, we may force him to act in the open."

Marcus regarded him for a moment, as if weighing old doubts against the dire need for unity. Then he inclined his head and signaled to the rest of the assembly. "The squads will deploy within the hour, after final briefings. We cannot wait for illusions to devour half the city. Prepare yourselves for disruptions in communication. The safe channels remain tenuous. If illusions bombard the fallback mirrors, we may lose contact, so keep your wards sharp."

A wave of murmuring spread among the watchers. Some looked determined, while others radiated apprehension. A few novices cast uncertain glances at each other, obviously fearing what lurked beneath the dark subways or sealed corridors.

Marcus raised a hand once more. "We stand at a threshold tonight. The illusions have brought Manhattan to a breaking point. Know this: if we fail, Sebastian's illusions will reshape the city in his image, and the mortal world will see a side of magic we have tried for centuries to protect. We cannot bow to fear. We must rise above it."

Off to the side, Zoe methodically checked the bandages on a guardian's forearm, ensuring that a nasty illusory burn had healed correctly. Keira closed her eyes, inhaling the faint lunar magic that always seemed to radiate from her presence, as if preparing for a night of continuous strain on her illusions-stabilizing spells.

Lila let her gaze drift around the courtyard. Hooded figures, novices, Council elders, and watchers of every rank formed a tense ring around Marcus. She recognized a few who had once greeted her with warm smiles. Now, they wore haunted looks that mirrored her own feelings. The illusions had battered them all. Trust felt like a scarce resource.

An older guardian spoke softly to Marcus. The elder nodded, then pivoted back to the crowd. "We move soon. Gather your recommended wards, double-check your gear. If you have not received your squad assignment, find me or one of the scribes. Dismissed."

The crowd pressed inward, watchers mixing with

novices to collect final details. Snippets of strategy whirled in the air. People swapped recommended incantations or illusions to watch out for. Lila saw Zoe approach a worried young witch, patting her shoulder and offering a quiet reassurance that illusions could be fought with the right mindset. Meanwhile, Keira conversed with two watchers about the nexus lines in the southwestern quadrant, ensuring no wards were overlooked.

Lila eased closer to Caleb, noticing a flicker of uncertainty in his usual calm expression. She touched a hand to his elbow, and he turned, exhaling as though he had been holding his breath.

"You alright?" she asked gently.

He gave a faint smile. "I should be asking you that. Leading a squad is not a small task."

Her stomach fluttered in uneasy excitement. "I know. But I'm ready. The illusions are out of control, and I have to do something."

"You will do well," he said. His voice softened. "Just— guard yourself too. Do not push yourself until you burn out."

She nodded, aware of the tension skating up her spine. "What about you? You're linking with

"Yes. We plan to track any large-scale illusions. If Sebastian tries to rally his loyalists in one location, we will move in. We need to push him to reveal himself."

A feeling of dread threaded through Lila at the idea. Facing Sebastian head-on meant far more illusions, far more risk. She felt an urge to pull Caleb in for a reassuring embrace. The swirl of watchers around them, though, allowed little privacy. She settled for squeezing his hand again.

Marcus's voice rose over the general clamor, "Final check, guardians. We deploy in five minutes."

A calm fell, reminiscent of the pause before a hurricane. The fear in the courtyard felt nearly physical, and Lila tasted its bitter tang in the back of her throat. Her eyes flicked around at the watchers, the novices, the few scribes hurriedly capturing notes. She saw Caleb rub the back of his neck, a sign of the tension he tried so hard to hide.

Some part of her felt a lingering pang that they might not see each other for hours—maybe longer—once the squads split up. The illusions would test every ounce of skill and resolve they possessed. But this was the plan. They had no choice.

Just then, Zoe and Keira approached Lila, armed with small pouches of wards and crystals that glittered faintly. "Ready when you are," Zoe said, her face set in calm determination.

Keira nodded. "The southwestern passages will require layered wards. Let us begin soon." Her voice was quiet, but her eyes burned with resolve.

Lila tried for a steady breath. "We are set."

The thought of leading them stirred an odd mixture of pride and dread. She mustered a firm nod and turned to Caleb. For a moment, the crowd's rush seemed to fade, leaving only the two of them standing in the flickering torchlight. She studied his face, memorizing the gentle line of his mouth, the way his blue eyes shone with unspoken promise.

He reached out, fingertips ghosting over her wrist. "I will find you as soon as we make progress," he said. "Stay safe."

She leaned into his touch, heart drumming faster than any illusions could force it to. "You too."

They held each other's gaze for a moment longer than was modest in front of so many watchers. She felt the tension intensify, as if every small movement echoed against the courtyard walls. Around them, the Council's authority felt close to breaking. The tension was thick enough to taste.

Then Marcus spoke again from the platform, voice ringing clear. "Squads, to your positions. The city will not wait."

Lila inhaled sharply, forcing herself to step back from Caleb. He gave a brief, resolute nod and moved toward his assigned group. She joined Zoe and Keira off to the side. The three formed a small circle, confirming details for the southwestern quadrant infiltration, exchanging final instructions about wards, illusions, and potential traps.

It felt like the eye of a storm, a deceptive stillness poised to explode the moment they all left these walls. Guardians stood with weapons or wands in hand, while novices clutched hastily scribbled instructions. Tension crackled with every breath.

Lila glanced across the courtyard. Caleb lifted his gaze, meeting hers through the shifting crowd. Even from a distance, she saw longing and fierce determination in his eyes—an unspoken vow that he would stand with her against whatever illusions threatened to tear the city apart.

Hours later, after the first wave of coordinated operations had been launched and the squads dispersed into the fractured city, Lila found herself back in the temporary warded safehouse near Gramercy Park. Her limbs ached, her illusion-stabilizing spells clung to her skin like smoke, and her nerves still hummed from what she'd seen in the catacombs—visions warped by Sebastian's power, whispers that scraped the edge of sanity.

She barely had time to shower and strip off her soot-dusted clothes when she heard the soft knock.

She opened the door to find Caleb, eyes shadowed and jaw clenched. "We cornered two loyalists. Interrogation ongoing. No major leads yet. I... couldn't leave without seeing you."

Lila pulled him in without a word, locking the door behind him.

The moment it clicked shut, something inside them both broke open.

He reached for her as if he'd been holding back for days. His hands found her waist, her face, her hair—all at once. Their mouths met in a rush of heat, frantic and starving. She pushed him back against the door, pulling at the buttons of his jacket, while he worked the hem of her worn cotton tee up and over her head.

"Lila," he murmured against her neck, breath hot and urgent, "you wreck me."

"Good," she whispered, fumbling for his belt. "Then we're even."

They kissed again—deep, consuming—and she felt the weight of the night fall away under the pressure of his hands on her bare skin. He scooped her up, carrying her toward the bed without breaking the kiss, then lowered her onto the sheets like she was something fragile even as his body trembled with restraint.

Clothes hit the floor in desperate tugs. His mouth followed every inch of exposed skin—thigh, hip, breast, throat—until she was gasping beneath him, her nails raking across his shoulders.

When he slid into her, it was slow at first, achingly intimate, their eyes locked, breath synced.

It wasn't just about release. It was about survival— proof that they were still here, still together, still burning brighter than anything Sebastian could conjure.

She moved with him, hips rising to meet his rhythm, letting herself unravel, letting the ache inside her spill over. Their bodies collided in a crescendo of movement and moaned whispers, a silent war cry against the chaos consuming their world.

He kissed her like a promise. She clung to him like a spell.

When they came together, it wasn't in shouts or gasps —it was a low, trembling, sacred thing. Her name left his mouth like a prayer. His breath caught in her ear. She felt the tremor roll through his body before his arms wrapped tight around her.

Afterward, they lay tangled in sweat-damp sheets, chest to chest, forehead to forehead. For a rare, fleeting moment, the world was still.

"I should go," Caleb whispered.

"Stay," she breathed. "Just for tonight."

He didn't answer right away. He just pulled her closer, kissed her temple, and let the silence stretch between them like a shield.

Outside, the city shimmered with unstable illusions and fractured loyalties. But inside this room, wrapped in each other's arms, they were real—and for now, they were enough.

THE STORY CONTINUES

The story continues in book three, *ULTIMATUM, coming soon to Amazon*

EXCERPT FROM ULTIMATUM

CHAPTER ONE

The soft light of dawn crept through the edges of the curtains, casting a pale glow across the room. Lila stirred, her cheek pressed against Caleb's bare shoulder, her limbs still tangled with his beneath the thin blanket. His arm curled around her waist, holding her close even in sleep, as if some part of him wasn't ready to let go.

For a few precious minutes, she stayed still, listening to the quiet rise and fall of his breath, memorizing the heat of his skin and the steady beat of his heart beneath her palm.

The world outside their window was fractured and dangerous—Sebastian's illusions still crept through the cracks of the city—but here, wrapped in him, she felt steady for the first time in days.

Caleb stirred beside her. His voice was husky with sleep when he spoke. "You're still here."

Lila smiled, brushing her lips lightly against his collarbone. "Where else would I be?"

He tightened his grip just slightly, burying his face in her hair. "I don't know. I guess I just didn't expect anything to feel...safe anymore."

She leaned up to meet his eyes, still shadowed with exhaustion but warm with something deeper. "It's not safe. But it's real. And that's more than I expected last night."

He cupped her face in one hand, thumb stroking her cheekbone. "I meant what I said. I'll find you, no matter what happens."

She nodded. "Just make sure you come back."

A knock echoed faintly from the outer hall. Duty was already calling.

They shared one last kiss—slow, quiet, unhurried. A promise.

Then they rose together, the spell of night broken, but the bond between them stronger than any illusion Sebastian could cast.

The glow of dawn filtered through the high-vaulted windows of the Council's assembly hall, revealing the exhausted faces of witches and warlocks who had barely slept. Lila stood near the center of the wide marble floor, her stomach churning as she watched clusters of guardians gather in tense conversation. The swirling lamps overhead provided a dim shimmer in the gray morning light, a reminder that wards and illusions danced in these halls even when the Council's mood turned grim.

Marcus, tall and composed despite the shadows beneath his eyes, stood on a raised dais. He rapped his staff twice. The sound carried across the hall, and murmuring guardians slowly turned his way. Lila inhaled carefully, hugging her arms for comfort. A restless crackle of magic charged the air, making her nerves flame. She brushed her fingertips over the silver amulet at her neck, seeking a steadying pulse.

"All of you have read the overnight reports," Marcus began, voice rough from hours of debate. "Our illusions watchers confirm more pockets of disruption have appeared around Midtown. Sebastian remains at large, and the city's wards strain under the pressure. We must unify if we hope to prevail."

A firm voice interjected, "Not if the threat is already in this room." A man in the front row, older and wearing an embroidered cloak, narrowed his eyes at Lila. "We have overlooked a simpler approach to controlling illusions. The Matthews amulet is a relic with immense power. If we take it out of a novice's hands, we reduce risk."

Heat rose against Lila's cheeks. She wanted to speak, to protest the injustice of that accusation, but surprise froze her tongue. She had seen the suspicion blooming among certain guardians in the last few days. A small but vocal faction had begun whispering that Lila's inexperience, combined with the amulet's strength, would inevitably trigger a calamity. Someone else—someone more seasoned—should hold it.

Caleb, stationed close to her side, spoke in a clipped voice, "That amulet belongs to Lila. No one else can wield it safely." His emphasis rang with finality, but the older man did not back down.

"How can you be so certain?" The question rang out from another watcher, a woman with braided hair twisted into a tight crown. "Our Council has traditions for regulating artifacts. With illusions soaring through the city, placing such a powerful object in untested hands invites catastrophe."

Lila's heart thudded. Her hands curled into fists at her sides. She forced herself to remain still, struggling to keep her breath even. The amulet felt warm at her collarbone, as though it sensed the threat.

Evelyn moved into the open circle, her posture as dignified as any Council elder's. "The Matthews lineage created the key that can tame illusions. This amulet does not accept a stranger's magic. We have centuries of evidence confirming that forcibly transferring it causes dire repercussions."

Zoe Blackwood, standing near Caleb, folded her arms. "I have studied similar binding attempts during my healing training. Few witches survive that process unscathed. If you do this, you risk unleashing the kind of magical backlash that would tear more than wards. You would tear people's minds."

An uneasy stir traveled through the crowd. Yet some watchers, apparently emboldened by rumor and fear, pressed forward. One woman, wearing the insignia of a mid-level enforcer, glared at Lila. "We do not suggest forcibly binding it lightly. But illusions have reached horrifying levels. Sebastian's illusions are cunning. If the amulet falls under his control, or if this novice fails to wield it properly, the results could be worse than anything we have seen. The Council must be practical."

Caleb's voice quivered with anger. "You do not get to brand her a threat when she has done nothing but attempt to help. She stepped forward, at great risk, to learn how to silence illusions. She has earned our trust."

A small group near the back snorted in disapproval. Lila's cheeks burned hotter by the second. She finally found her voice. "What do you think I have been doing these past days? Hiding? I have put my life on the line more than once, all to quell the illusions building in the city. I do not want to see Manhattan destroyed."

"Your intentions do not guarantee safety," a sharp voice countered. "We cannot risk illusions feeding off any misstep. A single uncontrolled surge could damage half the wards in Midtown."

Marcus lifted his staff again, but no one quieted. The tension in the hall spiked as more watchers spoke at once, and soon the entire assembly drowned in overlapping claims. Lila caught disjointed phrases: traitor, backfire, catastrophic. She swallowed thickly. The mention of a traitor among them made the hair on her arms prickle. All this chaos might be exactly what Sebastian wanted. If they kept fighting over who controlled the amulet, illusions would slip through the city's cracks.

Evelyn's eyes held a protective fire. "All of you should remember the underwriting principle of this Council— cooperation. If you suspect Lila could harness this amulet for darker aims, then you suspect the entire Matthews line. That is insulting, and more importantly, it is ignorant of the artifact's true nature."

At that, a tall warlock nodded in agreement. "Evelyn has a point. The family's direct resonance with the amulet is recorded in older diaries. Breaking that bond introduces unknown side effects."

"But if we do nothing," a hollow-cheeked guardian muttered, "we risk the illusions outrunning our capacity to hide them. We hear rumors every day of illusions capturing unsuspecting mortals, or illusions twisting entire streets. The Council is losing credibility. We must act boldly, or we fall."

Zoe stepped in, voice low but resonant. "Boldness does not equal recklessness. Especially not if it means trying to strip a family relic from its rightful keeper."

Another wave of arguing erupted from all sides of the hall. Several watchers turned to face each other, old grudges and half-acknowledged fears fueling their raised voices. One robed coven leader from the southern district began lecturing on the Council's failure to protect smaller enclaves near the East River; a second voice demanded an official vote on controlling the amulet. Lila's pulse hammered, each new accusation stinging like salt on an open wound.

Caleb caught Lila's gaze, eyes blazing. He touched her elbow gently, a silent offer of support. She exhaled, her chest trembling, and gave a shaky nod. Then she straightened her spine and cleared her throat. "Enough," she said loudly, though her voice shook. "We need to focus on the real threat."

Several watchers paused in mid-argument, turning to stare at her. She could feel her face burn. She had not planned to speak up in such a direct way, but she saw no other choice. Her next words emerged with surprising strength. "Bickering over who holds this amulet will not solve the illusions creeping into every corner of Manhattan. Sebastian must be laughing at how easily we tear each other apart."

Lila's heart slammed against her ribs, but she forced each breath to flow steadily. She clutched the silver amulet, remembering the faint glow it produced the last time she cast the chant with Evelyn's guidance. That power was real, and it was hers. Ripping it away would do more than cripple her. It might destroy the one advantage they had against illusions.

From near the dais, an older guardian glowered. "We only propose removing it because we fear rash mistakes. Sebastian's illusions have grown unstoppable. If you slip, we all pay the price."

Lila swallowed the tang of worry on her tongue. "You say you are afraid of my mistakes, but we have illusions spreading because your own wards faltered. Are you blaming me for illusions the Council could not contain?" She fought to keep her tone measured, though frustration laced every syllable. "I am trying to help. I do not pretend to be perfect, and I am not claiming my powers are fully trained. But if you strip this amulet away from me, you will get nothing but meltdown. Evelyn has explained the recoil that happens when you forcibly bind a relic to someone it does not accept."

"She speaks truth," Evelyn said firmly. "In centuries past, attempts to forcibly rebind could cause the artifact to misfire. It can lash out, sink illusions into the mind of the new host, or break wards in an uncontrolled quake. None of us want that."

Zoe pressed her argument. "If you let fear control your choices, you give Sebastian exactly the opening he wants. He thrives off chaos, divides us, and then exploits the gap." She glanced around, challenging watchers who bristled at her words.

A tense hush followed. But then a warlock near the left side broke the silence. "So we do nothing? We allow an untried novice to hold that power? If she fails, if illusions surge—"

"I will not fail," Lila cut in, voice cracking with emotion. "Not if the Council supports me the way it is supposed to. Do you believe I want to see illusions ravage the city? I take this as seriously as you do. I nearly lost everything the last time illusions flared." She refused to think of those frightening moments in detail. The memory of chaotic hallucinations still haunted her dreams.

"We do not question your will," another warlock said, "but your capacity."

Caleb bristled. "She has proven her capacity. The illusions in her apartment subsided when she performed the chant with Evelyn. She learned advanced warding in record time. Yes, she is new, but she is no incompetent child."

An older woman in Council robes snorted, but she did not contradict him. A hint of shame flickered in her expression, as though she recalled a recent moment when illusions nearly overtook her own team. A few watchers mumbled similar acknowledgments, though the air still felt sharp with mistrust.

Marcus slammed the base of his staff on the marble, mustering every ounce of authority. "All of you have voiced your concerns, but this bickering must end. We have no time for internal sabotage or division, not while illusions intensify every hour. If we tear ourselves apart over the amulet, Sebastian will crush the city unopposed."

He fixed a grave look on the watchers who had led the call for reassigning the relic. "No forced binding. That is final unless this entire assembly votes for it, and we have not reached that point. Focus on tangible plans—ward rotations, illusions detection, possible infiltration. We suspect a traitor is fueling these fears, stirring you all into panic. Until we identify that person, we proceed with caution. Understand?"

Several guardians looked away, some grimacing, others nodding reluctantly. The group that had demanded the amulet's removal exchanged quick glances, as if uncertain whether to press further.

Lila tried to swallow the dryness in her mouth. Her gaze flicked to the far side of the crowd, where rumors of a potential traitor had caused quiet speculation for days. If that traitor was present now, they were likely watching her every move. She clutched the amulet chain in a clammy grasp. That possibility made her skin crawl.

A man in a deep blue cloak cleared his throat. "Very well, Marcus. But do you realize confidence in the Council is fracturing too? Many watchers blame your leadership for letting illusions reach this point."

Evelyn spoke softly, "Pointing fingers at Marcus will not fix illusions, nor will blaming Lila. If you do not unite, illusions become unstoppable."

Caleb tilted his head toward Lila, giving her a barely perceptible nod. She inhaled, urging courage into her lungs. When she spoke, her voice was quiet but urgent. "Please, we need to stand together. Sebastian's illusions are powerful because he exploits every crack. The more we fight each other, the more room he gains to tear everything apart."

Her chest felt tight, and tears pressed at the corners of her eyes. She trembled with pent-up anger and anxiety. She refused to cry in front of everyone, but the tension was crushing. Caleb slipped one hand discreetly against her back. It was a small gesture and gave her the last bit of strength she needed to keep speaking.

"I take responsibility for what I must learn," she said. "You can question my skill, but do not undermine the only advantage we have. The amulet is active, it responds to me, and it can help us silence illusions if we work together on the chants and wards."

She could hear her own pulse in her ears, a rushing tide of emotion that threatened to spill. Around the hall, watchers exchanged uncertain looks. She sensed that some believed her, while others still let fear cloud their loyalty. Even so, the temperature of the debate seemed to waver. The force of the confrontation ebbed, almost as if her raw emotion had pierced their collective anger.

Marcus ran a hand along his temple, exhaling. "Well said. We will set aside the matter of removing the amulet. Instead, we will coordinate a more structured training for you, Lila, in case illusions escalate. The Council cannot spare further energy on disagreements. Sebastian is the priority."

Embittered muttering echoed toward the back. One or two guardians in the small faction retreated, grumbling about inept novices and short-sighted elders. Lila watched them stomp out of the assembly hall, their robes sweeping the floor in angry arcs. She doubted those individuals would accept the resolution so easily.

Caleb's hand remained on her back, a quiet reassurance that she needed desperately. Evelyn, meanwhile, stepped close enough to whisper, "Your words landed. Do not worry if some remain stubborn. The truth is on our side."

Zoe approached, her brow furrowed. "At least the immediate threat to tear that amulet away has subsided. But the Council's unity is thinner than ever. Did you see how many watchers glared at each other like enemies?"

Lila nodded, throat tight. "Yes, I did."

Marcus raised his staff, signaling the official end to the assembly. "We adjourn for now. Squad leaders, update your rosters for illusions patrol. Reinforce wards and look for infiltration. We will meet again by midday for further planning."

Groups of guardians filtered toward the exit, some in subdued conversation, others in heated debate. Tension clung to the corridors like an unsettling fog. A handful of watchers cast Lila apologetic glances, but most hurried off to their tasks, eyes averted.

She noticed the older man who had first demanded the amulet's removal. He lingered near a pillar, arms crossed. Sensing her glance, he shot her a glare, then turned on his heel and stalked away. Her stomach twisted with a fresh wave of unease. Even if the Council had decided to let her keep the amulet, resentment clearly simmered.

Furious murmurs rose from the far side of the hall, where two watchers cursed loudly about trust being an impossible commodity in this broken Council. Another coven leader rubbed his temples, muttering that everything was on the brink of collapse. Their voices carried just enough for Lila to catch the words.

OTHER FLORID ROMANCE BOOKS

To be notified of new releases and special promotions from Florid Romance, please join our email list:

https://floridromance.lmbpn.com/about/sign-up-for-our-newsletter/

For a complete list of books published by Florid Romance please visit our website:

https://floridromance.lmbpn.com/

BOOKS BY KELLI ROBYNS

The Enchanted Orchard
The Orchard (Book 1)
Family Curse (Book 2)
Crystal Heart (Book 3)
The Charmed City
Spellbound (Book 1)
Prophecy (Book 2)
Ultimatum (Book 3)

BOOKS BY MICHAEL ANDERLE

CONNECT WITH MICHAEL ANDERLE

Connect with Michael Anderle

Website: http://lmbpn.com

Email List: https://michael.beehiiv.com/

https://www.facebook.com/LMBPNPublishing

https://twitter.com/MichaelAnderle

https://www.instagram.com/lmbpn_publishing/

https://www.bookbub.com/authors/michael-anderle

www.ingramcontent.com/pod-product-compliance
Lightning Source LLC
Chambersburg PA
CBHW020246010826
48973CB00006B/1671